THE COLTON HEIR

BY
COLLEEN THOMPSON

MILLS & BOON

First published in Great Britain 2013
by Mills & Boon, an imprint of Harlequin (UK) Limited,
Eton House, 18-24 Paradise Road, Richmond, Surrey TW9 1SR

© Harlequin Books, S.A. 2013

Special thanks and acknowledgement to Colleen Thompson for her contribution to The Coltons of Wyoming miniseries.

ISBN: 978 0 263 90724 7

18-1113

Harlequin (UK) policy is to use papers that are natural, renewable and recyclable products and made from wood grown in sustainable forests. The logging and manufacturing processes conform to the legal environmental regulations of the country of origin.

Printed and bound in Spain
by Blackprint CPI, Barcelona

**"V.
want you to leave."**

"How can you," she asked, her still-raspy voice strained to the point of breaking, "when people have died because I stuck my head in the sand instead of going to the authorities?"

Dylan's boot heels crunched the gravel as he strode up behind her. "And once you realized what your husband had done, you gathered up your courage and you went to the authorities."

She wheeled around to face him, her vision blurred with tears. "And people *still* died—"

He took another step before reaching out to cup her cheek in his hand.

When his rough thumb stroked her flesh, her eyes slid closed.

His fingers touched her eyelids. "Open them for me," he whispered, his voice rough as his hands were gentle. "I want you to look into my face. This time, I want you watching when I kiss you."

The Coltons of Wyoming: Stories of true love, high stakes…and family honor

After beginning her career writing historical romance novels, in 2004 **Colleen Thompson** turned to writing the contemporary romantic suspense she loves. Since then, her work has been honored with a Texas Gold Award, along with nominations for a RITA® Award, a Daphne du Maurier Award and multiple reviewers' choice honors. She has also received starred reviews from *RT Book Reviews* and *Publishers Weekly*. A former teacher living with her family in the Houston area, Colleen has a passion for reading, hiking and dog rescue. Visit her online at www.colleen-thompson.com.

To everyone who has ever hugged a frightened child,
healed an injured animal or reached out
to help a heart in need.

Chapter 1

On the day her second life went up in flames, a female shopper stared out as the rain came sideways, driven by the high winds of a sudden squall. Just inside the automatic glass doors, she hesitated, watching another woman stagger beneath her umbrella before a gust blew it inside out.

With a murmur of sympathy for the drenched customer scurrying to her car, the shopper in the doorway wondered whether her frozen dinners would survive if she waited out the downpour. Or whether she would have at least thought of an umbrella if she hadn't been too miserable, too anxious, to check the weather forecast—or even look up at the sky.

A baby-faced manager trotted up to her, the loose knot of his necktie peeping out from beneath his plastic poncho. "If you'll point out your car," he offered, his Adam's apple bobbing, "I'll pull it right up to the front here by the overhang."

Her knee-jerk response was to clutch her keys even tighter, to trust no one, as she'd been warned. But the young manager looked so newly minted and so earnest, and she'd almost forgotten what it was to be offered such an uncomplicated kindness. Besides, this was small-town Iowa, a world away from everything she feared.

"Thank you," she told him before pointing out a small sedan so nondescript it might as well be invisible. Which was exactly why she drove it, rather than the sleek, eye-catching Jaguar she'd been given for her thirtieth birthday, a replacement for the Mercedes from the year before. "You're so sweet to do that for me."

Nodding, he turned quickly—though not fast enough to hide his blush—and dashed off into the rain.

Seconds later, she flinched as a boom shook the air, the lot, the entire building and a gout of flame erupted, so blinding that her first stunned thought was that the poor manager had been struck by lightning.

Behind her, screams competed with the sirens of a half-dozen car alarms, and several employees pushed past her to see what had happened. But she stood frozen, mute with terror, her panicked pulse pounding in her ears. With an almost-audible click, her shocked brain put together what she'd really witnessed. Not an act of nature, not a lightning bolt at all.

The flames pouring from her car's shattered windows and whipping in the wild wind had nothing to do with this storm. And everything to do with Renzo's favorite means of disposing of "loose ends."

Where would she go now, now that he'd found her a thousand miles and a new identity away?

Where could she hide this time—and who could be trusted with her life?

Two weeks later...

Huge, black and in a world of hurt, the bull was in no mood to be messed with. Inside the corral, nearly a ton of raw beef and attitude paced restlessly and snorted, his breath steaming in the freezing morning air.

"Easy, Nitro. Steady, boy," said Dylan Frick, noting the torn and bloody shoulder that Dead River Ranch veterinarian Amanda Colton needed to stitch up. Whether the massive creature had gotten caught on some barbed wire or fought with another animal, Dylan couldn't say. All that mattered was keeping ranch owner Jethro Colton's prized new Angus-Brahman cross strong enough to reinvigorate the herd.

Dying or not, the billionaire was still counting on Dylan, the head wrangler and renowned large-animal whisperer, to calm the massive beast enough so he could be treated. But as he told Bingo and Betsy, the ranch's two English shepherds, "Stay," and stepped inside the pen, he automatically shifted focus, slowing his movements and syncing both his brain and body with the huge animal's instincts.

Big universities had experts giving clinics in stock handling all over Wyoming and beyond, but Dylan had never needed any training to get started. He'd known what to do ever since the day he'd first toddled outdoors and slipped into the stall of a stallion so dangerously unstable that Jethro had given orders for the horse to be put down.

Dylan still remembered his mother's terrified cry, her ashen face as she'd rushed toward him. In crystalline detail, the memory unfolded, and he watched her fear give way, first to astonishment, then joy and wonder, when the "vicious" stallion lowered its head and nickered for him to scratch its silky neck, the first step in the valuable stud's rehabilitation.

But Dylan's thoughts zoomed in on the freeze-frame

image of his mother, the mother who had held him, raised him, loved him....

Who'd been murdered on this very ranch just four months ago, shot down by a kidnapper bent on taking Jethro's only grandchild. Racked with guilt that he had even considered for a moment the possibility that she was not his biological mother, Dylan soon found himself drifting, plucking at the edges of a life that threatened to unravel.

Nitro turned toward him and pawed the ground, still muddy with the remnants of an earlier November snowfall. Dylan looked away with feigned indifference, tracking a red-tailed hawk that flew out of the woods behind the stable. Then he strolled across the corral, his long-limbed body as loose and unhurried as his mind was troubled.

From the corner of his eye, he saw the bull instinctively veer away, trotting in the direction of the open chute door. Trusting that the huge animal would stay put once he found the hay, sweet feed and water Dylan had placed there, he wondered again why he had allowed himself to be talked into taking the damned DNA test in the first place. Though he had bigger goals, he'd been happy in the work that he'd felt born to do, content living in his Spartan room in the employee wing of Dead River Ranch's grand mansion. And he was proud, damned proud, to be the only child of widowed ranch governess Faye Frick, who had served as a loving mother figure for so many others. He didn't need cushier surroundings, and he damned well didn't want to find out he was actually Cole Colton, Jethro's only son, who'd been taken thirty years before and never seen or heard of again.

Worse yet, he didn't want to deal with the suspicion

that the woman, whose absence was still a raw wound, might have killed to claim him.

Outside the corral, Betsy and Bingo leaped to their feet barking and raced toward him. It was the only warning Dylan had about the high price of his distraction, his only chance to avoid the black blur hurtling toward him—and a pair of wicked horns. He leaped sideways, dodging death, but not even that instinctive action saved him from a glancing blow off his right shoulder.

The impact spun him, slamming him into the fence rails with force enough to rattle his back fillings. At his side in a split second, the shepherds leaped and barked, distracting the bull as he charged after first one, then the other, giving Dylan the moment he needed to roll beneath the bottom rail to safety.

Still on the muddy ground, he caught his breath and whistled for the shepherds. The brown-and-white female heeded instantly, with black-and-white Bingo giving the bull one last, defiant bark and following a moment later. Both dogs rushed to fill his arms, their frantic licks and wagging tails encouraging him to get to his feet.

"All right, you two. All right. Good dogs, *very* good dogs." Dylan stroked the silky heads and rose with a grunt, aching everywhere. Looking around to see if all the noise had brought anybody running, he sighed and told the pair, "There's an extra biscuit in it for you if you don't let this get around. Maybe steak, if I can sneak one from the kitchen."

As he headed for the stable to wash up, he clenched his jaw, scarcely believing he'd made such a rookie mistake as assuming that an already-agitated bull would rather munch some sweet feed than take out his aggression on the nearest target. If he kept it up, Dylan knew, his worries over this damned DNA test and all the recent criminal activity would be the death of him.

Leaving the dogs outside, he closed the stable door just behind him, then went to the big sink. Stripping to the waist, he washed off the ground-in mud and beading blood from the scraped skin of his lower left arm.

He didn't get much further when he froze, abruptly aware of the shuffling of hooves and a horse's nervous nicker. Turning off the water, he heard a thump against another stall, followed by the low rumble of another horse. An uneasy rumble, as if there were something—or someone—in this stable that did not belong.

He pulled on his shirt, his thoughts returning to his mother's murder. Though a young hand named Duke Johnson had confessed to the crime, no one yet knew who had put him up to it—or later murdered two other household employees. Except that, somehow, there was a woman involved, a woman who might very well be the mastermind behind it all.

Was someone skulking around now, maybe even doing something to the horses that Dylan spent so much time with that they felt like personal friends?

Too angry to take the time to grab his jacket, Dylan crept toward the row of stalls, his shirt still unbuttoned. Looking into the first doorway, he saw Gabby Colton's sweet old sorrel, his ears flattened and the rims around his brown eyes white.

"Shh," Dylan whispered, and almost instantly, the gelding quieted.

In the next stall, his own horse, a stocky buckskin he called Bushwhack, stuck his head out to give him a friendly nudge. Though the quarter horse was one of the most laid-back animals Dylan had ever worked with, he wondered, was he so distracted by recent events—or rattled by his run-in with Nitro—that he'd imagined an intruder?

He continued walking along the line of stalls, goose-flesh breaking out along his arms and shoulders. But it wasn't from the cold alone, for ahead, he heard more agitated stamping—and was that a female voice?

Unable to recognize the speaker, he crept past stall after stall, looking in on a gray, a palomino and then Amanda Colton's chestnut. What he saw in the next stall froze the air in his lungs—and made him completely forget his aching body.

A tall, clearly female figure had her back to him as she faced another chestnut, a troubled young mare that a neighboring rancher had asked Dylan to evaluate. Though there were other brunettes on the ranch, this woman's long, chocolate-colored waves and statuesque build made him absolutely certain she was a stranger, as he'd feared.

Dylan doubted that the intruder knew the fidgeting animal wasn't one of Dead River Ranch's horses, just as she wouldn't know that the flighty young mare had recently put an experienced cowboy in a body cast.

"Easy there," the woman crooned, her rich, sweet tones stirring a reaction in the pit of Dylan's stomach, a reaction he couldn't spare the time to think about.

"Who are you?" he asked sternly. "And what the hell are you doing in there?"

With a cry of alarm, she spun around, dropping a brush as her hand darted inside her jacket. Startled by the sudden movement, the young mare squealed and spun around, and a pair of steel-shod hooves flashed, aimed straight for the woman's head.

Reacting on pure instinct, Dylan wrapped his arms

around her waist and swung her out of the way. As he kicked the stall door shut behind him, he turned the stranger around to face him, then noticed, for the first time, the small, snub-nosed revolver in her trembling hand.

A gun pointed straight at his thundering heart.

For over a year now, she had been telling herself that, when the moment came, she wasn't going to go down without a fight. In her mind, she'd run through dozens of scenarios, preparing herself to scream, to claw, to stab or shoot—whatever it took to survive to get justice as she'd sworn to and reclaim some semblance of a normal life.

Yet faced with the bare-chested man, she froze for a crucial moment, as stricken by his serious blue eyes as the fact that this particular "assassin" had just saved her from the supposedly gentle horse she had been grooming.

Close as he was standing, the moment's hesitation cost her. Before she registered his movement, he'd snatched the gun from her hand and turned it on her.

"Don't. Move," he warned, digging into his jeans' back pocket with his free hand. "I'm calling the police."

"No. Please," she begged, realizing that this gorgeous specimen, with his tight, toned abs and his unforgiving gaze, hadn't come to kill her. But if he sounded the alarm and called in the authorities, anyone might arrive, and there would be a lot of questions. Questions that were bound to leave her just as dead.

A memory detonated in her mind, an image filled with rain and fire, with the horrifying reek of burning metal, gas and—at least in her imagination—human flesh. The knowledge that that fate had been meant for her, that it could follow her here, too, revved her panic even higher.

"He'll find me if you do! He'll kill me this time for certain."

He glanced down at the phone and swore, and she noticed the cracked, black screen. As he tucked the broken cell back inside his pocket, the devastating blue eyes narrowed. "I asked you before. Who are you? And who sent you? Tell me now."

"I'm H-Hope. Hope Woods," she stammered. "I work here. Look, I'll prove it."

Her hand jerked toward her jacket's zipper, then stopped abruptly at the harsh, metallic click of the pistol's hammer being cocked.

"No sudden moves," he warned her. "And what do you mean, you work here? I've been on this ranch for almost thirty years, and I've never laid eyes on you."

"I'm the new maid," she said, her voice shaking. "I have the uniform, see?"

"Stand still," he ordered as he stepped closer. Close enough for her to smell the sharp scent of the soap he used, with the background aroma of hay, hard work and saddle leather. The combination was a far cry from the expensive colognes and exotic aftershaves worn by the men she'd once imagined she knew, but she decided on the spot she liked the honest smell of horse and cowboy better.

Flicking a look at her eyes, he reached for the tab of the zipper and slowly worked it downward, his breath warm against her face.

"So you've got the uniform," he conceded, nodding toward the ugly gray dress, with its stiff, starched fabric. "But that doesn't explain anything, not why you're out here messing with the horses and certainly not why you pulled a gun on me."

"You startled me."

"You said something a moment ago, something about someone who was going to kill you if I called the police. Why? What're you being coerced to do here? And what else have you done for this person already? Who have you killed?"

Fresh alarm ripped through her. "No one! I swear, I haven't hurt anybody." Her eyes stung as she remembered the young manager, with his bobbing Adam's apple and his blush when she had thanked him. And his was only the latest death she carried on her conscience. "I haven't hurt anybody here on the ranch. I was, um, I was cleaning the back wing and I—I needed to get away, just for a few minutes."

Thanks to Jethro Colton's obnoxious grown stepson, Trip Lowden, she had. In the three days she had worked here, she'd found that though Trip wasn't a real Colton, the big blond jerk was all too happy to lord his "position" over the help. But she had bigger worries right now than his constant leering. Namely, convincing this cowboy, with his darker hair and his searing gaze, that she wasn't lying to him.

"I had to find someplace quiet," she explained. "Out here with the animals, I can almost breathe again. I can almost—almost forget…."

She pinched her lip between her teeth, making one last, desperate effort to keep from totally dissolving. To keep from blurting to a stranger the words that would surely get her killed.

Grabbing her by the arm, he said, "You're coming with me. Inside. To find a phone to call the police and let them figure this out."

"You can't." Tears streamed down her face, and her

shaking knees gave way completely. But she didn't fall, for in one swift and fluid movement, the cowboy wrapped a strong arm around her waist to support her.

In his blue eyes, she saw a glimmer of compassion. Praying it was more than wishful thinking, she whispered, "You can't tell anyone...because I'm in hiding."

"In hiding from what?" he asked, speaking with a gentleness that stood out in stark contrast against his chiseled features and hard muscles. "I'm Dylan, Dylan Frick, the wrangler here, and I swear I'll see that you're kept safe, Hope, no matter who's been threatening you."

"It's my husband," she murmured, and once she started, there was nothing she could do to stop more from leaking out, like the air from a punctured balloon. "My ex-husband, I mean. He wants me dead so I can't testify against him. He's already tracked me down once. Or his assassins did, Witness Protection or no Witness Protection."

Dylan's tanned face drained of color. "What the—the Witness Protection Program placed you *here?* At Dead River Ranch?"

"I'm not in WITSEC any longer. I can't—can't trust them anymore, not since my car was blown up. A man was killed—an innocent man in the wrong place at the wrong time." More tears welled at the thought of him and all those others hurt by her decision to come forward. The father left to worry about her disappearance, the friends who had meant so much to her. And then there were the other victims, the ones who'd paid the price for her own selfishness and fear.

"So you ran?" the cowboy asked her.

She nodded. "I did. To the only place left for me to

turn. You see, Amanda Colton was my college room-mate."

He looked confused. "You two went to veterinary school together?"

"No, not vet school. It was just for a few months back in our sophomore year...." After winning the Miss New Jersey pageant at nineteen, Hope had had to take off for the remainder of the year. She'd had duties to attend, a bigger competition to prepare for. The memory of those bright lights shimmered, a beautiful illusion from the wreckage of her life. "We were a lot different, but Amanda and I really hit it off. We both loved animals, for one thing."

"And she'll back up this wild story?"

"She will," Hope swore. "I'm telling you the truth, Dylan. And Amanda told me it would be okay to come here. She said I could hang out with Prince William any-time I wanted."

Hope still thought it was an odd choice for a horse's name, but she was far too grateful to her friend to say anything about it.

"Prince William?" Dylan sounded surprised. "That's not PW you were in there brushing."

"Sixth stall down. The chestnut, Amanda told me."

"You picked the seventh, with a half-crazy chest-nut *mare*," he corrected, a chill coming over his voice, "which is why Chica here nearly kicked your head off. And why we're going to go and find out if you really know Amanda Colton as well as you claim."

Chapter 2

The longer Dylan listened, the more he wanted to believe the woman calling herself Hope Woods.

All his life, he had been drawn to damaged creatures. Wherever he saw suffering, he felt compelled to help. Though horses and cattle were his specialty, he was aware he had a reputation around the ranch as a good listener and a better friend, the kind of guy that even the humblest of employees could turn to in a pinch. And everything about this woman, from her trembling to her tears to the desperation in her strained voice, screamed she was in trouble. The kind of trouble he couldn't help but want to fix.

He had to admit, too, it didn't hurt that Hope was a knockout—not just a pretty girl-next-door, either, but a certified stunner whose slender curves couldn't be disguised by even the most shapeless of dresses. Each time he looked into those deep brown eyes of hers, framed by long lashes beaded with tears, his instincts shouted that he should be offering his protection, not holding her at gunpoint.

But even if she hadn't first pulled the gun on him, recent events had made him wary of trusting his own instincts. After all, he'd figured Duke Johnson, who'd admitted to firing the bullet that had killed his mother, for a decent and promising young hand. And Dylan knew the nightmare was far from over, as long as the person behind all the killings remained at large, possibly hiding among those he'd known and worked with his whole life.

"Amanda ought to be outside by now," he told Hope. "She was supposed to meet me by the corral."

"Wait," Hope said nervously. "Before we go, I need to— I have a hair clip and my glasses in my jacket. I just don't want you freaking out and shooting me when I reach inside my pocket."

"You wouldn't be carrying an extra gun, then?"

"Not unless you'd count the AK-47 and flamethrower I keep stashed there."

When she cocked a wry smile, he laughed, amazed that she could joke while staring down the barrel of a pistol, that she could smile at all considering what she claimed to have been through.

Tension broken for the moment, he nodded his permission and waited while she slipped on a pair of big tortoiseshell-framed glasses and wound up and secured her long hair.

"Is that supposed to be a disguise?" he ventured, wondering if she imagined for a moment she could make herself appear plain. At best, she'd downshifted her look from pinup fantasy to sexy librarian, but a woman like her couldn't blend in if she wore a paper bag over her head.

She frowned. "It'd work a whole lot better if someone wasn't always walking up behind me while I'm dusting and pinching the clip to let my hair down. Thinks it's hilarious."

"Who does?" Dylan asked, irritated that someone would bother a new employee while she worked.

She waved off the question. "Never mind that. It's the least of my worries right about now."

After retrieving his own jacket where he'd left it by the sink, Dylan put it on and dropped the pistol into his pocket. "Let's go."

She looked surprised. "So you're not going to march me outside with my hands up?"

"You planning on making a run for it?"

"And going *where,* exactly?" she asked as he pushed open the stable door.

"Cheyenne's only forty miles," he offered, gesturing toward the woods and pastures beyond, "as the buzzard flies."

Narrowing her eyes at the bright sunshine, she speared him with an annoyed look and kept walking.

They met Amanda Colton by the corral, where she was watching Nitro snort and charge at every shadow. As usual, she wore her long, brown hair in a messy ponytail, and she was dressed for the tough and dirty business of working around livestock, her boots, jeans and barn jacket more functional than stylish.

Her golden eyes flicked toward Dylan. "Thought you were going to get Nitro in the chute first thing this morning so I could suture him up."

"I'll take care of him in just a minute. But first…"

Amanda was already looking past him, blinking in surprise when she noticed Hope. "What's going on? Is something wrong, Auror—"

"Hope," the woman by his side corrected. "Hope Woods, the new maid. We both have to remember, that's who I am now."

Casting a worried look from "Hope" to Dylan, Amanda nodded. "I'm so sorry. It's just—you both looked so tense, and I thought that maybe you'd seen—" She cut herself off, looking uncertain.

"I caught her in one of the stalls," Dylan reported, "a second before she pulled this gun on me." He drew it from his pocket, keeping the muzzle pointed at the ground.

Amanda shot a horrified look at her friend. "You brought a gun to my home and nearly shot one of our most trusted people?"

Dylan glanced away, her words echoing through his head. *One of our most trusted people.* Would he start talking like that if he, too, turned out to be a high-and-mighty Colton?

He reminded himself that he'd never been on the receiving end of a moment of snobbery from Amanda or her sisters. Still, though the distinction went unspoken, it hung in the crisp, chill air: on this ranch, you were either the family or the help, no matter if you'd all grown up in the same house. And sick as he was, Jethro Colton would send packing any employee who forgot it for a moment.

Burrowing deeper into her jacket, Hope said, "I'm really sorry, both of you. I'm a little jumpy lately. Okay, a lot jumpy. Besides—" she shrugged, her contrite expression giving way to the kind of smile that begged them not to hate her "—I'm still a Jersey girl at heart. We all feel naked without a little steel insurance."

"How much did you tell him?" Amanda demanded, clearly in no mood for humor.

Dylan said, "She gave me some half-baked story about Witness Protection and a car bomb. And a mad ex-husband with a long reach."

Amanda's striking gold eyes turned on Hope. "You *told* him?"

"I had to. He was going to call the police, get everybody stirred up," Hope said, her Jersey-girl bluster giving way to welling tears…and a far more cultivated accent. Her hand shook as she wiped away the moisture. "I couldn't let that happen. Couldn't let trouble follow me here, too."

"So it's true, I take it?" Dylan frowned, though some part of him was relieved that Hope hadn't been lying.

Amanda nodded. "I'm afraid so. Hope's an old friend—"

"So she told me."

"I couldn't say no when she came here, so desperate for help. And the maid's position offered perfect cover— though I seriously doubt that Hope's ever cleaned a house before in her life."

Hope argued, "I've *watched,* plenty, and Mrs. Perkins was nice enough to show me how to fix the vacuum cleaner. Who knew those things have bags that need changing sometimes? Or that you're not supposed to use the scratchy side of the sponge to clean a marble surface?"

Dylan snorted, trying to imagine the kind of world Hope must have come from. Back East in New Jersey, she must've been some type of Colton, too. A far prissier brand, for certain—one who couldn't be more out of place here on a working ranch.

"So Mathilda Perkins knows about her?" he asked Amanda. Though he'd never worked directly with the head housekeeper, everyone knew she ran a tight ship when it came to household staff. But the trim, fiftysomething woman was just as quick to defend "her girls" in the employee dining area if one of the hands teased a pretty housemaid or criticized the cooking.

Amanda nodded. "She does, and we've also informed the new police chief, Harry Peters, too. But no one else can know, Dylan. Hope's life could depend on it."

"And not just *my* life," Hope said. "My ex's men have already killed one other person while they were trying to get to me. I couldn't stand it if my being here put anyone else in danger, so please—"

"You have my word," he said.

Amanda reached out and squeezed her friend's hand. "Then you don't need to worry anymore, because when Dylan Frick gives his word, he always keeps it."

Hope sighed. "Thank you, both of you, but I suppose I'd better get back inside before anyone sees me out here. That back wing doesn't clean itself, especially not with those tacky stepsiblings of yours messing it up as fast as they can."

Amanda frowned, as she often did at the mention of Trip and Tawny Lowden, or their mother, Jethro's ex-wife from his third marriage. "Yes, you'd better go, Hope, and don't come back to the stable again until your workday's over. Otherwise, the other employees will all start wondering why Mathilda doesn't fire you."

"All right," Hope agreed, "but there's one more thing."

Both looked at her expectantly, but Hope's focus had turned to Dylan.

"Now that we've cleared this up, you think I could have my gun back?"

"Not a chance," he told her, returning it to his own pocket. "I don't want you getting jumpy and blowing someone's head off the next time they surprise you."

Amanda backed him up, saying, "You're perfectly

safe here on the ranch—and I really don't like guns in the house."

Dylan supposed Amanda was thinking of her seven-month-old daughter, Cheyenne, who was just beginning to crawl. But whether or not the nervous new "maid" went around armed, none of them were really safe here, he knew, not in the long run....

Not until he found and stopped the mastermind whose botched attempt to kidnap Amanda's baby daughter, Cheyenne Colton, had resulted in his mother's death.

Once Hope was out of earshot, Dylan told Amanda, "Let me take care of that bull now."

He whistled for the English shepherds, who came running moments later. They sat at his feet expectantly, tails wagging and gazes bright and eager.

Amanda held a hand up, her expression serious. "Wait, please, Dylan. I just wanted to tell you, I'm really sorry about Hope pulling that gun on you. You could've been killed."

"She's no killer," he said. "She froze instead of shooting first and asking questions later."

"Thank God."

"Yeah," he said, his voice rougher than he intended. "You wouldn't want to lose one of your *most trusted people*."

Frowning at him, she said, "You know you're more than that. To all of us. And if this test turns out to show that you're really family—"

He stiffened. "I don't want to talk about that DNA test, except to say it's all a bunch of bull—"

"However it turns out, it'll be fine. And I for one would be proud to call you my bro—"

"I'm no Colton," he said, the words as sharp and cold as chips of ice. "I'm Faye Frick's boy, the ranch wrangler. And that's plenty good enough for me. You got that, Dr. Colton?"

Seeing her flush, he was instantly ashamed of the way he'd flung her kindness and acceptance back in her face, along with her desire to find a possible marrow match to save her father's life. He knew he was behaving as irrationally as Nitro had this morning, lashing out because of pain. But the apology she deserved remained knotted tight in his throat, so he climbed back into the corral and did the one thing he was good at. The only thing that calmed the doubts and the anger and, yes, even the fear roiling inside him.

He turned his attention to the injured bull, but this time, he refused to give in to distraction. Taking his cues from the animal's eyes and the way he held his body, Dylan used his own subtle movements and the dogs' silent assistance to gently pressure the bull into the chute.

In under two minutes, he had the gate closed tight, and moments later, Amanda scrambled up on a rail and leaned in to give Nitro an injection to help calm him.

"Careful there," Dylan warned, still regretting his rudeness. "Big sucker just about squashed me flat a little bit ago."

Nitro kicked the chute's slats and bellowed, though it was probably more from finding himself trapped than the needle's pinch.

Backing off to give him time to settle, Amanda looked Dylan up and down, her gaze lingering on the mud ground into his jeans. "You've had a rough morning, haven't you, tangling with both Nitro and Aurora?"

Grateful she was still speaking to him, he said, "That's

Hope's real name, huh?" though he'd guessed as much from Amanda's earlier slip.

She nodded and confided, "Since you already know the rest, yes. It's Aurora Worthington. Our new 'housemaid's' an East Coast socialite and a former Miss New Jersey."

"Well," he said drily, thinking how far out of his league she was. Not that he had the time, the energy or the interest to pursue some spoiled beauty queen. "I guess the judges for that pageant didn't ask a lot of questions about biology."

"Why would you say that?"

He grinned. "Instead of going to visit with your gelding, your little princess accidentally picked that wild little mare in the next stall. Nearly got her head kicked in for her trouble."

"Oh, dear. Just what we need. Between that and nearly shooting you, 'Hope' needs a full-time keeper...." Amanda pursed her lips, looking thoughtful. "I need a favor from you, Dylan. A serious favor."

"Name it," he said, eager to put their working relationship back on track.

"I want you to keep a close eye on her, close as you can. When she's sitting around the table eating with the rest of the staff, try to steer her around conversations that'll get her into trouble, and when she's out around the animals, make sure she doesn't wander into danger."

He nodded, then asked, "She's really important to you, isn't she?"

Amanda hesitated, leaving him to wonder if he'd crossed a line by asking. Amanda might be unassuming, but she was still a Colton, and except for occasionally gushing over Cheyenne's latest development, she'd never been the type to talk about her personal life.

Looking ill at ease, she finally answered, "To tell you the truth, I didn't even like her at first. She was so popular, so gorgeous. Compared to her, I felt like—" Cutting herself off, she shook her head. "But she figured it out fast. Somehow, she just got me, and she did everything she could to make me feel like I really mattered, like I was special, too. It may not seem like much, but at that time, in that place, it meant everything to me."

Surprised to realize that being a Colton hadn't made her immune to the same self-doubts that plagued mere mortals, Dylan nodded soberly. "Then I give you my word, Amanda. As long as I'm on this ranch, I'll make sure Hope stays safe."

It took forever for Hope to clean the mess Trip Lowden's sister, Tawny, had left in her bathroom. But as aggravating as it was to pick up the piles of damp towels thrown haphazardly on the floor and scrub the makeup spattered across every surface, Hope was happy to be out of Trip's range and happier still that his slob of a sibling and her hypercritical mother were both out for the day.

As she rubbed at a stubborn spot left on the mirror, Hope couldn't help but wonder. Had she been as inconsiderate of her own maids? Not anywhere near as rude or messy—a person would almost have to *try* to come even close to Tawny—but as casually indifferent? As heedless of their efforts?

Though she'd always asked after her maids' families and given liberal bonuses, she knew she'd never really respected how hard they worked to keep strangers' living spaces gleaming. And to Hope's surprise, there was an entire array of tips and tricks she'd never had the chance to pick up, as she'd begun to appreciate while cleaning her own rented room in Iowa.

After finishing the bathroom, she moved on to the bedroom, where she stripped and remade Tawny's bed once she'd moved her open laptop to the nightstand. Remembering her financial situation, Hope thought of using the computer to look up local pawnshops. While she weighed the risks, the screen automatically refreshed.

Heart pounding wildly, she barely stifled a shriek at the image peering back at her—a face looking out from beneath the banner of a well-known gossip site.

It was her, the younger, blonde her, crowned with a tiara and giving her brightest smile and her queenliest wave as she stood in her shimmering, cobalt evening gown, onstage in Atlantic City. Taken twelve years before, the photo might be dated, but her cheekbones remained as high, her chin as delicate. And underneath her contacts, her eyes were the same striking blue.

Stricken as she was by the sight of her own picture, it took her a moment to calm down enough to notice the headline just beneath it, a headline that sent her bolting to the bathroom, where she was sick in Tawny's spotless sink.

"Oh, no, no, no," she whimpered. "You couldn't do that, Renzo. Please tell me you didn't."

But a return to check the story confirmed that her ex-husband *had*...

And raised the toll of death and destruction that followed her disastrous decisions. A toll that shattered every last trace of her courage as it dropped her to her knees.

Upset as she was, Hope knew she couldn't stay here, couldn't risk letting Tawny catch her staring at a computer image of her own face. Couldn't explain why she was weeping over an article reporting the death of a missing New Jersey woman's father.

Hope forced herself to stand, to go about the business of gathering soiled towels and linens. Thanks to her unauthorized break in the stable earlier, she would be hours late taking her basket to the basement laundry—and lucky if the laundress's wrath didn't strike her dead.

Even though Mrs. Black's sharp tones and harsh stares frankly scared Hope, she didn't make it five steps down the hallway before she ran into another delay as Trip Lowden stepped out of a little alcove, his perfectly white teeth bared in a predatory smile.

"Well, hello, pretty lady. Funny we should run into each other like this again."

In what was undoubtedly meant to be a rakish gesture, he swept his expensively styled blond bangs out of his brown eyes. Hope didn't like what she saw in them, and worse yet, she was so upset, she didn't know how to hide her own revulsion.

"Is something wrong?" he asked, feigned compassion oozing from him like an oily slick. "You look like you've been crying."

Gritting her teeth, she lowered her gaze. "I don't want to trouble you, sir, and I'm already running late with my work."

"If anyone says anything, you just tell them you were with me." He moved in closer, crowding her personal space the way he had this morning, when he'd crept up on her as she was neatening his bedroom. "After all, I'm Mr. Colton's stepson. There's so much I can do to help if you'll just let me."

When she'd still been Aurora Worthington-Calabretta,

Hope had known exactly how to deal with a handsy little wannabe like Trip Lowden. But now, as the most junior maid on the staff, her skin broke out in gooseflesh as she tried to think of how to put him in his place without losing hers.

She murmured, "I'm sorry, Mr. Lowden. I really have to go now. I'm not feeling well and—"

"Don't go."

When he reached past the laundry basket she was holding, she shifted to balance it on one hip, every muscle tensing in preparation for his touch. He might be bigger and more powerful, but considering the amount of private self-defense training that her father had insisted she take, she had every confidence that she could lay out the twerp. Which would mean she could kiss her cover—and Dead River Ranch—goodbye.

Reminding herself she *had* no other place to go, she somehow managed to keep still as Trip removed her glasses.

"I don't know why you hide that beautiful face of yours behind these," he said.

"To see, sir. Just to see." She stuck her hand out, her eyes welling as she imagined her poor father seeing her reduced to this. "Give them to me, please. So I can get back to my duties."

He chuckled as he peered through the lenses. "Why, they're as clear as window glass."

Her heart thumped as she grappled for some explanation. "The prescription's slight, I'll admit. But they help keep me from getting a headache when I—"

"You really *are* hiding," he said, sounding so sure of it she wanted to scream. "Deliberately hiding your face from—"

"I don't like to be bothered," she blurted as panic coiled tight inside her. What if Trip figured out who she was? What would he do with that knowledge?

"By men, you mean?" he asked.

She nodded, her face burning, and then tried to slip past him.

He blocked her way, his face lit up like a little boy's on Christmas morning. "You mean, you prefer women? You're a *lesbian?*"

She stared in disgust, for there was no mistaking his excitement. Or the suspicion that he'd pursue her all the more aggressively if she relied on such an excuse. *Pervert.*

"No, sir," she answered slowly and carefully. "What I *said* was that I don't like being bothered. By anyone, sir."

"You might fool those others, but you're not fooling me, Hope," he said, reaching out to skim her cheekbone with his fingertips.

She jerked away, skin crawling. "Leave me alone," she warned, then tried another lie. "I'm feeling really— I think I'm going to be sick."

Clapping her free hand over her mouth, she whirled around and started running. As she made for the stairwell, she willed herself to keep hold of the laundry basket, for there was no way she was coming back upstairs to reclaim it.

Maybe Trip was afraid she'd make good on her threat and heave all over his black cashmere sweater, or maybe he'd simply tired of his game. Whichever the case, he didn't follow, allowing Hope to calm down enough to make it to the basement without further incident.

She crept downstairs as quietly as possible, praying that Mrs. Black's poor hearing would protect her. Her back turned, the older woman was grumbling under her breath as she ironed the freshly washed sheets, except for those Hope had neglected to bring downstairs by the appointed hour of three o'clock.

Her pulse thrumming in her ears, she quietly set down the basket and backed toward the steps. But her hopes of a quick escape were dashed when the laundress whipped around, her steel-gray ponytail flying, to glare at her with the most intimidating gaze that Hope had ever seen. It didn't help that the woman's left eye had filmed over, turning it an opaque, milky white. The younger maids swore that Mrs. Black, who was said to have Native blood flowing through her veins, used that pale eye to see things that no one else could. Apparently, those things included the lowliest new maid's attempt to slink away.

"I'm sorry I'm so late," Hope offered, struggling to keep her teeth from chattering. "Is there anything I can do to help you?"

The stare lengthened, and Hope saw that the older woman was keenly aware of its effect on others.

When she did speak, her contempt echoed loudly through the basement. "Learn to read a clock, for starters. I'll be here half the night, sorting all this out, no thanks to you."

"I could help," Hope tried again, her stomach squirming.

"You could what?" the laundress asked, cupping a hand to what must be her better ear.

"Help you. Or you could go home right now, and I'll take care of—"

"Get. Out," the laundress warned.

Hope didn't wait to be asked a second time, but fled upstairs, her face so hot and her skin so clammy that she nearly barreled over a black-haired maid named Misty Mayhew on her way to the back door.

"Well, excuse you!" the younger woman snapped, her brilliant blue eyes sparking.

Hope didn't waste a second on an explanation. She just kept running, fast as she could, all the way out to the stable.

Chapter 3

A solidly built male traveler in his late thirties exited the 737, relieved to finally escape the whining brat who'd been kicking at his seat back for the past two hours. As desperately as he'd wanted to whip around and scream at the kid's mother to keep her whelp in line, Joey Santorini had been forced to keep his mouth zipped.

The last thing he could afford was to get hauled off this plane and interrogated for hours, maybe even locked up if the TSA saw through his fake ID. As bad as it would be to find himself back in custody, things would rapidly go downhill when word got out that he had screwed up.

Screwed up just like last time, with the car in Iowa.

Sweat beading on his meaty forehead, Joey remembered his cousin Luca, his partner on the job for years, desperately trying to explain how there'd been no way to predict that some lust-struck grocery-store punk would give his all for customer service. Only hours after their return to Jersey, Joey's cousin had abruptly vanished, and it was understood that asking about Luca's fate would be seriously unhealthy.

Instead, Joey had been given a last chance to make things right, to visit an old friend of Aurora Worthington's—a connection so obscure, so remote, she hadn't yet been checked out—to finally silence the one woman who threatened everything.

As much as Joey hated working with strangers this far from his home turf, he'd been forced to rely on free-lance local talent to get into the location. But the man had come highly recommended, so Joey picked up his pace, his dark glower parting the teeming school of fellow travelers like so many frightened fish.

He clenched his jaw, telling himself it wasn't the terminal's other passengers who needed to beware of him, but the sleek, blonde bitch who'd put all this in motion. For four years, she'd never had a bit of trouble prancing from one glitzy charity event to the next, showering her much older husband's money on the sick kids, homeless puppies or abused women she'd adopted as her causes. But let her find out where that money really came from, and she couldn't betray the man who doted on her fast enough, along with the organization he'd built up from the ground floor.

Joey Santorini swore to himself he was going to make good on this chance, to recast himself as the hero rather than the scapegoat. After all, this friend of Aurora's had not only the land, but money enough to keep Aurora in the style she'd always expected as her due.

Time you got taken down a notch, he thought as he stepped out into the bracing Colorado air. For his own sake, as well as in memory of the cousin whose name he must never again mention, he vowed he was going to give the pampered blonde bitch everything that she had coming.

Spotting the white panel van with the Elite Electrical logo as it pulled up to the curb, he grinned savagely, eager to begin the drive into Wyoming. And even more eager to spend a little quality time with Miss New Jersey, where he would teach her that sex didn't always have to come with roses, diamonds and a fancy set of silk sheets.

Sometimes it came with fear and blood and death.

Though he'd spent countless hours eating, talking and laughing around the communal dinner table with the ranch's other employees, Dylan had grown to hate it lately. He was all too attuned to the measuring looks that kept darting his way—looks that told him the word had gotten out about his DNA test and that some were already wondering if the results would transform him from the hard worker they knew to an entitled princeling. And wondering as well if he would replace Amanda Colton as Jethro's heir apparent.

Their curiosity was bad enough, but he'd noticed a few resentful glances from those jealous of his possible good fortune, an "honor" he'd happily hand over to any one of them if he could only go back to knowing who he was and where he came from. But when the normally straitlaced new maid, Misty Mayhew, started batting her lashes at him and the head cook loudly insisted that he should get the choicest chop from the platter, he pushed back from the table, his face on fire and his appetite gone. "Dammit, that's enough of that. I'm finished."

Only after he had stormed out of the kitchen did he realize he had just made a complete fool of himself. And that the newest of the ranch employees, Hope Woods, had not shown for dinner at all.

Cursing under his breath, he stalked upstairs to his room to grab his jacket on his way back out to the stable. Though he was in no mood for conversation, let alone fit company for some pampered prima donna, he could at least do one thing right this evening and keep his promise to Amanda by looking for her friend.

As soon as he stepped outdoors, the postsunset chill hit him, a biting harbinger of the colder months ahead. Used to it, he stuffed his hands into his pockets and picked up his pace.

Bingo and Betsy bounded up, seemingly from nowhere, and this time, he let the two dogs follow him inside. Though one of the stable lights had been left on, he saw and heard no sign of any human presence.

Just in case, he called, "Hope? It's Dylan. Are you out here? Thought you'd want to know you're missing dinner."

There was no answer, except from both of the English shepherds, who shuffled their feet and licked their chops, as if to remind him of his debt from this morning.

"Sorry, you two beggars," he said. "There was no steak to swipe this evening, but how about some rawhide?"

Wagging their fringed tails, the two dogs barked in unison, then plopped down on their wriggling rear ends to await their treats. Once he returned from the feed room, where he kept some rawhide stashed, Dylan left them chewing happily and went to check PW's stall. The chestnut looked up from the hay he had been munching, but Hope was nowhere in sight, and there was no response when he called for her again.

So where the heck had she gone? Up to her own room, on the floor above his?

Come to think of it, he realized, he had never seen her dining at the employees' table. Did she think she was too good to eat among them, or was she scared that she would stand out, like a brightly colored orchid among a bunch of prairie weeds?

One thing was for certain: every red-blooded man among them would have noticed her. The women, too, he suspected, at least enough to wonder how someone who scrubbed and swept and changed linens for a living maintained her elegant manicure.

Snorting at the thought, he had almost convinced himself to go back inside, maybe even apologize for his outburst, when he heard the sound of a soft sniffle. Not an equine sound, but one as human as it was distinctly female.

Following it, he crept nearer to an empty stall, where the hands stacked straw for bedding. There he found her sitting on a bale in the spill of dim light, her shoulders hunched and shaking, and no wonder, for she wore only the ugly maid's dress and a sweater far too light for the evening chill. Her wavy hair was down again, the horn-rimmed glasses missing, as if this was the only place where she could be herself.

Though he made no effort to move quietly, she didn't even look up when he came inside. Forgetting his anger and frustration, he slipped off his own jacket and laid it over her shoulders. "You'll freeze out here like this. It's getting colder by the minute."

She didn't say a word, only stared straight ahead, the misery rolling off her in waves as black as midnight.

He sat on the bale beside her and saw how wet her face was. Trying again to get some reaction, he asked, "Didn't you hear me call you?"

Once more, no response.

Worry contracted low in his gut. Worry that she might have cracked under the strain of starting over in another new place. Could she have taken something to ease her stress?

He enfolded her ice-cold hand in his warm one. "Hope, you need to answer." His voice dropped to an urgent whisper. "Aurora?"

Her spine straightening, she jerked her head toward him and sucked in a startled breath. "Dylan? I didn't hear you. Didn't—" Pulling her hand from his, she patted the jacket. "This is—this is yours?"

"You looked so cold," he said quietly. "Are you all right? You haven't taken a sedative or something, have you?"

"No. Of course not. Why would you think—"

"Well, for one thing, you were wound up so tight this morning that you nearly shot me. Then you're not at dinner, and when I come looking for you, I find you nearly catatonic."

"I'm not on drugs, if that's what you're thinking. I just needed—I needed someplace private." Her hands shook as she pulled off the jacket and handed it back to him. "Here. You take this back. You'll need it."

"I cut my teeth on Wyoming winters. A little early frost won't kill me," he said. "So put the jacket back on, and tell me, what was it that upset you enough to bring you out here like this? Was someone bothering you again while you were working?" If so, he swore he would damn well put a stop to it.

"It's not that," she said, teeth chattering as she slipped her arms inside the jacket's sleeves. "And thank you. The cold kind of crept up on me, but now that you mention it, I really am chilled. Maybe we should go in."

"Tell me first," he said, catching her arm when she started to get up. "What is it? What's happened?"

"You mean, *besides* having my whole life in ruins, hit

men on my trail and an ex-husband who knows I'm the only thing standing between him and freedom?"

"I'm sorry," he said, realizing that just as he might be soon, she'd been ripped out of her own life. Ripped away from everything she'd ever thought she was.

Another sniffle followed, then a spill of bitter words. "And to think I loved that man once—or loved the man I thought he was. And now he's—he's—"

"He's what, Hope? You can tell me."

"He's had my father k-killed. The only family I had left."

As she choked out the words, she fell apart completely, her sobs coming in soft gasps, as if she'd gotten in the habit of muffling her tears. Gathering her to him, Dylan stroked her hair, her back.

"I'm so sorry," he said, and though he'd soothed a thousand animals, he felt clumsy and inadequate against this woman's pain and grief. Grief that he identified with all too closely.

When the worst of it was over, he reached into the pocket of the jacket she was wearing and came up with a clean bandanna, which he used to blot the tears from her face.

"Th-thank you," she said, faltering through a sad smile. "And I'm sorry if I got your shirt all wet. Tough guy or not, you were probably cold enough already."

"Not now I'm not," he said, liking the feel of her in his arms. Liking it far too much. Her tight curves were getting to him, her clean floral scent making it difficult to breathe, reminding his body painfully how long it had been since he'd been this close to a woman. And how wonderful it would be to shed his pain, to lose himself inside—

He let go of her, embarrassed by his physical reaction. Told himself to have some decency. She'd just found out about her father's death, for heaven's sake, and here he was thinking about leaning her back on the bales and taking advantage of her grief.

As the blood returned to his brain, sanity flooded back. She had to have found out about her father somehow—in some way that might have put all of them in danger. "You didn't risk a phone call, did you? Or an internet search, maybe?"

"No, of course not. I just— I was cleaning Tawny's room, and it was splashed across her computer. An old photo from my pageant days—"

"Your picture?" he asked, alarmed to think that others on the ranch might see it, including a few that he could think of who wouldn't lose a moment trying to figure out how to profit from her presence. Whether the result was blackmail or a phone call to some sleazy tabloid publication, Hope would be in danger. She could be in danger anywhere.

"A twelve-year-old photo—I look completely different," she assured him. "But there was a headline..." Her voice quavered, and her eyes closed. "Father of Missing Beauty Queen Found Dead in Burned Home."

"I'm sorry." He remembered the first hours of his own grief, remembered friends looking as helpless and stricken as he felt now, each of them wishing there were better words, stronger words to show compassion. "Very sorry he's gone—"

"Because of me, I know it."

"You're sure? Did you click through and read the article?"

She nodded. "I did. I had to, but it just said the cause

of death is still under investigation. And the fire in his house, too. He'd just moved to Florida last winter. He loved to fish and play golf. I thought he'd be safe there if I stayed away from him. I thought— I should have realized that when Renzo couldn't get to me, he'd punish me by…"

Hearing her quiet gasps, he took her hand in his and filed away the ex-husband's first name for future reference. "You don't know that. Not for certain. It could've been an accident—"

Her gaze shot up to meet his. "Don't patronize me, Dylan. It's all my fault. I know it. Sometimes, I wish I'd never found out about my husband's family business. Wish I could go back to living in blissful ignorance."

He thought of his own hunger to learn the truth about his mother's background. "Do you? Do you really?"

She considered for a moment. "No, I don't. It's just…a year ago, I was so happy. So in love. I had lots of friends, good friends who supported me when my mom lost her remission. And I still had my dad."

"Were the two of you close?" he asked.

Her sigh was heavy with regret. "Not as close as I wish. My father had his fishing, his golf and his club friends. I always knew he loved me, but—why did I never take the time to know him better?"

He gave her hand a squeeze. "I know what you mean. I've been asking myself that same question lately."

After a long silence, she ventured, "I heard about your mother. When I passed by the kitchen, the cook and her two helpers were talking. Talking about you."

"Yeah," he said cautiously, the hair rising behind his neck. Though she had seemingly been cleared, there had been whispers about the head cook, Agnes Barlow. Dark suspicions that she might be the mastermind behind the recent crimes. Though Dylan, who'd known her for decades, couldn't bring himself to believe it, he wondered what else a careful listener might overhear inside the mansion.

"They said your mom was murdered, right here on the ranch this summer. I'm sorry for your loss, too. But maybe you could tell me. Does the pain—does it ever get…where you can swallow without feeling like there's a razor blade stuck in your throat? Where you can eat or breathe or smile?"

He decided she deserved the truth, no matter how tough it was. "It comes and goes. Sometimes you'll forget, for a few minutes or an hour. Then it all comes crashing down, how there's no going back. And no way in the damned world to undo what's happened."

He felt the warmth of her sigh against his skin.

"Worst part is," he added, "that, like you with your father, I have a lot of questions about my mother's death. And so far, I'm not liking any of the answers."

"Tell me, Dylan," she whispered. "Please. I need something else in my head besides my own guilt and anger. Otherwise, I'm likely to get on the first plane out of Cheyenne and fly back to give interviews—tell the media, tell the whole world everything I found out."

"What *was* that?" he asked her. "Who was this man you married?"

"A successful businessman, I thought. Well regarded, generous."

"Who was he really?" Dylan asked her.

"A scheming, murderous monster." She pulled her hand from his, her voice shaking with anger. "One I owe it to my father to do everything I can to stop."

When she started to her feet, he grabbed her arm and pulled her back down. "You can't do that, Hope. Can't go charging in and let him kill you, too." Though she hadn't told him who this "Renzo" was, Dylan had heard more than enough to know the man would find a way to get to her if she resurfaced.

"Let go of me."

She tried to jerk free, but he held fast, saying, "You're not thinking straight now. You've had a shock, a huge blow—"

"So distract me, Dylan," she whispered, her voice too close to breaking. "Tell me, what have you found out about your mother that's upset you? Because if I don't get my mind off what I've done, I'm leaving. I'm packing my things up and calling a cab right away."

Finding a taxi to come all the way out to the ranch after dark would be damned near impossible, but Dylan couldn't find it in himself to refuse her. Maybe because her pain and anger reminded him so sharply of his own, or maybe it was because he needed a sounding board, someone to hear him out who was a stranger to the ranch's caste system and its people.

Whichever was the case, he soon found himself talking, barely noticing how still and cold the air was growing. Barely noticing anything as the pent-up words came, first in awkward clumps, and then as steadily and relentlessly as a February snow.

"So let me see if I have this right," she said. "You found out that your mother—who may not have been your biological mother after all—*killed* a woman when you were just a baby? Who?"

"*Might* have killed her," he stressed. "Her name was

Desiree Beal. She was a sister to Jethro's first wife, Brittany—"

"The missing Colton baby's mother?" she asked, trying her best to follow along.

"Right. First, though, Brittany left Jethro and her baby, then got herself killed driving drunk."

He spoke in an oddly flat voice, but Hope would swear she felt the walled-off scorn behind it, the pain of a rejection he wasn't ready to contemplate, let alone acknowledge.

"Maybe Brittany was aware she had a problem and didn't want to put her own child at risk," Hope suggested, painfully aware that things weren't always as they appeared.

Dylan gave a noncommittal shrug before adding, "A couple of months later, Brittany's kid disappears from the ranch, and no one ever finds a trace. Except that not long afterward, Desiree shows up looking for work in Jackson, a little tourist town way up in the northwest corner of the state. The diner she applied to was managed by my mother, who was apparently calling herself Faye Donner at the time."

"Her maiden name?"

"There's no record she was ever married, but according to another waitress who once worked there, Faye felt sorry for Desiree on account of the baby she had with her and her story about being widowed. She even had the wedding ring to prove it."

Hope frowned, marking it all down on her mental scorecard. "So Faye—your mother—hires this woman, who later turns up dead. Robbed and murdered in the diner parking lot just before the baby she had with her and your mother both disappear."

"That's what I can't wrap my head around. I'm supposed to believe that my mom, who was the sweetest, gentlest woman I've ever met, was a kidnapper, or maybe even a killer? She would never do it. Never. That wasn't the woman that I knew."

"Everybody has a breaking point," Hope ventured. "What if she were trying to protect someone, or even save her own life?"

When he was quiet for a few seconds, she took it as permission to continue. "Maybe she found the baby in danger after the robber murdered Desiree."

"She would've turned him in to the authorities," he insisted, "would've done the right thing."

"What if she thought the 'right thing' was keeping this baby out of the system and with someone who had already come to love him?"

"Or maybe Desiree had already gotten rid of this baby somehow before she was killed," Dylan said. "It's a terrible thought, but she might've done away with the Colton baby out of fear that she would be caught and imprisoned. Kidnappers panic sometimes."

"There's another possibility, as well. What if Faye somehow figured out that the baby wasn't really Desiree's? Maybe there was some kind of confrontation."

"What are you suggesting?" he asked.

"That if Faye really was the person who killed Desiree, it could have, *must* have, been self-defense. After all, didn't your mother lose her *life* protecting another infant?"

"That can't be right," he argued, "because if it were, why on earth would Faye *Frick* show up here, of all places, months later, with the same story about being widowed and a baby in her arms?"

"With *you*," she whispered, and whether it was the darkness or the cold or the bond of grief between them, she moved closer, reminding herself that she still wore his jacket. That she could, at the very least, share some of her warmth.

But in her heart, she knew that it was only an excuse. That after so many lonely months, months where her secrets had left her too afraid, too anxious, to forge a single real connection, she was starved for the comfort of a simple human touch. Especially tonight, when she'd never needed it more.

"Yeah, me," he acknowledged. "But I couldn't possibly be—"

"Maybe not," she allowed, mostly because he needed to hear it. "Faye could have had her own child, though the timing's—"

"She lied to me about my father," he admitted, "said he was a cowboy at a dude ranch out in Cody, that he'd died in a bad fall from his horse not long before I was born. I'd always figured I inherited my need to work with animals from him, that it was in my blood. Except that no one at the Bar None had ever heard of my 'dad.' It seems the man never existed."

"Could she have come up with that part because— forgive the suggestion—she'd found herself pregnant out of wedlock?" Hope asked. "Maybe she was involved with someone she couldn't talk about, a married man, or even someone with a checkered past. She could have made up the rest, could have kept your birth from others in order to protect you."

"I plan to drive out to Jackson to do more research, but there's no birth record on file under either her maiden or her 'married' name. And if what this waitress who worked there told my friends on the phone is true, she always made a big fuss over any kids the customers brought in, but she never even had a boyfriend, much less..."

"She could have adopted," Hope offered, though even to her ears, the idea sounded like a long shot for a single woman. *But not impossible.*

"I've gone through all my mother's things. The birth certificate I used to get my social-security card and driver's license? Turns out it's a fake. And there's no adoption paperwork, no baby pictures of me, either, not from my first year."

"What if the adoption was informal? From a friend in trouble or a family member, maybe even a teenage waitress from her diner who wanted to keep things quiet?" Hope said, remembering what it had felt like to need to grasp those final straws. To fight off a truth so huge it might've drowned her, if she hadn't found her own way to float past her denial.

But at what cost?

Dylan blew out a long breath. "Then what really happened to Desiree's child? According to the sheriff up in Jackson, there was no record of any baby being found after Desiree Beal's murder. No unidentified small bodies found within that time frame, either, thank God."

"So let's suppose, just for the sake of argument, that child was...that *you're* Cole Colton."

She felt him tense beside her, every muscle tightened.

"I'm no damned Colton. I can't be. Because if my mother knew I was Jethro's son, why wouldn't she report it? Or at least give her boss back his child?"

Hope ran her fingertips across the back of his hands, the soft pads skating over the rough bumps of his knuckles. "Maybe she was afraid, afraid that she'd be charged with Desiree's murder. Or maybe she came here with the best intentions. She meant to give you up when she came, but by then it was too late."

"What do you mean, too late?"

"She'd already fallen in love with the child she'd always wanted." Shoving aside her own fears, she touched his strong jaw, slightly prickly with the light beard of a day's growth. "With the *son* of her heart, the baby boy she called Dylan. With you."

He grasped her wrist roughly, then began to shove it away from the hard planes of his face. But in the span of that split second, his eyes caught hers and something flared to life between them, something as bright and hot as the stall was dim and cold.

A silence filled the narrow space, a stillness so complete, she heard the rush of her own blood, the stutter of her heart. She'd gone too far, presumed too much, she realized. Angered a man so much larger and more powerful, a man she'd never met before this morning.

Yet it wasn't fury radiating from his gaze now, but a brand of hunger that sent a shock of pure anticipation streaking through her.

Turning her wrist over, he ran his callused thumb along the delicate, pale skin there, focused his whole being on the tiny spot, so exposed and vulnerable. She shivered, her every nerve ending tingling with awareness...and a memory of his bare chest, all hard muscle and deep tan, as if he sometimes stripped to the waist when working with the animals.

It was enough to make her mouth go dust dry, to remind her with a jolt that once upon a time, she'd loved the act of making love...and that that part of her life need not be over.

The thought was followed by a rush of guilt, followed by the realization that she didn't really know him.

He could be anyone—including someone who had heard of the bounty on her head. For all she knew, the convoluted tale that he had told her could be no more than a distraction, meant to engage her until the real killers could get here.

You're being ridiculous, she told herself. *Amanda said I could trust him,* and her former roommate was a woman who didn't trust lightly.

Hope's instincts, too, were insisting he was honest, her heart telling her he was as lost, as hollowed out by grief, as she'd been feeling this past year. But her heart had been wrong before, so tragically wrong, it was unlikely she would survive it, much less reclaim the happiness she dreamed of.

Still, she couldn't move as he drew her closer, couldn't do a thing but gasp as he ducked his head and pressed his warm lips to that scrap of tender flesh. Her eyelids closed, the heat of twisting flame behind them, and her only protest was a whimper when his mouth found hers.

Chapter 4

Dylan knew insanity. He'd seen it in Nitro's eyes this morning, when the bull had meant to kill him. He'd seen it dozens of times, in that mad moment when a wild stallion reached the intersection of testosterone and pain.

He was on the brink now, helpless to stop himself from claiming a kiss, from pouring every last bit of pent-up loneliness and longing into the connection. The stable light flickered and then died, but Dylan barely noticed, his attention on the murmur low in her throat and the way she tipped back her head.

Inflamed by her response, he pulled her even closer, his lips parting hers and the answering inferno burning through his stress, his grief and what was left of his self-control. Already rock hard, he leaned her back against the stacked straw, wanting nothing but her breasts cupped in his hands, her skin bare and sweating beneath his.

It wasn't sweat, however, but the hot trickle of a tear from her face that restored him to his senses. That had him remembering how much fresher her loss was than his own.

Swamped with shame, he stammered, "Sorry, Hope—so sorry. I wasn't thinking, didn't mean to—" A lie, he knew. Kissing her had been no accident. But that didn't make it right.

In the darkness, she turned from him, her voice muffled, perhaps with the bandanna. "I just wanted to forget," she said. "Forget everything, except…my dad's gone. Gone forever, Dylan, and here I am, in your arms, as if I could erase it."

The pain in her words had him aching to reach out to touch her, but he didn't dare for fear of the attraction still crackling between them. "What happened here tonight— this wasn't your fault. It was all mine, but it stops now, and I swear, on my honor, it won't happen again."

When she sniffled in the darkness, it sickened him to think he was the cause of such regret.

"What happened to the lights?" she asked.

Before he could answer her, he heard the creak of the stable door, followed by soft footsteps.

Dylan straightened, senses on alert for trouble, until a familiar voice spoke.

"Hope Woods, are you out here?" called the ranch's head housekeeper, Mathilda Perkins, who was even more of an institution around here than his own mother had been. "I brought a plate to your room, but you weren't there, so I thought maybe…"

As he came to his feet, Hope stood up beside him. A moment later, she was stripping off his jacket and shoving it back into his hands.

"She's warned me about fraternizing," she whispered, "told me I'd be sure to blow my cover."

"Don't let Mathilda fool you," he said, keeping his own voice low. "She's always warning the maids about us wild and woolly cowboys."

"After tonight, I see her point," Hope said, but Dylan

heard the fear behind the attempt at humor and mentally kicked himself again.

When Mathilda called her name once more, Hope answered, "I'm sorry, ma'am—I must've fallen asleep. I came out here to be alone, and—"

He stepped behind a stack of bales, hiding himself an instant before the beam of Mathilda's flashlight found Hope. Above it, he could just make out the head housekeeper's short, silvery-blond hair and worried face, floating in a sea of darkness.

"The power's gone out," she said. "I was worried. Didn't want you stumbling around or getting yourself hurt trying to find your way back inside."

"That was very kind of you, ma'am," Hope said, "but how did you know to look for me out here?"

"Someone mentioned seeing you head this way."

"*Who* mentioned it?" Hope answered, her voice strained.

"I believe it must have been— What's that in your hand, dear?"

A cloth fluttered behind Hope's back, so quickly that it took Dylan a moment to register the navy-and-white pattern of his bandanna.

He bit back a curse when Mathilda held out her hand expectantly.

"Show me," she said, in the voice of a woman used to having her orders heeded.

"You mind lowering that flashlight?" Hope asked, in the voice of a woman little used to taking orders. "The light in my eyes is giving me a headache."

The bright beam didn't waver, but there was a long, tense pause before Mathilda said, "Your face is flushed. And damp, too."

"That'll happen when a girl cries." Hope pulled the crumpled cotton square out from behind her back. "It's just somebody's old bandanna. I found it lying here, and it looked clean enough, so I used it to wipe my face."

"Oh, you poor thing." Compassion thawing her chill, Mathilda lowered her light and stepped forward to touch Hope's hand. "You're cold to the bone, dear, and after everything you've been through, I should've guessed you'd be upset. I just thought for a moment—"

"What did you think?" Hope asked.

"I imagined that you might've come out here to meet someone. I'm sorry. I know you're not— I know a woman of your background could hardly be interested in the likes of ranch hands. But you're such a pretty thing, and these young men can be quite charming when there's something they're after."

Her tone left no doubt what that *something* was, not that the head housekeeper's starched decorum would ever allow her to say the word.

"Believe me," Hope said with a bitterness that sliced straight through Dylan, "the last thing I want in my life right now is another charmer. At least not until I'm certain I'll live through the last one."

Gently ushering her toward the stable door, Mathilda said, "You heard what Miss Amanda told you. You're perfectly safe here on the ranch."

"Like Faye Frick and the last maid?" Hope challenged. "There was a young kitchen worker, too. At least that's what I've heard."

"Their deaths have nothing to do with you, I'm certain," Mathilda reassured her. "There's no need to worry."

"You really think so, ma'am?"

"I know so," the older woman said firmly, but kindly.

"Now come back inside and have some hot tea in the kitchen. Surely, someone will start up the gas stove, and you'll feel so much better once you've warmed up."

"Thank you," Hope said, risking a final glance in his direction....

Before robbing both the stable and Dylan of all light and warmth when she left him there alone.

Her lips still tingling with Dylan's kiss, Hope followed Mathilda Perkins toward the house in silence. Her thoughts careened wildly from the death of her father to her lapse in the barn—how right she'd felt, encircled by the wrangler's strong arms, and how very wrong she felt now, how sick with guilt and worry.

Your father's murdered, and the first thing you do is lock lips with some cowboy you met just this morning? But in that dim stall, cocooned in the intimacy of their conversation, Dylan Frick had felt less like a stranger than a refuge...a refuge she had known for years.

Her mind a thousand miles away, she nearly ran into Mathilda when she stopped abruptly to stare at the dark bulk of the mansion. An instant later, the kitchen door flew open, and members of the staff came pouring out. In pairs and small groups, they chattered among themselves. Hope couldn't make out their words from this distance, but she heard the undercurrent of anxiety crackling through their conversations. And cold as the night was, none of them had taken time to grab a jacket.

Heart thumping, she hurried after Mathilda, who made a beeline for another of the senior staff members, a short, plump redhead Hope recognized as the head cook, Agnes Barlow. During the past few days, Hope had heard her underlings refer to the woman as The Dragon Lady...but only after checking over their shoulders to be certain she was out of earshot.

Casting a look at the younger kitchen helper with her, Agnes snapped her fleshy fingers. "Over there, and quickly now. It's no safety drill this time." She gestured with her flashlight toward the paddock area, where a couple of the hands and another maid were heading.

As the young woman scurried off, Agnes called after her, "And be sure you don't go wandering off where I can't find you."

Ignoring Hope, who lingered just behind Mathilda, Agnes said, "Mr. Lowden came upstairs from the basement to tell us it's full of smoke down there—a burned, electrical smell you could make out from the kitchen. He said everyone in our wing should exit, nice and orderly, until we're given the all clear."

"The family, as well?" Mathilda asked. "Have they all been told? And what about poor Mr. Colton? This cold could make him sicker."

"Miss Amanda's seeing to it that everyone's informed, and she's sent one of the hands to help Dr. Colton move his father if it comes to it."

Concerned as she was about Amanda, Hope couldn't stop wondering what Trip Lowden might have been doing in the basement. Certainly, he wouldn't have gone to visit with the laundress, who barely tolerated intruders in her domain. Not even Coltons and their near relations, from what Hope had heard.

Her stomach crawled toward her throat as she wondered if Trip might have sneaked down on the chance of catching her there, or at the very least, finding out where his new "pet project" had gone.

"Has the fire department been called?" Mathilda

asked, turning back toward the door. Neither smoke nor flames were visible, but a few fat snowflakes spun like dancers through her flashlight's beam.

Agnes sniffed. "The whole place could go up before they get a fire truck out here, but Mr. Black grabbed an extinguisher from the kitchen and ran straight down to see what he could do about it."

At the mention of the ranch's maintenance man, Hope sucked in a sharp breath, remembering his wife's unsettling stare. "Is Mrs. Black still down there? The last I saw of her, she was lighting into me for being late with the laundry. Told me she'd be working half the night because of me."

Agnes blinked in surprise, as if a fence post had suddenly begun to speak. "You don't think she could've started the fire with an iron or a dryer, do you?"

Intimidating as the laundress was, Hope was more concerned about her safety than whether she might be to blame. "What if she's been burned or overcome by the smoke? Someone has to check."

Before Hope even realized she was on the move, Mathilda grasped her arm to stop her from charging toward the house. "Surely, her own husband will look for her down there. Now, you'd best get over by the paddock with the others. It's our designated staff meeting spot in case of an evacuation."

Hope turned her head to look. "But Mrs. Black's not there. And it'll be my fault if she's—" She cut herself off, unable to bear the thought. With the weight of grief and guilt already haunting her, she couldn't imagine having one more death on her conscience.

"You leave it to Mr. Black and Mr. Lowden, and just do as you're told," Agnes insisted, fisting one hand on an ample hip and scowling when Hope didn't move fast enough to suit her. "Have your ears frozen off, girl, or is it your brain that's iced over? Don't just stand there staring. Come along with me now, and leave Mrs. Perkins to her duties."

Hope shot a pleading look toward Mathilda, but the housekeeper was already turning and ordering two of the hands to gather some scrap lumber for a small fire, to warm the coatless group.

Out by the paddock, someone had set up and lit several lanterns, which cast an eerie flickering light over the small knots of employees, many of whom paced and stamped their feet against the cold. Hope wondered, would the family soon join them? Or would they meet in one of the barns, where they'd stay dry and warmer, too?

The moment she could, she slipped away to join another of the maids, the younger woman she had nearly run over on her way out to the stable.

"Sorry about before," Hope offered. Though the prim-and-proper Misty Mayhew—who had made several disparaging remarks about the quality of Hope's work—was hardly her favorite person, she needed to keep the peace. Especially if she wanted her help.

Misty tucked an escaping black curl back into the bun she wore and narrowed her blue eyes. "What were you doing earlier, bursting out of the basement like a bat out of you-know-where?"

Normally, Hope would have laughed at Misty's euphemism. But it was hard to find anything amusing tonight, particularly the suspicion she heard in the maid's voice.

"To tell you the truth," Hope said, "I was half-afraid Mrs. Black was right behind me, coming to tear my head off. You should've heard her down there."

Misty winced. "Late bringing down the laundry, were you? That old troll's such a horror!"

"I won't argue with you there, but I'm still worried. Have you seen her? If the smoke was really as bad as I've heard, she surely would've had to come out."

Misty shrugged her shoulders. "For all we know, she has a secret bunker down there—or she's set the fire herself to smoke out any visitors."

Seeing she would be no help, Hope turned to scan the small group, spotted Dylan trotting their way and ran over to tell him about the smoke coming up out of the basement.

"I've heard as much," he told her, nodding toward the two hands returning with armloads of dry wood. "I'm heading in to see what I can do to help Amanda."

"But we're supposed to stay out here."

"Not me, this time. Head of ranch security asked me to keep an eye on things while he's away for a few weeks—*Hope?*" he studied her face, his forehead creasing. "What is it?"

After once more explaining her worry over Mrs. Black, she added, "I can't let anyone else die because of me."

He laid his warm hand over hers. "You can't blame yourself for everything that happens, either. Here, you take this back now." Stripping off his jacket, he draped it over her shoulders. "I'll check on her and let you know as soon as I can."

"Thank you, but be careful. I don't—I don't trust Lowden."

"Trip?" The look that crossed Dylan's face spoke volumes. Dislike and suspicion, even a hint of resentment.

"He went down there with Mr. Black, right? Though it's hardly like Lowden to make himself useful."

"He was the one who came up to report the smoke and tell everyone they needed to evacuate the servants' wing."

Dylan hesitated. "That *is* strange. I've never seen or heard of him going down there for any reason. Thanks for the heads-up."

Before she could say another word, he left her, heading toward the mansion.

As the snowflakes settled gently, Hope wrapped Dylan's jacket tightly around her, and a trace of his masculine scent enveloped her, reassuring on some level.

But when she looked up, she noticed Misty in her maid's dress, rubbing at the gooseflesh along her bare arms. And staring straight at her with eyes so angry that Hope couldn't help but wonder: Did the gorgeous wrangler have a history of meeting other women inside dark stalls and haylofts?

Inside the house, Dylan walked through the dark kitchen, his borrowed flashlight cutting through faint layers of smoky haze. He smelled it as well, a sharply acrid odor that reminded him that the mansion's electrical panel was in a tiny utility room at one end of the basement.

The idea that the fire had started there made sense, considering the power outage that had preceded the evacuation. He only hoped that Mr. Black would be able to stop the smoldering before it ignited the whole mansion. As for Trip, well, maybe the walking parasite could at last make himself useful by holding a flashlight or something…unless his purpose in being down there was as sinister as Dylan couldn't help suspecting.

The real question was, could Trip be in league with the female mastermind seen running from the scene of an assault last month? It certainly made sense, if the culprit was his sister, Tawny, or their stepmother, Darla Colton. With Jethro Colton dying, all three must know their years of living large on the ranch were about to come to an abrupt end.

Then again, thought Dylan, there was always the chance that he was looking for any excuse to lean on Trip, who seemed bent on being as obnoxious as possible to every employee he encountered. As if he'd done a damned thing to earn his position.

A few steps from the basement door, Dylan found Amanda Colton holding a folded kerchief to her mouth.

"What are you doing here?" he asked her, wishing he had another bandanna of his own. "I thought everyone was heading outside."

"I sent the baby outside to the barn with Tom Brooks," she said, referring to the bodyguard she'd hired to look after Cheyenne in the wake of the kidnapping attempt. A former marine and cop, the grandfatherly but still-robust man had fallen for Amanda's daughter the moment he had met her. "But most of the others are holding off since there's no visible fire, and this is the only area besides the basement where there's smoke."

"So you're standing guard?"

She nodded. "Waiting to hear what Mr. Black says before I give the word to people in the other two wings."

He nodded, seeing the sense in that and not in the least surprised that the eldest Colton sister would take charge. "If it comes to that, I'll help you round up everybody. With the intercoms all out, that'll take some legwork."

"So far, the phones are working, but I'd still appreciate the help," she said.

He shared Hope's concern about Mrs. Black.

Amanda shook her head. "I haven't seen her, either. Maybe Mr. Black knows where she's gone."

Opening the basement door, she shouted down the stairs. "Mr. Black? Trip? Everything still okay down there?"

There was no answer, only an echoing clatter, as if someone had dropped a tool on the concrete floor. It was completely dark, too, but with the utility room at the basement's far end, it wasn't surprising to Dylan that he and Amanda couldn't see Trip's or Mr. Black's flashlights.

"Mrs. Black?" he called, his deeper voice echoing. "Are you still down there?"

Again, there was no response.

"I'd better go check on them," Amanda told him, her golden-brown eyes worried.

"Let me get this," Dylan told her. "If Lowden's up to something—"

He cut himself off, wondering if he'd said too much. Trip might be a worthless sponge of a stepbrother, but he was still Amanda Colton's family in a sense. And until—unless—it was proved otherwise, Dylan was a mere employee.

"It's okay to say it to me," she assured him. "I've been wondering about Trip and his sister a lot lately. So be careful down there, will you? And if there's anything you need, just call out, and I'll come help."

He shook his head, wishing he hadn't locked up Hope's gun in his room, but unwilling to take the time to go upstairs to retrieve it. "Don't even think about it. If you hear me yell, you call some of the hands and send them down here. Or Levi or whoever you can round up."

"Whichever *man,* you mean," she clarified.

Dylan didn't deny it, for if things came down to a hand-to-hand fight, he wouldn't want to see her hurt. "I'll let you know what I find," he promised before stepping through the doorway and starting down the stairs.

The smoke was thicker here for certain, the striated bands hazing in the flashlight's beam and causing him to cough. But it grew easier to breathe and see as he descended, assuring him that the worst of it had risen to the level of the basement ceiling.

Still, beyond the bright tunnel carved by his light, the darkness was complete and the cavernous basement far too quiet. He took a few steps forward, into the laundry area on his way to where the utility room lay, beyond several rows of shelving used for storage.

He swept his beam across the tools of Mrs. Black's trade: the gleaming surfaces of high-end commercial washers and dryers, a clothespress and an ironing board that pulled down from the wall.

He almost passed the iron itself, lying on its side on the floor behind a clothes bin. Without touching it, he looked more carefully, his gut twisting when he saw the wine-dark drip near its sharp tip.

Was that blood? The thought jolted through his body, leaving a sick chill in its wake.

"Mrs. Black?" he called, keeping his voice low enough so it wouldn't carry. "Mrs. Black, are you here?"

His body tensing, he counted down the pounding beats of his heart until he heard— Was that the scrape of movement just behind him?

He spun toward the sound, raking the flashlight's

beam across the staircase, but there was no one there, and he heard a male voice from the direction of the utility room.

It sounded upset, maybe angry, though he couldn't make out the words. But the speaker had a loud voice, which made him think of Mr. Black, who tended to overcompensate for his poor hearing.

Telling himself he'd only imagined the scraping noise before, Dylan moved with the quiet confidence he'd mastered trying to keep spooked cattle from stampeding. Schooling his breaths, he stepped around the seething knot of his emotions and found the calm, still center he relied upon, the heart of who he was.

Taut with tension, Mr. Black's voice reached out to him with icy fingers. "It's been tampered with, Mr. Lowden. See here. Someone's taken off the deadman panel—that's a safety panel to keep folks from electrocuting themselves—and set it over here. Then he used magnets to put this metal bar across the inside of the outer cover."

Sabotage. Dylan's calm shimmered and then dissolved like the mirage it was. Had whoever tampered with the power killed the sole potential witness? But as urgent as it was for them to locate Mr. Black's wife, Dylan hesitated when Trip began to speak.

"So this was definitely done on purpose?" he asked.

"Oh, yes, sir. I'm sure of it. By somebody who knows what he's about, too. See that broomstick by your feet there? I'd bet anything he used it to push the outer cover shut."

"Why a broomstick?"

"Wooden handle won't conduct electricity and fry you half as easy. You see, sir, soon as he shoved it closed,

there would've been an awful lot of arcing and sparking—
see those darker burned spots? The whole thing's melted
down."

"You can get the power back on, can't you?" Trip
sounded whiny and petulant, as if all of this had been
done to inconvenience him. "You've got a spare one of
those whatchamacallits somewhere, don't you?"

"A whole electric panel, with all the wiring to replace
what's burned up?" The maintenance man sounded in-
credulous. "No, sir, and even if I did, I'm not licensed
to install it. But I'll have Miss Amanda put in a call to
the electricians we have on retainer and the police, of
course."

Trip made a scoffing sound. "Oh, right. Like those idiots are batting a thousand lately solving crimes around
here."

Dylan wanted to drag the pampered fool out by the
scruff of his neck and rearrange his pretty-boy face, but
he kept his peace, willing Trip to say something to explain his presence here—or, better yet, incriminate himself. And wishing that Trevor Garth, the head of ranch
security, hadn't picked this week to try to reconnect with
the supposedly reformed father who'd abandoned him
years earlier. The former foreman, Dylan's good friend
Gray Stark, had left, too, after asking Dylan to keep an
eye on things here on the ranch.

"Those electricians need to get out here right away,"
Trip continued. "We'll need heat and light, and there's
the football on tonight."

As much as Dylan despised the freeloader, he had to
admit that Trip sounded, true to form, more self-absorbed
than malicious. Besides, there was no way he had the

smarts to sabotage the electrical panel without turning himself into a smoldering heap of ash.

Pleasant as that thought was, Dylan didn't linger on it, announcing his presence by calling, "Mr. Black? Mr. Lowden? Miss Amanda sent me downstairs to make sure there's no fire."

Mr. Black poked his graying head out of the cramped utility room. "What smoldering there was is out now," he reported, hefting a small extinguisher to show Dylan. "But we'll be without power for a day or two—and that's if we can get the electricians out here on the double."

"They'll get it fixed tonight if they mean to keep our business," Trip grumbled.

"Oh, no, sir," Mr. Black said, the gaps from several missing teeth looking even starker in the near darkness. "That's impossible. There'll have to be a special panel this size brought in out of Cheyenne, or maybe even Denver. And we'll need a complete inspection before we can risk switching it back on."

"I'm afraid we have a bigger problem," Dylan said. "I can't find Mrs. Black."

Mr. Black stiffened. "Bernice isn't outside with the others?"

"I didn't see her anywhere," Dylan said. "Could she have gone home to your cabin?"

"Not without me, no. I have our truck's keys right here in my pocket."

"She might've walked," Trip speculated.

"No, sir." Mr. Black walked out of the utility room, shaking his head emphatically. "Not my Bernice, not after dark, in this cold, and never once in all these years without a word to me."

"We'll find her, sir," Dylan swore, though in light of

the previous murders of ranch employees, he couldn't promise that Mrs. Black would still be breathing.

Especially not when he kept picturing that dark red drop, gleaming on the sharp steel tip of the iron. And he couldn't help but wonder what damage that humble instrument might have done if used to strike a human skull.

Chapter 5

Hope was standing slightly apart from those huddling around the bonfire, so immersed in her own grief and worry that she paid no attention to the approaching footsteps. Until she recognized the hiss of Misty's voice behind her.

"Must be nice to be all cozy wearing that warm jacket. You earn it on your knees, Hope? Could *that* be why you were in such a hurry to get to the stable earlier?"

Hope whirled around to face her, wanting to scream at her to shut her filthy mouth. She swallowed back her angry words, reminding herself that Misty's disgusting suggestion had nothing to do with the kiss she'd shared with Dylan in the stable. A kiss she would swear he'd needed as desperately as she had. "He was only being kind. And unlike you, he listened when I told him Mrs. Black might still be downstairs."

"You might be new," said Misty, hugging her own arms for warmth, "but you're not stupid. I'll give you that. You found out he could be coming into money, didn't you? Heir to heaven only knows how many millions."

Hope snorted and waved her off. "If he is, he's welcome to them."

"Don't pretend you don't care. That you wouldn't want to be rich as a Colton."

"Then don't pretend you'd be interested in Dylan if he turns out to have the wrong DNA to suit you."

Misty's blue eyes narrowed. "I'll tell Mrs. Perkins what you're up to! I'm her favorite, you know. I know how to make a room gleam and never sneak off to do heaven knows what when I'm supposed to be inside working."

Hope wondered, would Mathilda see through Misty's jealousy or believe her? After all, the head housekeeper had been instantly suspicious when she had spied the blue-and-white bandanna in Hope's hand. But surely Mathilda would know Hope was far from the type to be dazzled by the prospect of money and status.

Or would the housekeeper believe she was desperate to find another wealthy man? Desperate enough to pursue Dylan for his potential windfall rather than settle for a life filled with hard work, an ugly uniform and a bedroom smaller than her old shoe closet?

"Tell her whatever you like," Hope said, refusing to be reduced to squabbling with this grasping little idiot. "I'll be busy praying that everyone gets out of that house safely."

And praying, too, that this fire was only minor—and a mere coincidence. Praying that it didn't mean her ex's capos, as he called his lieutenants, had somehow managed to track her here and torch the Colton mansion, too.

Ignoring Trip, Dylan spoke to Mr. Black directly. "Your wife has to be down here somewhere. Surely, someone would have seen her if she'd have been forced upstairs or carried."

"Let me go up and tell Amanda," Trip suggested. "She

can send some servants down here to give you a hand looking."

"You're not going anywhere," Dylan said firmly. "I'll tell Amanda and come right back. You can stay with Mr. Black and help him look."

"Just who do you think you're talking to?" Trip demanded.

"Someone who's probably never seen the inside of this basement before he came down here this evening. Why is that?"

"You're forgetting your place, wrangler. I don't have to explain myself to the employees."

Dylan shrugged. "Fine, then you can talk to the police about it. And your stepfather, too, because I'm absolutely certain everyone will be wondering why you'd dirty your hands down here."

"If you must know, I was looking for something I'd had brought down and put in storage."

"What?" Dylan challenged. "What was so important you wouldn't send a servant for it, *Mister* Lowden?"

Trip glared at Dylan's impertinence before snapping his fingers.

"I know what's gotten into you. I've heard these insane rumors." Trip's lip curled back in a sneer. "The very idea that some stupid hand who spends most of his day stinking of manure could be an honest-to-God Colton. We laugh about it in the family wings, how you're wasting precious hours dreaming of dollar signs when you're bound to spend your whole life mucking stalls and—"

"None of that. Not now, sir!" Mr. Black burst out, clearly beside himself to interrupt even a shirttail relation of the Coltons. "You've got to help me find my Bernice! She could be hurt, or even…"

But it was Dylan's curled fist Trip was staring at when he abruptly said, "Of course I want to help. Where do we start, Mr. Black?"

Dylan took a deep breath, willing his pounding heart to slow. Mr. Black was right; finding his wife quickly was a lot more important than getting sucked into Trip's bull.

"I've searched the laundry area already," Dylan told them. "And I'm sorry to tell you that I found an iron, with what might be a little blood on it."

"But no sign of my wife?" Mr. Black asked, sounding as if he might break down any moment.

Dylan shook his head. "You might start there, though, then check out the storage area. There are a lot of places where someone could—" He cut himself off before finishing what he'd been about to say: *where someone could hide a body.*

"Stick together," Dylan reminded them, "in case whoever did this is still down here. And don't touch anything, especially that iron. There may be fingerprints."

He finished with a hard look into Trip's face. "I'll be back before you can miss me."

With that, he hurried upstairs and quickly apprised Amanda of the situation. "You can let everyone come back inside, but be sure to send down four or five good people—people we can trust not to lose their heads— with flashlights or electric lanterns to help us search. Might want to make a couple of 'em strong men, just in case."

"I'm coming, too," Amanda told him, splashes of color staining her cheeks.

"I wish you wouldn't," he said. "You're needed up here to make sure the police are called and everyone stays calm. And one more thing. I want you to send Hope straight to her room. Just a while ago, she learned her father's been killed—"

"What?" Amanda clapped her hand to her mouth before recovering enough to drop her voice to a whisper. "Was it her ex-husband? Did he find some way to—"

"No one knows for certain, but she's convinced he was behind it. As upset as she is, people might get suspicious and start asking questions."

"Thank you, Dylan. I'll take care of her. You just concentrate on finding Mrs. Black—and keep a close eye on Trip, too, while you're down there."

"Don't worry. I'm not turning my back on him for a second," he said, already wondering, as he started downstairs, if Trip could have been faking his ignorance about electrical parts. For all Dylan knew, the mastermind or another of her lackeys may have given him a recent crash course.

Halfway down the stairs, Dylan heard a shout of alarm close by.

"Bernice! Bernice, sweetheart!" Mr. Black cried.

Dylan hurried downstairs and turned to look behind the steps, where Mr. Black had shoved aside some plastic storage bins to kneel beside his wife. She lay on her side, with her knees drawn toward her thick waist. Her long, iron-gray hair had come loose from its ponytail, and her arm was covering her face, as if the beam from Trip's flashlight hurt her eyes.

"She's conscious?" Dylan asked.

"Bernice," Mr. Black said, "can you speak to me? Say something."

A low moan was her only answer.

"Don't move her," Dylan said. "I'll get help."

Running back to the staircase, he shouted for Amanda.

"We'll need Dr. Colton down here. Mrs. Black's been hurt."

Amanda wasn't at her post, but she had stationed Mathilda Perkins there in her stead. Working with her usual efficiency, the head housekeeper quickly found Levi Colton and relayed the message.

Within minutes Levi came hurrying downstairs, his medical bag in hand. A lean young man with a serious expression, he'd only recently returned to the ranch to help treat Jethro—reluctantly, Dylan thought, since the old man had previously ignored his illegitimate son.

For just a moment, Dylan mentally compared the two of them. Levi lacked the tan and the brawn Dylan had earned working outdoors with livestock, but he looked to be about the same height as Dylan's own six-two. And despite the doctor's lighter hair and the hazel eyes, there was something familiar in the way those eyes were shaped, or maybe it was the jawline.

Could it really be possible Levi was a half brother, as closely related as Amanda, Gabby and Catherine Colton? Or was Dylan deluding himself, imagining a family where he had none, a connection with those who were sure to see him as some kind of pretender to the throne?

No, no... He shoved aside the unsettling thoughts, reminding himself this was no time to let his doubts—or Trip Lowden's cruel words—get under his skin.

As Levi reached the bottom of the staircase, he asked, "Where is she?"

"Right over here." Dylan led him to the spot, saying, "Looks like she was hit on the back of the head, with an iron, I think."

"Excuse me," Levi said to Mr. Black, who was on his knees and holding his wife's hand.

"She's in terrible pain," the older man said, still blocking Levi's way. "Please, Doc, can you help her?"

Levi touched his arm. "I promise I'll do all I can. Now, why don't you run upstairs and see if there's any way Agnes can brew us all up some fresh coffee? This could be a long night."

"I—I'll see what I can do about getting a backup generator on line for the kitchen."

Dylan understood at once that Levi was getting the distraught man out of his way, but Mr. Black looked grateful to be given something useful to do, something that, even in a small way, would aid his wife's recovery.

Trip, on the other hand, already looked so antsy that Dylan suggested—none too politely—that he ought to go upstairs as well, and see what he could do to help Amanda. Most likely, he'd duck out on the "help" option and simply go whine to his mother and sister about being forced to miss his precious football game instead. But better that than keeping him here, irritating Dylan every time he opened his mouth.

Later, though, he'd track down Lowden, or better yet, suggest to the police chief that he question Trip more closely about what had happened.

Mrs. Black was sitting up now, holding her hand to the back of her head as she told the doctor, "Don't touch it again, and keep that damnable light out of my eyes."

Dylan couldn't help but smile, relieved to hear that a clout on the head hadn't cost her the special brand of "charm" she was so famous for.

"Can you tell me your full name?" Levi asked her, followed by questions about the time of day and her location.

Glaring with her mismatched eyes, Mrs. Black snapped

out the answers, right about all except the time, which she guessed to be just after lunch.

Levi asked her to follow his light with her good eye, stretch out her arms and then touch her nose with each index finger, but she finally lost patience when he asked her to smile.

"You tell me what I have to smile about and I'll be glad to!" she barked.

Dylan interrupted the examination to ask her, "Do you remember anything about what happened or who hit you?"

The laundress struggled to answer before admitting, "I don't know. I can't remember anything past bringing a roast-beef sandwich and an apple downstairs for my lunch."

"After a head injury," Levi explained, "retrograde amnesia's very common."

"Retro-*what?*" she asked, gingerly touching the sore spot.

"It means you have no memory of what happened just before the blow to your head. The memories might be gone forever, or they could return."

"For Mrs. Black's safety," Dylan suggested, "maybe we should all stick to saying she doesn't remember. Otherwise, whoever did this might try to—"

"To shut me up forever?" Mrs. Black's eyes widened and her already-pale skin went paler with the thought.

"If you remember anything," Dylan said, "you could tell one of us or police chief Peters. No one else, Mrs. Black, not even your husband. Because if it gets mentioned to the wrong person…"

Levi nodded, his expression more serious than ever. "That's a good idea, and let's get you away from the ranch for a while, too. I'll want you to go to Cheyenne Memorial for a CT scan. I don't have privileges there, but I'll make a few calls and see that you're admitted for overnight observation, at least."

She protested emphatically, complaining about the long drive and waste of money even after Levi assured her the cost would be completely covered since she was injured on the job.

"And they're sure to stick me with a dozen needles." She shuddered visibly. "That's what all your kind do. When they're not prescribing enemas."

"There'll be no enema, I promise."

How Levi managed to keep a straight face, Dylan would never know.

The argument ended when Mr. Black returned, a mug of coffee in hand, and heard the doctor explaining that an undetected brain bleed might cost Mrs. Black her life. Taking charge, the maintenance man insisted she was going and helped Levi get her upstairs and into the Blacks' pickup for the forty-minute drive.

Dylan, meanwhile, stopped the two hands and the pair of housemaids Amanda had sent to help him search the basement.

"Now that Mrs. Black's been found," he told them, "it's better we all stay upstairs. The police won't want us disturbing any evidence that might have been left down there—or leaving any extra fingerprints they'll need to sort through."

Misty Mayhew shook her head, her blue eyes wide. "But won't some of us already have our fingerprints down there? We can't be blamed for the places our duties take us!"

"Surely, they'll take that into account," said Hilda

Zimmerman, an older maid who spent her nights at home in town with her husband. "Won't they, Dylan?"

He hurried to reassure the kindly woman, whose sweet demeanor reminded him so much of his mother's. "Of course they will," he told her. "You've got nothing to be concerned about."

Unless your prints are on that deadman panel, the broomstick or that iron—the way I'm guessing Trip's will be.

Chapter 6

From the moment Amanda caught her eye, Hope knew Dylan must have said something about her father's death. The sympathy in her friend's gaze was nearly her undoing.

As she came inside with the others, Amanda spoke quietly in her ear. "Go wait in my solarium, and I'll come as soon as I can. Do you remember where it is?"

Her emotions too close to the surface to dare speaking, Hope nodded, recalling the quiet little sunroom off Amanda's suite. With its beautiful white wicker furnishings and its potted tropical plants, it reminded her of the cozy little childhood nook where she'd hidden away to read sometimes or simply bask in the weak sunlight of a winter day. There was even a gorgeous, long-haired orange cat, a purring, tailless cutie Amanda called Reyna, a reminder of happier times when Hope had had pets of her own.

But the best things about Amanda's solarium were the powered louvers that could be closed to cover up the windows. No one would see or hear them speaking—a conversation Hope felt certain would end with Amanda asking her to leave.

About twenty minutes later, Amanda came in carrying her daughter, Cheyenne, who lay sound asleep with her head on her mother's shoulder.

"She's adorable," Hope managed, though she couldn't trust herself to look into the baby's face without losing it completely. *If I hadn't wanted a child of my own so badly, hadn't let it blind me...*

Fortunately, little Cheyenne didn't stir when Amanda put her down in a portable playpen off to one side and covered her with a light blanket. Crossing the room, Amanda hugged Hope tightly. "I'm so sorry about your dad."

"It was a fire," Hope said, fresh guilt knifing through her. "And a fire here today, too. He *knows,* Amanda. Renzo's found me again."

Amanda gestured toward a love seat. "You don't know that. You can't."

Tired of her own pacing, Hope forced herself to sit. "While I was walking over here, I overheard your sister Gabby telling Mathilda that the power was sabotaged. That's what caused the fire, she said."

Amanda perched on the edge of a chair, her mouth pressed in a grim line. "That's true, but we've had a lot of other issues on the ranch lately. So there's no way to know if this has anything to do with—"

"I don't believe in coincidences this big. I can't afford to." Crossing her arms tightly, Hope wished for the comforting warmth of Dylan's jacket. To avoid more unwanted attention, she'd hung it on the rack outside the employee dining area, despite the mansion's growing chill. "My father's gone, Amanda. Horrible as it is, I can't do anything about that. But it's not too late to leave here before anyone else ends up dead because of me. It's bad enough that Mrs. Black—"

"So you heard that she was found?"

"Found hurt, I understand. Will she be all right? Do you know yet?"

"Most likely, she'll be just fine. She's awake and talking. Levi only sent her to the hospital as a precaution."

"Thank God. I couldn't stand it if— I know she doesn't like me much, but—"

"Probably as much as she likes anybody, if it's any consolation."

Hope tried to smile at Amanda's wry face, but she couldn't pull it off. Not tonight. "Does she know who hurt her? Did she see anything?"

When Amanda shook her head, Hope sighed in relief. "I hate to ask you this, but if I could get a ride to Cheyenne and borrow enough to cover bus fare…I wouldn't ask, but I used almost everything I had on me after the bombing to hide out and then get here, and there's no way I can risk accessing my own money."

She had a trust fund from her mother and money she'd saved from a string of commercials she'd done for local businesses following her pageant days, including a car dealership owned by the friend of Renzo's who had introduced them. Though she'd transferred every penny of it in the hours before she'd left home, she couldn't touch it until she testified, nor could she risk pawning the diamond ring she'd so carefully sewn into her bra. In a town as small as Dead, one of Joey's men could have easily bribed the local pawnshop owner to be on the lookout for her.

"You're not going anywhere." Amanda straightened her spine, a fierce determination lighting her golden eyes.

A feeling of déjà vu shivered through Hope. Where was it she'd seen that same look so recently? Shoving aside the odd thought, she argued, "But I can't stay. I can't possibly put you and your family and everyone in danger—"

"You aren't getting on a bus. That's crazy. If your ex's people tracked you this far, the Cheyenne terminal would be the very next place they'll look. And they'll find you, Hope. They will. Because you might be wearing those big glasses and that shapeless gray dress, but your walk, your speech, even the way you stand— You can take the girl out of the pageant, but you can't take the pageant out of the girl. Or maybe it's the socialite. I'm not sure. In either case, you're noticeable. Memorable, especially to men."

Hope frowned. "I could always strap down my bazoombas."

Amanda snorted. "Yeah, right. Just how much duct tape do you think we keep around this ranch?"

Hope couldn't help herself. She laughed, a desperate sound closer to hysteria than humor, then burst out weeping moments later, her emotions tumbling quick as thought from grief to guilt. How could *anything* be funny right now, with her father lying dead? With all the lives lost to her string of bad decisions.

Amanda, to her credit, didn't try to stop her. Instead, she brought a box of tissues and waited with infinite patience for the storm to pass. As she did, her cat rubbed past her legs purring like a coffee grinder and the baby slept, oblivious to the turmoil around her.

Hope dabbed at her eyes, though she suspected her mascara was already a lost cause. "Sorry. I know you always hated it when I acted like such a girl."

"Believe me," Amanda said, "I've shed some tears of my own since the two of us were roommates."

Hope knew there'd been an attempt to kidnap baby

Cheyenne, just as she knew Amanda's little daughter was the love of her life. The thought set off a pang of pain and longing, and the wish that they could really talk about the events of this past year.

But there were some secrets Hope couldn't bear to divulge to anyone, and besides, she knew how fiercely private Amanda had always been, to the point where she hadn't even mentioned the child's father. So Hope let her change the subject, let herself be talked into staying.

"At least until we know for sure," Hope reluctantly conceded.

Amanda refused to let it go at that. "Even if we find out you're right, there's no way in this world I'm going to let that sick SOB hunt you down like an animal and kill you. I've got your back, Aurora, no matter how hard things get."

It was only afterward, when walking back toward the servants' wing, using an armload of soiled towels as cover, that Hope realized why it was that Amanda's stubborn loyalty, her fierce determination to do the right thing by an old friend, had seemed so strangely familiar. Earlier this evening, she'd seen the same look already, the same posture, the same mannerisms in another person.

In Dylan Frick.

Could it be because the two of them had practically grown up together, then worked so closely as adults? Or was the similarity genetic?

Were they really half brother and sister, after all?

Early the following morning, Dylan took a deep breath and braced himself before knocking. In years past, Jethro Colton had summoned him any number of times: to talk about this horse or that heifer, to get his take on a new breeding or vaccination program.

But never before had he been invited to see Jethro in his private suite. And never before had he been forced to report to the man who might just, heaven help him, turn out to be his father.

"Come on in," called the familiar voice. Brusque, impatient, no different than Dylan had heard it a thousand times before.

He stepped inside a sitting room that served as an entryway, softly lit with a pair of oil lanterns. The greens and golds and dark, espresso-colored wood looked comfortable and masculine…and nothing like the jeweled and gilded throne room he and his friends had imagined growing up here as employees' brats.

One of the room's framed photos caught his eye, this one of a beautiful young woman—Jethro's first wife, the late Brittany Beal Colton—holding a tiny baby swaddled in a blanket embroidered with the name *Cole.* Dylan stared at both, feeling a trace of sadness to think of two young lives wasted, for the more he thought about it, the more firmly he believed that the missing child must be dead. Tragic, yes, to imagine Desiree or perhaps some coconspirator murdering an innocent, but it had happened years ago, and he felt nothing to indicate the woman was anything more than a stranger to him, just as he felt no particular connection to the infant in her arms.

Not me, he thought, relief cascading through him, for in his line of work, Dylan had learned to rely upon his instincts. To trust them with his life or pay the consequences.

"All the way in. Don't just stand out there," Jethro ordered from the adjoining bedroom.

"Yes, sir." Dylan walked in to where Colton sat in one of two wingback chairs in front of a blazing fireplace.

The massive, four-poster bed behind those chairs looked freshly made, though Jethro still wore his thick, black robe over fleece pajamas, along with a permanent scowl.

"You're looking well, sir," Dylan told him, though his employer—his boss and not his father—was thinner than before and clearly frailer, his tanned skin faded to a bruised translucence.

Could the leukemia's ravages be stopped, even reversed, with a transplant of bone marrow from a matching donor, or was it already too late? Even if a perfect match were found, Dylan knew there was no guarantee that Jethro, who had fought treatment at every step of the way, would change his mind and consider a transplant, no matter how his daughters pleaded.

"Looking well, my ass." Judging from the scowl on Jethro's face, the possibility of a miracle cure was the furthest thing from his mind. "You don't get paid enough to stand here lying to me, so sit down, boy."

Dylan felt his body go stiff at Jethro's gruffness, a painful reminder of his recent refusal to pay the ransom of a mere employee's infant girl, even though the baby was only taken after being mistaken for Jethro's granddaughter, Cheyenne Colton. And even though Dylan's own mother had died defending her, Colton had never once acknowledged the loss. "I'd just as soon stand if it's all the same to you. Sir."

"It's not. Makes my neck ache looking up at you."

Dylan conceded the point, lowering himself into the chair and waiting for Jethro to get around to the reason he'd been asked here. He knew very well that the old

man had already demanded—and been given—reports
on the basement fire and power outage by Amanda and
the police chief, neither of whom had shared the details
of the investigation with Dylan.

"So tell me," Jethro said, "what the hell is really going
on around the ranch these days?"

"We've finished separating out the weanlings from
their mamas," he said, speaking of the beef cattle he
knew so well, since he'd been acting as the ranch's temporary foreman, "and we've put the young stock on the
feeding program you approved last summer. Weights are
looking good so far, and we've had zero mortality this
year, down from—"

"That's not what I meant and you know it. Tell me
about what happened in the basement. I heard you were
down there before anybody except Horace Black and
my stepson."

Dylan shook his head, unwilling to discuss his suspicions about Trip and Tawny without hard evidence. And
there was no way in hell he was sharing details about
Hope's situation—or her ex-husband's apparent penchant
for settling scores with arson. "I honestly couldn't say."

Ailing or not, Jethro fixed him with a look that contained every bit of his old shrewdness. "Couldn't? Or
won't?"

"If you're looking for a spy to share the latest half-
baked speculation, you've got the wrong man," Dylan
answered. "If I were you, I'd be more inclined to listen
to what the cops have to say once they process whatever
evidence they collected."

Jethro chuckled, and if Dylan didn't know any better,
he'd almost swear he saw a glint of fondness in Colton's
flinty eyes. But then, Jethro had been the one to take

note of and capitalize on Dylan's talents, back when he was still a half-grown kid. From time to time, Dylan had overheard him boasting of his "large-animal whisperer" to other ranchers as well, though the old man had never praised him to his face.

"I figured that's what you'd say," Jethro admitted.

"Then why call me in here?" Dylan asked.

"Because there's something I needed to say to you. Something I've neglected far too long."

Dylan's mouth went chalk-dry, and his palms grew clammy. Had Jethro found out about the DNA test he had taken? Had he somehow intercepted the results—or bribed some lab technician into giving him inside information? Unable to speak, Dylan simply waited, the sound of his own heartbeat crashing in his ears.

"I just wanted to tell you that I'm sorry. About how your mother died."

Dylan stared back in confusion, his thoughts jumping from the sweet woman who had raised him to the photo in the sitting room. Could his instincts have been wrong about Brittany Beal Colton? Could he actually be…?

Jethro stared into the fire, waiting, and Dylan sensed that he was being tested. Being played, perhaps, by a man eager to find out just how interested a mere employee was in claiming a portion of the Colton empire. An empire spun from thin air, as far as anyone had figured. Oh, everyone agreed that after his initial purchase of the ranch, Jethro's shrewdness, his business sense and the fortunate discovery of a natural-gas reserve beneath the ranch's rockier northwestern portion had amplified his fortune, but not even that could entirely account for his billionaire status. And where on earth had he gotten close to a million dollars to buy the ranch in cash in the first place?

As stubbornness and loyalty joined forces, Dylan finally responded. "She was a good woman. And the *best* mother any kid could've asked for." *A woman who loved me so much, she might have been willing to kill to raise me.* "And you're about five months late with your condolences…*sir.*"

"You're right." The words twisted Jethro's lips, as if he'd rarely had occasion to admit such. Or was he disappointed in Dylan's reaction? "Faye Frick was a fine employee and a caring teacher to my children, to all the children on this ranch. A beautiful woman, too, back when she first came here."

Dylan blinked in surprise, remembering his mother as a plump, matronly figure who kept her dark hair plainly styled and wore little makeup. Come to think of it, he realized he had never seen a photo showing her in her younger years, and his early memories of her were a blur.

"I see you don't believe me," Jethro told him, "but she was a real beauty then, almost as pretty as my first wife, Brittany." This time, the old man's probing look left little doubt that, though he'd been kept isolated to protect him from infection, he clearly had heard something about the suspicions swirling around his ranch wrangler.

"Tell me about her," Dylan said, wondering which of the employees had been currying favor by feeding Jethro bits of information. "I've been curious about your first wife." *Curious why she'd abandon you and her kid, then get herself killed in a one-car accident a few months later…*

"Why would you be?" asked Jethro bluntly, clearly wanting him to admit that he knew she might be his birth mother.

But Dylan wasn't ready to give him the satisfaction. "Because someone's tried to kidnap your heir, Miss Amanda's daughter. And judging from the number of attacks and killings these past few months, there's no indication this is over. So if there's an answer somewhere in your past, a way to stop this violence and figure out who was behind my mother's murder—"

"It was nothing to do with Brittany or—" Jethro coughed, sounding like a truck with a bad starter, and his face reddened. "Nothing to do with her or the boy, either one."

This is the point where Amanda and her sisters would want you to back off, Dylan told himself, *to avoid upsetting Jethro.* But there were questions far too important to allow to go unanswered—or to be taken to the grave.

"Sir, I think it just might. Please. My mother *died* in one of these attacks, and you waited five long months to say you were sorry."

"I've been a little damned distracted lately, in case you haven't noticed," Jethro answered, his face growing a shade redder. "And you're still an employee, at least for the time being."

Dylan didn't know whether Jethro was referring to the DNA test or threatening him with dismissal, but he no longer cared. "All I'm asking for are a few answers." *I wouldn't take another damned thing from you if you begged me.*

Jethro scowled fiercely, a look that would have once made Dylan back off. But this morning, he felt reckless— or desperate—enough to hold his ground.

Jethro looked away first, glaring back into the fire. "She was a real beauty, that little Brittany. Prettiest girl I'd ever laid eyes on. Young, too. So damned young and so sweet. And dumb enough to imagine she'd be happy out here in the middle of nowhere with no company but a baby and a man too busy building an empire to spend time worrying over how she'd feel about every little thing."

"So it was the ranch life that made her leave? That was it?" Had it driven her to drink, too, an issue that eventually caused her to swerve off the road, or was Jethro, difficult as he was, to blame for her defection?

Jethro answered with a deeper cough, only this time, Dylan went to a small table at his bedside and poured him some fresh water.

"You all right?" he asked as Jethro drank from his water glass and repeatedly cleared his throat. "You need me to get Dr. Colton?"

Jethro waved off the suggestion. "It's just this fireplace, drying me out. I'll be fine—fine for a dying man, that is—as soon as those electricians get their tails out here and get the power back on."

Dylan nodded, making no mention of the night he and many other employees had spent shivering beneath extra blankets in their cooling rooms. Some had bedded down on the floor of the great room instead, after the Colton daughters had suggested they light the huge fireplace to keep warm. If the power wasn't back by tonight, he imagined he would join them, under the imperious gaze of the huge portrait that hung above the mantel, of a virile, vital Jethro Colton in full rancher regalia. As if they were a bunch of damned supplicants, worshipping at his altar.

But since this might be his only chance to speak to Jethro in private, Dylan ventured another question. "So she never contacted you again? Never called to ask about her baby after she—"

Jethro stiffened. "I'm not so damned sick I don't know impertinence when I hear it. And I'll remind you, wrangler, the last fellow who got delusions that he might be entitled to a share of Colton money found himself very much mistaken on the matter. That Jagger journalist fellow took us all for a ride."

Stunned by that assumption, Dylan blasted back, "Everyone knows that was never Jagger's intention, and it's sure as hell not mine."

"*Out.* Now. And take your questions with you." Jethro broke into—or faked—the loudest, longest coughing spell yet.

Moments later, there was a tap at the door, and Misty Mayhew came in, pushing the cart of cleaning tools and supplies all the maids took with them to their assigned areas. After darting an alarmed look from Dylan to the still-hacking Jethro, she said, "Let me get Dr. Colton. I think he was coming up the hall right behind me."

He must have been, for Levi arrived quickly and pulled a stethoscope from his medical bag to listen to Jethro's lungs.

"I'm not hearing any rattles," Levi told him. "Your lungs sound clear for now."

While Jethro reached for his water glass again, Dylan explained, "He said the dry air from the fire's bothering his throat, or maybe it's the woodsmoke." *Or my questions.* "Let me see if I can find someone to help me crank up a portable generator outside, and we'll snake a line and an extension cord either up the stairs or through the bedroom window."

Normally, Mr. Black would have done more to make the family comfortable by now, but as far as Dylan knew, he was still in Cheyenne with his wife.

Levi nodded. "Definitely do that, and we'll get space heaters and a humidifier going. Also, could you see about getting the infirmary back on line, too, just in case I need to treat him there?"

"Sure thing, Levi," Dylan answered before leaving disappointed, dead certain he'd just blown what might be his last chance to get the answers that could lead him to the mastermind.

And hoping like hell he wasn't related to either Jethro Colton or the woman who had left her infant, seemingly without so much as a backward glance.

Hope worked more quickly than usual, counting on her exertions to help warm her. She wore a light cardigan sweater over her dress, but despite the mansion's chill, Mathilda Perkins was unwilling to relax her strict dress code further to allow any of the maids to wear long pants—as if Amanda Colton or her sister Gabby would have an attack of the vapors at the sight of the household staff in jeans.

Come to think of it, Tawny, who was packing her stylish designer overnight bag in the next room, might. But soon, she would be gone, driving to Denver with her equally snobbish mother, where they would check into a five-star hotel until the power was turned back on at the ranch.

With any luck, they'd convince Trip to leave with them, too, and he'd become so engrossed watching sports—or porn—and ordering room service, he'd forget to come back home.

Smiling at the thought of their absence, Hope scrubbed at some stubborn spatter on Tawny's bathroom counter. When she saw that she was making no headway, she glanced back at her cleaning cart. What was it that Hilda Zimmerman had suggested would do the trick?

Frowning at a white bottle with a torn label, she went ahead and sprayed, but before she could put a sponge to the problem, she heard a sharp tap at the suite's hallway door a moment before it was opened.

"Hey!" said Tawny, sounding as annoyed as ever. "Did I tell you you could come in?"

"Sorry, miss. Excuse us," called a male voice. A voice that made Hope's vision swirl as the blood rushed to her head. "Electricians. Mr. Colton wants the whole place gone over to make sure everything's unplugged so we can—"

Every cell of her being shrieked at Tawny: *order them to go away! Throw a giant tantrum! After all, it's the one darned thing you're good at.*

But Tawny only said, "About time you people got here. Think you'll have it fixed soon?"

Heart pounding like a snared rabbit's, Hope looked frantically to the bathroom window, with its smoked glass. But it wasn't made to open, and even if she smashed it, she'd have a bone-shattering drop to the ground from up here on the third floor.

"Two, three days," said another male voice, one Hope didn't recognize. Was he another of her husband's soldiers, or a freelance hit man the organization had contracted just for this job? Or had she been wrong about the first man, the one who sounded exactly like— What was his name? Oh, yes, Joey Santorini, the one she'd once naively imagined was nicknamed "The Jawbreaker" because he liked the candy.

"Makes no difference to *moi*," said Tawny. "I'm off

to Denver, or maybe I'll fly into New York City, if the shopping gods are with me."

Hope might have rolled her eyes if she weren't so concerned with trying to keep herself from screaming. Or being killed, if she'd been right and it was really Joey, here to find her. Joey, who was plenty smart enough to bribe someone to start last night's basement fire in order to gain access to the mansion.

"Well, you have yourself a good time," the first speaker told Tawny.

Her head spinning and lungs burning, Hope eyed the shower and wondered if she could be seen inside it if she hid there. But its glass-brick construction offered little in the way of cover. Where, then? Where could she go? The linen closet—yes! Maybe she could stuff herself beneath the bottom shelf.

"Oh, I intend to," Tawny purred. "And don't mind my maid. She's just finishing her scrubbing in the bathroom." Raising her voice, Tawny added, "And *this* time, do a better job, or I swear, I'll have you fired!"

More quietly, she confided in the electricians, "You can't imagine the incompetence I'm forced to deal with."

Caught halfway through the act of squeezing herself into the cramped space, Hope wanted to explode. Or faint. That would be so much better, to be unconscious when the two men stained the freshly mopped floor with her blood.

But she didn't faint. She couldn't, and her pounding heart didn't burst like a balloon in her chest, either. So rising from the linen closet, she decided to try to bluff her way out, counting on her rumpled appearance and her disguise to see her through.

Except that no one buys it.

What was it Amanda had said to her last night? About her posture and the way she moved giving her away?

Hope forced herself to take a deep breath. To channel the energy of some of the battered women, when they first came into the shelter where she'd volunteered back in New Jersey. Beaten down, defeated, vulnerable to whatever abuse might next come their way.

Put yourself in their shoes. Imagine you never had a champion, never knew a parent who had taught you to believe you could accomplish anything.

At the thought of her poor father's fate, she found her shoulders slumping. Mop in hand, she trailed through Tawny's room, her head down as she shuffled toward the door—and her sole hope of escape.

"What're you doing?" Tawny shrieked at her. "You're dripping dirty water on my nice rug."

"Sorry." Hope's voice rasped as if she were coming down with something. "This old mop needs a new head."

"Why don't you try replacing yours, too, while you're at it?"

Tawny laughed lightly at her own wit, and Hope wondered if she would have time to strangle the little witch before Joey and the other man recognized her. But instead of taking her best shot, she murmured, "Yes, Miss Lowden," and resumed what felt like an endless journey toward the door.

When two sets of men's work boots came into sight, her stomach roiled and tiny white dots exploded like phantom popcorn across her field of vision. But dizzy as she felt, she couldn't afford to faint now, not this close to freedom.

"Excuse me, sirs," she managed, "and I'll be out of your way."

One of the two sets stepped aside, but not the other.

Scuffed, dark brown and enormous, the boots in front of her didn't give an inch.

Chapter 7

It was sheer suspense that broke her, that forced Hope's gaze to rise above the level of the work pants of the huge man who stood in her way. To look into the smirking face of a blond stranger with a heavy jaw and thick neck.

"Forgot the magic word, did ya?" he asked, shooting a grin toward Tawny and his partner.

"*Please* excuse me," Hope murmured, her heart bumping its way into her throat as she recognized the even larger hulk that was Joey Santorini dressed in workman's coveralls.

The question was, would he know her, too? Would he kill her here and now, and maybe gun down Tawny, too, before leaving their bodies to be discovered later?

When the blond man laughed and got the door for her, Hope shuffled out with her mop. They hadn't recognized her—either of them! But then, they were looking for Aurora Worthington-Calabretta, not some drudge to be mocked and tormented.

She wanted to weep for joy, or scream, or at the very least, run from this spot as fast as she could. But she'd only walked a few sedate steps when Tawny moved into the hall behind her. "You forget something?"

Hope turned to face Tawny, who had her overnight

bag slung over one shoulder. And a brand-new mop head, wrapped in plastic, in her outstretched hand.

"Honestly, they should change your name to Hope-*less*," she said. "I found this on your cart. And by the way, that bathroom stinks to high heaven. You'd better go rinse off whatever it is you were using in there before it melts the paint off the walls."

When Hope didn't move fast enough to suit her, Tawny jabbed at her midsection with the mop head. "Here. Take it and get back to work. I don't have all day to stand here."

Nodding, Hope took the bag.

"You're shaking like a leaf," Tawny noted. "What's wrong with you today?"

"Can't seem to get warm," Hope lied, her voice even raspier. "My room was so cold last night."

Tawny hesitated, and Hope swore she could hear gears whirring as she thought through the explanation. Did she realize Hope's shivering had far more to do with the "electricians" in the room behind her?

"You know," said Tawny, a strange look twisting her mouth. "I—um—there's a box just inside my walk-in closet, clothes I'm getting rid of to make room for this year's styles. There's a good wool sweater in there, nice and heavy. Take it. Put it on. Then get that stink out of my bathroom."

"Thanks," Hope managed, as though Tawny's rare act of charity might not be the death of her.

Behind them, the door opened, and the two men came out of Tawny's suite. Neither spared her a glance as they wished Tawny good shopping and strode toward her mother's suite two doors down.

Stomach heaving, Hope ducked back inside of Tawny's room and raced into the bathroom to splash cold water onto her face. She ducked over the sink, gulped in several deep breaths before she was slammed with the harsh chemical reek Tawny had complained of, an odor she had been too upset to notice after she had sprayed the cleaning solution seconds before the arrival of the "electricians."

Rinse it down, she thought, remembering what Tawny, of all people, had suggested. But by this time, the white popcorn had burst back to crowd her vision, and a wave of dizziness brought her to her knees.

From there, it was only a short drop to the floor.

Luck was on her side, as the one referred to as the mastermind caught sight of the thick-necked blond man before he spotted her. Cursing under her breath, she cautiously followed, wondering what her old partner and his huge friend were doing in the mansion.

Up to no good, she was certain, despite the coveralls that both were wearing and the small toolbox the blond was carrying. She was certain because she knew he'd never done an honest day's work in his life, the man she'd teamed with to dupe old people into coughing up thousands for repairs that never happened.

She knew, too, that if he saw her here, he'd find a way to ruin everything. Maybe he would try to blackmail her with the threat of going to her employers with what he knew about her background. Or maybe he would threaten to tell police about another time, when a too-talkative senior had told them enough about his churchgoing habits to entice them to break into his house to relieve him of a valuable coin collection he couldn't help but boast about. Except the old chatterbox hadn't been feeling up to church that Sunday, and so had surprised her while her partner was in the next room.

He'd ended up dead on the floor for his trouble, a strangulation death that had been utterly missed by a medical examiner who had presumed that the octogenarian with known heart trouble had died a natural death. With no close relatives to press the matter—or notice the missing box of coins—they'd gotten away clean, and there was no way she was allowing that old crime to come back to haunt her now.…

Not when she was so very close to achieving everything she had worked for, everything she wanted and deserved. So she crept along, following the two men— neither of whom seemed to know the first thing about stealth—until her blond "friend" popped out of a room and asked his partner, "Ya wanna show me her picture one more time?"

"You mean you haven't memorized it by now?" asked the big man, whose harsh accent sounded as if he might be from New York, or somewhere right around there. "It's not like you didn't spend enough time staring at her last night in the motel room."

"What? You really think I was spendin' all that time in the bathroom lookin' at her *face?*"

The two men laughed at the crude joke, which only made her lip curl.

"That one we spotted on the family wing, the brunette. Could the bitch have dyed her hair?"

"Not unless she also found a way to make herself look taller and do some serious— Whatcha call it? That's right. Breast reduction."

"Cuttin' down a pair like that's a crime against man and nature.…" quipped her former partner. A partner she had learned the hard way could never be trusted, when he had beaten and threatened to betray her unless she let him take the valuable coins.

"A capital offense," agreed the big man, in a voice that made her shiver. But she knew now whom the two of them were hunting. Had to be the clearly nervous new girl, the one who took such pains to dress in a way that hid her generous cleavage.

Certainly, it wasn't the red-haired Gabby Colton, or anyone well-known here. Anyone who would be missed.

But as long as the new maid, the one calling herself Hope Woods, remained at Dead River Ranch, the mastermind would never be safe. Not unless she found a way to permanently rid herself of the problem before the bimbo drew more trouble.

"See there, Chica?" Dylan told the young chestnut mare that he was riding around the corral in a smooth jog. "You were never really mean or crazy. Only scared and confused, that's all—"

The chestnut dropped her head and bucked, kicking out with both rear legs.

"And maybe just a little ornery," he admitted as he struggled to regain control. It took him a few minutes to prove to the horse she wasn't going to pitch him, but finally, he had her loping around the enclosure, completely under his control.

"Thought you'd given up bronc busting," called Amanda, who was watching from the rails.

"So did I." Dylan smiled at the reminder of his younger years, when he'd taken a couple of years off to ride the rodeo circuit. As much fun as he'd found the cheering and the beer and the buckle bunnies—as the cowboys called their more aggressive female fans—he'd been a disaster as a bronc and bull rider, so in tune with the animals that they almost instantly calmed down and cost him points. "But Chica here had other ideas."

Finished for the moment, he pulled her up and dismounted, then patted the sweaty, red-brown neck.

"So what can I do for you?" he asked Amanda, studying her for any signs of tension. When he noticed the tightness in her shoulders and the grim line of her mouth, he added, "Listen, I'm sorry about upsetting your dad before. That was never my intention."

"You went to see my dad this morning?" She sounded genuinely surprised.

As he opened the gate to lead the mare out, he admitted, "I did. Got a call first thing saying he wanted to see me. Wanted to question me, it turned out, on what I thought was going on." If asked about it in detail, Dylan wouldn't lie, but he decided not to volunteer the information that her father had somehow heard about the DNA test.

"So he's playing the detective now?" She shook her head. "Somehow, that doesn't surprise me. But I didn't come about him or about work, either. I wanted to check on Hope, to see how she's doing since her father… Have you seen her anywhere around this morning?"

He shook his head, worry snaking up his backbone. He'd looked for her this morning, but she hadn't been at breakfast. When he'd discreetly asked Mathilda, she had informed him Hope hadn't been among those who had camped out in the great room. "I haven't caught a glimpse of her all day, but Mrs. Perkins told me she'd gone straight to her duties."

"I called the rooms back on the wing where she's assigned," Amanda told him, "but Trip says he hasn't seen her, either."

"Trip..." Dylan's gaze drifted with the thin clouds as he remembered what Hope had told him about someone sneaking up behind her and letting down her hair while she worked. Of course that had to be Trip. "Damn it all. Sorry for the language, but I think Trip—uh, Mr. Lowden—could be lying. Hope didn't come right out and say it, but I think he could be harassing her. Sexually, I mean."

Amanda blew out a breath. "Why wouldn't she tell me?"

"You've both had a lot on your mind. And maybe she figured she could handle things." He didn't add that Trip's position in the household would make such an accusation awkward, and dependent as she was on Amanda for her cover, Hope might not feel she could afford to take the risk.

"Would you mind having someone see to Chica here? Then I'll go check on Hope. Even if I have to go through Trip to find her."

Amanda shook her head. "You just can't go barging into the back wing. Maybe I should—"

"Do you really think Trip will give you a warm welcome after he's already told you that Hope's not there?"

Amanda's cheeks flamed. "But it's *my* house. My family's, I mean."

"But that particular part of it's your father's ex-wife's and her two children's. Have you ever so much as set foot there since they've been living there?"

"No, and I'd love to know why on earth my father would allow that situation to continue," she said as she took the mare's reins from his hands. "You're right,

Dylan. You need to go and find her. Make whatever excuses you have to and get her out of there. And whatever Trip says, whatever he does, don't you be the one to take the first swing."

Dylan snorted. "If he takes a swing at me, it'll be his *last* one."

"Seriously, Dylan," she warned, "you know how my father is about employees and the family. He has to know you're worth at least a hundred Trip Lowdens, but Dad'll still feel compelled to make an example of you. For one thing, he has no idea that you might be—"

"I'll make sure you're informed as soon as I find her."

When she stiffened slightly, he realized he was doing it again: being short with Amanda because of his own issues with the DNA test. Before he could think how to apologize, she had recovered from the interruption.

"If anyone gives you static," she suggested, "you can tell them that I sent you. Say I answered a phone call for her, from a family member with an urgent message."

"I hope to hell she's really in the back wing cleaning. Because considering what happened to her father and the fire here last night—"

Amanda shook her head. "It can't be her ex-husband's people. We've been so careful."

"I imagine the Witness Protection people thought they were being careful, too."

The color drained from Amanda's face. "Find her, Dylan. Find her quickly, will you?"

"Yes, ma'am," he answered, and as he hurried toward the mansion, he wondered if he'd ever again be able to return to the easy, natural relationship he'd once had with her. Maybe it was time for him to reconsider one of the two jobs he'd been offered during the past few months, standing offers he'd refused to think about until the person responsible for his mother's death was behind bars.

By the time he made it inside, those worries had been crowded out, displaced by memories of the way Hope had filled his arms last night, the compassion in her voice when he'd told her a story he couldn't imagine sharing with any other woman, much less a near stranger....

And he thought, too, of his vow to keep her safe no matter what.

Hope cracked open her burning eyes to find that everything was spinning: tile, glass brick, bathroom cabinets, all whirling around so swiftly, she might have been sucked into a storm's vortex.

Must have banged her head when she fell, for it was pounding, throbbing sickly, and her fingers came away gummy with half-dried blood when she tried to touch the sore spot on her forehead.

Fumes, she realized, as she registered the high-pitched rasp of her own wheezing. Pain shot through her lungs with every inhalation.

Still only semiconscious, she knew she couldn't stay here. If she did, she'd die on this floor, poisoned by... Had something unexpected been inside that white bottle with the torn label? Something meant to harm her?

But right now, the how of it made no difference whatsoever. The only thing that mattered was getting out of this room. Because no one would come looking for her, at least until tonight, when she failed to turn up for...

Would anyone even miss her then? Afraid her nervousness—and last night's weeping—would lead someone to suspect her, she'd given the other employees a wide berth. Except for Dylan…

Her mind flooded with a memory of his voice in the darkness. And the physical sensation of his arms as they'd held her.

Except she couldn't afford to wait for him. And wouldn't ever again fall into the trap of counting on a man. Eyes streaming from the stinging fumes, she crawled across the tiled floor. Fresh pain shot through her chest with the exertion, but she forced herself to go on, to haul her weakened body to the foot of Tawny's bed.

There, she tried to pull herself to her feet, but agony detonated more of the white dots in her vision. Afraid she would pass out again, she continued crawling toward the hall door, thinking that if only she could reach it, someone was bound to find her.

She prayed that someone wouldn't prove to be one of the "electricians" who had come to kill her.

But as she crawled closer to the door, she realized it was Trip, arguing with someone. Trip, who for all she knew might try to grope her if he found her unconscious on the floor.

Surely, she thought, he wasn't arrogant enough to molest a woman in front of a witness. She should be safe enough—unless he was out there haranguing Joey Santorini and his partner about the continuing lack of power.

Deciding she had no choice but to risk it, she tried to call for help.

Barely a hiss escaped from her mouth, a strangled sound so painful that tears poured down her face and the room spun all around her.

The voices in the hall were receding, taking with them her last hope of rescue. Refusing to let it happen, she fought through waves of pain to pull off one of the low-heeled black pumps she'd been wearing.

To hurl it at the door with every bit of strength that she possessed.

The loud thump down the hall surprised both men—and served as the last straw for Dylan.

"Someone's in there. Out of my way," he ordered Trip, who had been arguing that his mother and sister were both gone and there was no one else on the floor since the electricians had left an hour earlier.

"What the hell?" Trip asked, looking startled as he turned to the noise.

Dylan shouldered his way past him and threw open the unlocked door.

His heart jerked in his chest at the sight of Hope lying prone on the floor. The moment he stepped inside, a caustic, chemical odor made his eyes water.

"Is she breathing?" Trip asked, still standing in the doorway, his hand covering his mouth and nose.

"Hope, wake up," Dylan said as he grabbed her arm. She didn't respond, but her skin was warm to the touch and he could hear her wheezing.

"She's alive." He fought the urge to cough to tell Trip, "Go get Dr. Colton—fast."

For once, Trip didn't argue, disappearing in an instant.

His eyes burning, Dylan took hold of Hope's shoulders and dragged her from the room. Dangerous as it was to move a potentially injured person, he had no doubt whatsoever that continuing to breathe the bad air inside the frilly, pink suite was the greater risk.

Hope groaned when he moved her into the hall and tried to swat at him. After kicking shut the door behind them, he caught one of her hands and squeezed it and then noticed the bloody, bruised spot on her forehead.

Remembering Mrs. Black, he asked, "Hope, it's Dylan. Did someone hit you?"

The strangled sound she made when she spoke might have been a *no*. "Cleaning chemicals," she rasped. "Got dizzy."

"Doctor's on his way. He'll have medicine to help you," he assured her, trying not to panic at how very weak her voice was, how shallow her breathing. Her half-closed eyes were red, too, burned by the fumes, he realized.

Would Levi have the right tools here to save her?

"Stay with me," Dylan told her, brushing a stray, chocolate-colored lock from her face. Somewhere along the way, she'd lost the horn-rimmed glasses, but with her lips and eyelids swollen, she scarcely looked like herself. "Stay awake, Hope."

Her lashes fluttered and she reached up toward her face. "Eyes. My eyes are burning. Contacts hurting so bad."

"Don't touch," he tried to tell her, but she was fumbling with her left eyelid, then popping out a contact…

And revealing a vibrant blue eye, a shade made far more startling against the redness of her corneas.

Another layer of disguise gone, he thought as she removed the second brown contact. "Close your eyes," he told her as he heard the thumping of footsteps coming up the staircase. Though Levi would have to see her new eye color, there was no need to allow Trip to get a look.

"If I d-don't— You have to tell my— Tell him that I love him, Dylan… Tell him I'll always…" Her head tipped back, her spine arching as tremors racked her body.

"Dr. Colton, over here!" called Dylan, trying to catch at her flailing limbs.

"Step back, please," Levi said as he knelt on the floor beside Hope.

The movements stilled in seconds—the longest seconds of Dylan's life—and the doctor rolled her onto her side and quickly checked her pulse and breathing.

"She's moving air," he said, "but not much. What the hell is happening?"

Dylan quickly gave him a rundown on her symptoms and what she'd said about the cleaning chemicals. "I think she might've banged her head when she fell," he added. "When I asked, she told me no one hit her."

Levi called her name, but she must have passed out once more, for she was unresponsive. He lifted her hand and peered down. "She's seriously constricted. Cyanotic, too. See right here. The nail beds are bluish, like her lips."

He was right, Dylan thought, stunned to realize that instead of improving with the fresher air, Hope was still deteriorating. "Is it from the chemicals?" he asked. "The whole suite reeks like—"

"Like strong bleach," Levi agreed as he peeled back Hope's eyelids and shone a flashlight in each pupil. "I can smell it from here. Could be she mixed bleach with some kind of acid. It's a relatively common accident."

"Can you save her?" Though he thought he'd given up on praying, he found himself silently sending up a plea. *Don't let her die, too, not after everything she's been through.*

Rather than answering, Levi told him, "We'll need to get her down to the infirmary, stat. I've got a nebulizer down there to deliver the breathing medication she'll need, and I can administer oxygen, as well. Let me call downstairs to get a—"

Before he could finish, Dylan lifted her in his arms, unwilling to waste a single second to get her what she so clearly needed.

"I was going to say 'a couple of strong hands and a backboard,'" Levi finished, "but I can see you've got it covered. Let's go."

"Need some help?" Trip asked, belatedly appearing at the top of the stairs. He looked more anxious than last night, to be certain. Was it because this "accident" had hit too close to home?

"I'm fine, thanks," Dylan told him, not trusting Lowden not to drop her. And not wanting Hope to catch his attention if she chanced to open her eyes again. "Just let Mrs. Perkins know, if you would."

"Sure thing," Trip said, going for a hall extension.

Certain that Mathilda would alert Amanda to her friend's condition, Dylan carried Hope down two flights of stairs, not even slowing his pace when Misty Mayhew stopped to ask him what had happened.

Trailing him, Levi opened the door to the infirmary and flipped on the lights, and Dylan thanked God that the doctor had asked him to find another generator to get the ranch's small clinic back up and running earlier.

"Let's put her over here," Levi said, motioning to the hospital bed he kept rolled off to one side, rather than the exam table. "That way, if she has another seizure, we won't have to worry about her falling."

As Dylan laid her down, however, Hope didn't move a muscle, which somehow scared him even more. "What can I do?" he asked. "There has to be something."

"You can step out of the way," Levi ordered. "Maybe go ask Agnes to whip up a fresh pot of coffee for us."

Dylan didn't give a damn if Levi *was* both a doctor and a Colton. "You're not going to run me off. I'm staying."

"Then sit down and be quiet, will you?" said Levi, and he pulled a wrapped unit containing a plastic mask and tubing from a cabinet drawer. "Or better yet, go look on my desk and see if you can find the number of the MedFlight helicopter service in case we need her air-lifted. In case this is beyond what I can do for her here."

He unlocked another cabinet and opened a box containing plastic ampuls of some clear medication. Breaking open one, he poured it into a small chamber underneath the mask, which he strapped over Hope's face.

As he turned on the nebulizer, Dylan dug through a small stack of papers until he found a card whose logo boasted: For All Your Critical Care Needs.

His heart hammering, Dylan prayed he wouldn't have to call the number. Prayed that the fledgling doctor could save Hope Woods' life…

Even though, lying in that hallway, she had confessed that she still loved the ex-husband who wanted nothing more than to see her in the ground.

Chapter 8

There was a background hum, a hiss, but it was the light that Hope first became aware of. Painful. Inescapable, as she couldn't even close her watering eyes to get away from it. She reached up to bat clumsily at her face, to push away whatever was prying open each lid in turn.

"It's all right, Hope," a male voice reassured her as he gently caught her wrist. "Just checking your corneas for damage."

Confused, she forced herself to lie still, though she could do nothing to control her shaking. Was she still at the ranch, or in a hospital, where soon, someone would come looking for her insurance and ID cards?

Remembering that "Hope Woods" had no credentials, she fought to sit up until not one but two sets of hands pushed her back down.

"Easy there." Dylan's voice somehow took the edge off of her panic. "Don't fight Dr. Colton. He's just trying to help you."

Dr. Colton. That must mean... Blinking furiously, she blurted, "I'm—I'm not at the hospital?"

Her voice echoed strangely, muffled by... Slipping one hand free, she felt the mask strapped over both her nose and mouth.

"You're at the ranch infirmary," Dr. Colton told her, "but you will need to be hospitalized." Vision still blurred, she squinted to take in the two shapes hovering above her.

"Your pulse oxygen's much better," explained the doctor, who had dirty-blond hair and a surprisingly young face, "and I think your eyes will be fine. The contacts you had on may have saved them."

"C-contacts," she rasped, her heart pounding out a frantic tattoo. "You mean—"

"Those beautiful blue eyes of yours are safe," Dylan interjected, a warning that zinged straight through her. "You took your contacts off upstairs, remember?"

She did—sort of—but how was she going to possibly explain a total change in eye color to anyone who noticed? Some would, she was certain, for her natural eye color was a vivid hue, one that made her far more recognizable. Which meant if her ex-husband's henchmen came around again…

She shivered at the thought, wanting desperately to warn Amanda or Dylan about the "electricians." But she didn't know this doctor, and though she thought she'd heard someone refer to him as Amanda's half brother, she couldn't take the chance of allowing her secret to spread any further.

"Still," Dr. Colton continued, his gaze serious, "I'd feel more comfortable having a specialist take a closer look at—"

"Can't go to the hospital." Shaking her head rapidly, she dug her nails into her own palms. "Won't."

"Your lungs and trachea are burned," explained the young doctor. "Chemically burned, most likely as a result of mixing some form of bleach with another cleaner, possibly ammonia. You created a type of chlorine gas when the—"

"Chloramine… The decomposing bleach formed hydrochloric—" She coughed, wincing at the pain in her lungs. And at the realization that she should have figured this out far earlier. "Hydrochloric acid that reacted with the ammonia and formed—"

"That's right," the doctor confirmed, and to her irritation, both men looked surprised.

With a shrug, she explained, "I started out studying chemistry, back before I got sidetracked." Sidetracked by her mother's urging her to enter the Miss New Jersey pageant.

She had gone along with it, if only because she knew how much her mother would have loved the opportunity when she was younger. And once Hope had gotten past the silliness of the idea, she'd started having fun meeting her fellow contestants and spending quality girl time with her mom. Time she wouldn't trade for all the sashes in the world.

"You were a chemistry major?" Dylan asked.

"Try not to look so shocked, cowboy. Just because I'm—" She glanced at the young doctor, cleared her stinging throat and tried again. "Just because I'm the world's worst maid doesn't mean I'm terrible at everything. And I *never* would've mixed those chemicals on purpose."

"So what're you saying?" Dylan asked her.

Unable to compete with the hissing hum of the machine, she reached up to remove the mask from her face.

"Don't even think of taking that off," Dr. Colton warned. "Your lungs are very fragile. Though judging from how well you're speaking, maybe we can forego that trip to the hospital after all."

She sighed, allowed him to check her vitals before he turned away to jot some notes in a file.

"How do you think it might've happened?" Dylan asked her.

"Someone said I should try the white bottle whenever my usual cleanser didn't work. But the one on my cart— the label was torn off it."

"*Who* told you to use it?"

Hope tried to wave off his suspicion. "I was standing around with some of the other maids, rinsing our mop buckets, when I mentioned how hard it was to get off—" She swallowed painfully, her mouth full of a sharp chemical taste. "How hard it was to get the makeup off of everything in Tawny's bathroom. Then Hilda Zimmerman suggested that I try the— She couldn't recall the name, but somebody else remembered the color of the bottle."

"Who said that part?"

"I'm not sure. Could've been…" Her face contorting, she cried out as sharp pains shot through her lungs.

Dr. Colton reappeared, telling Dylan, "That's it. That's enough talk for now." Looking to Hope, he added, "If you won't go to the hospital—"

She shook her head emphatically and said, "C-can't. Please, don't—" But she couldn't manage to force out another word, or plead with him to let her speak in private to Amanda.

The doctor frowned a question at her, but it was Dylan who explained, "She can't because she's on the run."

Glaring through tears, Hope mouthed the word *No!* Just because he'd kissed her didn't give him the right to share her secrets without consulting her first.

"She's a victim of domestic violence," he continued, ignoring her growing panic, "and she's afraid to risk her ex-husband hunting her down. He's a powerful man with a long reach, and he could easily find her if she checked into a hospital."

At the moment he heard the half-truth, Dr. Colton's expression softened. "All right. I understand now. But if you're going to stay here at the ranch, you're going to have to do things my way."

Relieved that Dylan hadn't told him everything, Hope nodded her agreement. Though she still wondered who on earth had died and left him in charge of her life.

"I'll want you right here in the infirmary where I can watch you, on complete bed rest with no talking, for at least a couple of days."

"With her eyes covered," Dylan put in. "She'll definitely need to have them bandaged."

Hope stared at him in shock.

"What are you talking about?" Colton asked him. "She doesn't need—"

"She does," Dylan insisted, "at least until her new colored contacts get in. When she arrived here, she had brown eyes, and the old contacts are ruined. But don't worry, Hope. I'll have Miss Amanda put a rush on a new pair for you off the internet."

"So Amanda knows about this?" the doctor asked him.

Amanda. Hope reminded herself that not only her own safety might be at risk, should the phony electricians once more find—and this time recognize—her in the mansion. For everyone's sake, she had to somehow warn her friend that Renzo's assassins might still be here—even if it meant letting the doctor in on another facet of her secret.

Making the decision, she pointed to the pen that Dr. Colton was still holding and mimed the act of writing. But neither man was looking her way at the moment.

"She knows. They're old friends," Dylan confirmed before patting her arm. "Just lie back and try not to worry, Hope. I'll take care of everything."

Gritting her teeth, she clutched his sleeve and refused to let go until he paid attention to her gestures.

This time, Dylan nodded, finally understanding, and Dr. Colton gave her a small pad of paper and his pen. With her every exhalation, a puff of steam rolled up to obscure her vision, and the faster she tried to write, the harder her hands shook.

"The shaking's from the medication," Dr. Colton told her. "Just slow down for a moment. Don't try to move so quickly, and you'll be fine."

It was easier said than done, and Hope's normally neat script was a mass of knotted loops and squiggles, but when she handed the note to Dylan, he frowned at it only a few moments before asking, "You're sure about this?"

She nodded.

"What does she mean?" Colton asked, as he read over Dylan's shoulder.

"It means I'd better damned well hurry," Dylan told them. "I'll fill you in when I get back."

As Dylan headed for the service entrance, he prayed that Hope was right, that the man she'd recognized hadn't had a clue who she was. Maybe her disguise was better than he'd first imagined, or the thugs searching for her had been so focused on finding the sleek blonde princess they were looking for that it had never occurred to them to look for her among the mansion's staff.

But then again, it was altogether possible they had only been pretending not to know her…and that they were planting an explosive somewhere in the mansion. An explosive that, as with the car bomb back in Iowa and yesterday's fire in Florida, could kill not only their intended target, but anyone and everyone who might be in the way.

As adrenaline spiked through him, he wondered, should he recruit help to search the mansion? Betray Hope's confidence to stop what might turn out to be a bloodbath? Surely, the safety of everyone who lived and worked here trumped one woman's secrets. But what if Hope was wrong? If the scrawled note she'd written had been based on a hallucination rather than reality?

He pictured her lying in the upstairs hallway, her back arched and her body racked with tremors. Worried as she'd been about her ex-husband's people tracking her here to kill her as they had her father, was it possible her oxygen-starved brain had manufactured their appearance?

He hesitated for a moment, then decided he would look into this himself before stirring up more trouble by prematurely sounding the alarm. On his way to the rear entrance, he followed the yeasty scent of baking bread to the nearby kitchen, where Agnes and her assistants were working.

"Excuse me," he said, his stomach growling as Agnes pulled a pan of fresh rolls from the oven. "Has anyone seen the electricians yet this morning? With Mr. Black gone, I've been asked to check on how they're coming."

Clearly, none of the kitchen staff had yet heard about Hope, for rather than asking what had happened, the red-haired cook set the pan down on the stovetop, her round face scrunching as she considered. "Have you checked the basement, where all the trouble is? Or was it your nose that led you here, as usual, when I'm baking?"

He tilted a smile at her. "You know me better than I know myself. But I really do need to find those two workers. Did you *see* them head down?"

"I think I did." Though she would have bitten the head off any other cowboy who dared to ask for one, Agnes tore one steaming roll apart from the others and pulled it open before adding a generous yellow dollop of butter for him. "At any rate, they walked right past here."

Dylan wondered if the two might be downstairs at this very moment, rigging the electrical panel for a deadlier explosion. But the more he thought about it, the more ridiculous the idea sounded. Why would two professionals risk killing dozens, with no certainty whatsoever that their quarry wouldn't escape?

Before he could grab the roll on his way to check them out just in case, Kate McCord, the pretty pastry chef he'd known a few years, gave a shake of her dark curls.

"They're gone already," she told Agnes. "When you stepped out for a moment, I saw both of them leaving."

"Leaving?" Agnes fisted a hand on one broad hip, her face reddening. "You aren't telling me those lazy lumps are out on a lunch break while we're all left to shiver in the darkness?"

With a humming generator just outside the noon-bright window and mostly gas appliances, the kitchen was by far the warmest, best-lit spot in the house, but Dylan was far too interested in hearing Kate's response to point that out.

"I assured them we'd gladly feed them lunch," she said, "but they said they'd have to run back to town to pick up some part they needed. Something about an oscill-regulator, I think."

"A *what?*" While Dylan was no expert in such things, Mr. Black had taught him enough over the years that he was almost positive that no such device existed.

"I'm sure it was the oscill-regulator." Kate gave a little shrug. "Whatever on earth *that* is."

"What exactly did these guys look like?"

Kate described the two large men wearing coveralls and work boots. Neither sounded like anyone he'd seen on the ranch before.

"Did you happen to see the vehicle they left in?" he asked her.

She thought for a moment before nodding. "I saw a white van backing out, with Elite Electrical on the side. Why? Is that important?"

"I'll let you know. Thanks, Kate," he said, forgetting about food as he rushed toward the service entrance. As he stepped outside, a silver van was just pulling into an empty space in the small lot. Had Katie been mistaken on its color? Were these the same two workers, already returning?

Two men climbed out of the Elite Electrical vehicle, one of them a dark-skinned, middle-aged man whose belly strained his coveralls and the other a younger, slimmer version, so similar in appearance that he had to be the man's son. As Dylan approached, the younger man, who couldn't have been older than twenty, opened the back of the silver van, while the older walked up and offered Dylan a worn and callused hand. "Sorry we're so late getting here this morning. We always hate keeping Mr. Colton waiting, but we had to run to Laramie to pick up the only one of these panels Junior here could track down in the state."

Dylan shook his hand and introduced himself, realizing the man, who passed him a card bearing a greasy fingerprint and the words *Leon Nelson, Elite Electrical,* looked familiar. Probably because Nelson had been coming to the ranch to deal with various electrical concerns for years.

"Mr. Colton appreciates you sending that other team out earlier," Dylan said, to test his working theory.

"What other team?" Nelson's dark brow crinkled. "Our only other unit's out wiring a new commercial project going in next to the—"

"Driving a white van?" Dylan interrupted.

"No, sir," Nelson told him, sounding adamant. "My brother Emmett drives a silver one, just like this, only it has a magnetic sign on the side."

"So what do you know about a white van that came here earlier, with that same logo?" Dylan pointed to the side of the van and noticed the son looking at him from around the open rear gate....

He noticed, too, how Junior avoided eye contact, his dark brown eyes shifting nervously.

Leon Nelson shook his head emphatically. "We don't own a white van, and I'd swear on the nearest Bible my brother's working on that new service station back in town."

"They left not long before you got here. You didn't pass a white van on the way here?"

"No, sir, Mr. Frick. Like I told you, I did not," Leon said hotly. "If somebody else was out there this morning, they're nothing but poachers—out to steal my service contract with Dead River Ranch."

"They certainly didn't impress anybody by walking all through the mansion and then leaving to pick up an 'oscill-regulator.'"

Leon's gaze narrowed, and he cut a look toward his son, who quickly ducked back behind the van.

"They weren't here to fix any power, and they certainly weren't electricians," Leon told Dylan. "Sounds like they were a couple of low-life thieves, out to case the place to rob it later."

"Low-life thieves with one of *your* magnetic signs on their van's side," Dylan ground out. "Which has me wondering exactly what the connection might be."

Once more, Leon glanced toward the rear of the van, his expression anguished. "Son, you might as well come on out and tell me what you know about this. Whatever it is, we'll find a way to straighten things out, just like we did the last time."

The metallic rattling of tools was their only answer.

"Son?" the father called. "I asked you to explain this. Now, don't you figure you owe me at least that much after all we've been through?"

When Junior didn't respond, Dylan stepped around the back of the van. And barely ducked in time to avoid the huge wrench swinging toward his head.

"Junior, no!" the father shouted. "Whatever it is, it isn't worth this."

His face a frozen grimace, the son advanced on Dylan and took an even more determined swing. This time, Dylan blocked it and slammed his lighter, younger opponent just beneath the breastbone. With a grunted exhalation, the air exploded from Junior's lungs and he staggered.

"Please don't hurt him," begged the father.

But with the son still clutching the wrench, Dylan had no choice but to hammer him a second time, striking both his jaw and shoulder.

As fights went, it was the kind that Dylan liked best: short and heavily weighted in his favor. Junior made one last, desperate swing for Dylan before the wrench clattered to the ground and the younger man went to his knees. An instant later, he fell to his side, where he lay holding his midsection and struggling for breath.

With one booted foot, Dylan kicked the wrench out of the younger man's reach. "You'll be all right in a second, son. Wind's just knocked out of you, that's all."

The elder Nelson knelt beside his son and shook him. "What did you do, boy? What did you do with the extra sign? Because if you've cost me my best customer, I swear on your mother's grave I'm finished with you."

Junior coughed and choked and breathed again, panting heavily. And seething with resentment as he eyed his father.

"I didn't do a thing. I swear it," he choked out. "You're always on me, always believing any random stranger— all because of one mistake!"

"Nobody's buying what you're selling," Nelson ground out through his clenched teeth.

"Damn straight," Dylan put in. "You nearly took my head off with that wrench. Why?"

Junior pushed himself to a seated position but remained on the cold ground.

"Well?" his father answered.

"I just knew I was about to get blamed, that's all," Junior blurted. "'Cause I'm always the one blamed, always the one pulled over, always the one the cops bring in for questioning."

Moisture sheened the furious brown eyes, and pain, too, if Dylan was reading him correctly. But that didn't mean the kid wasn't up to his neck in this mess.

"Me and my friends was only sixteen when we busted into that house," Junior told him. "Just a punk kid stunt, that's all. We didn't even know it was the police chief's. Doesn't make me no career criminal."

"Only the biggest idiots in Dead," his father said.

"So you took a swing at me because...?" Dylan pressed.

"Because I'm done with takin' the rap for stuff I never had a thing to do with."

"Huh." Nelson turned his gaze as if he couldn't bear to look at his own flesh and blood another moment. Or as if he'd heard that same excuse once too often in the past.

"I could press charges for assault," said Dylan. "Could wreck your father's business with one word about this to the old man."

"If *you're* the one who was assaulted," Junior said defiantly, "how come I'm the one down here with all the bruises."

"Nobody ever said that you were *good* at it," Dylan countered. "Which gives me hope for you. And your father's business, too, if you tell me who conned you into handing over one of your company's magnetic signs. And exactly who it was you told how to sabotage that electrical panel in the first place."

At this point, Junior completely clammed up, refusing to say another word or look at either of them. While his father cursed him for a stubborn fool and threatened to tell the police to "throw the key away," Dylan thought he saw something beyond belligerence in the younger man's dark eyes.

Was it fear he read there? The fear that telling what he knew could have more serious consequences than jail time?

Dylan walked back inside still shaking his head, wondering if he had just made a deal with the devil by allowing Junior Nelson to leave with his father.

But Leon Nelson had sworn to get to the bottom of whatever was going on. If he failed, the man knew he would lose the business he'd spent decades building. And he would lose his only son as well, the young man who, for all his missteps, was all the father had left of his late wife.

Though Dylan didn't like it, he liked his alternatives even less. If he had Junior arrested, word was likely to get back to the assassins, considering that someone who lived on or worked at the ranch must have also been in their pay. But who the hell had that been, and could this saboteur have anything to do with the "accident" that had led to Hope's collapse? Certainly, it made more sense than the idea of the mastermind trying to kill a new employee.

At the thought of Hope, he shuddered, remembered her lying on the hallway floor and rasping the words *"Tell him that I love him."*

Could she have really meant it? Could she still have feelings for the man she'd called a murderer, the man who had sent hired killers after her?

Dylan tried to shake it off, telling himself that he had no right to care how Hope felt about anything, that he was only looking out for her safety as a favor to Amanda, in spite of his lapse of judgment in the stable last night. With that in mind, he started up the stairs with the goal of solving at least one mystery.

Halfway up, he met Hilda Zimmerman and a younger brunette maid named Fiona, who was handling a cleaning cart with Hope's name printed on it in black marker.

Eyeing the cart carefully, he saw no sign of the white spray bottle, but there was a trash bag tied to it. A trash bag that might well contain the evidence he was looking for.

"What are you two doing up here?" he asked, not wanting to alarm them by immediately demanding they turn the cart over to him.

"Cleaning up, of course," said Hilda. "Mr. Lowden insisted we get everything picked up and aired out, for his safety."

Of course he had. "*Before* anyone could come investigate what happened?"

"Investigate? It's not—" Fiona's eyes widened. "Please tell me Hope hasn't—she hasn't—"

Shaking his head, he answered, "She's very much alive—no thanks to whoever told her to mix two reactive cleaning products."

"So it was an accident?" Fiona was practically pleading, and he didn't blame her, considering the number of homicides among the staff these past few months.

But Hilda's face had gone red. "Surely, she didn't— She wouldn't be so foolish as to mix two fluids without checking the label?"

"Hard to do when someone's torn it off," he said.

Pulling out a handkerchief, Hilda dabbed at her damp eyes. "But Mrs. Perkins asked me to look out for her, to give Hope a hand since she was new to the work. I was only trying to help. She must have misunderstood me."

She looked up at him, one corner of her mouth twitching. "I won't— I'm not in any trouble, am I?"

Fiona wrapped a protective arm around the older woman's shoulder. "I'm sure she didn't mean it. Anyone who knows Hilda would know it had to be an accident."

Not wanting to frighten the women, he patted Hilda's arm and lied, "I'm sure that's all it is."

"So, will—will she be all right?" Hilda asked him.

"She's holding her own now," he said, "but Dr. Colton wants to keep her in isolation in the infirmary for a few days until the burns in her lungs and eyes begin to heal."

"In isolation? It's that serious?" Fiona interjected.

Dylan nodded, trying to think of a reason strong enough that the two would put the word out for everyone to stay away. "He says she's extremely susceptible to infection right now, like Mr. Colton, with his leukemia."

He felt a twinge of conscience, especially with poor Hilda looking so guilt stricken. But he reminded himself that what he'd said might actually be true—and that this way, Hope would remain much safer, not only from anyone who might note her jewel-bright blue eyes, but from whoever might have orchestrated this accident in the first place.

"Is there anything we can do for her? Anyone I need to inform?" Hilda managed.

"I'll take care of it," he told them, thinking that he'd have to fill in Amanda, "as soon as I run up and check to see if I can find Hope's glasses for her."

"I found them on the floor next to Miss Lowden's bed," Hilda volunteered. "I have them right here." She pulled them from her pocket.

"Excellent," Dylan said, collecting the glasses before adding, "and how about you let me take that cart down for you while I'm up here? I'm sure you two ladies are eager to get back to your other duties."

Hilda's and Fiona's gazes met, confusion in their faces at his odd offer. But when he slapped on his most charming smile and grabbed the handle, Hilda responded, "You know where this goes?"

"I sure do," he told her. "And I'll be sure to put it in the right spot."

As soon as I've checked the contents of that trash bag for that missing bottle.

Chapter 9

The following evening, the back wing lay silent as a tomb as a bright beam tunneled through the darkness. The soft pad of footsteps followed, the footsteps of a man well practiced in treading lightly.

Trip Lowden hesitated for a moment, his heart pumping with anticipation, before he opened the door to his sister's suite of rooms. If anyone were to confront and question him, he would claim that he was only making certain the housekeeping staff had gotten the place cleaned properly, no matter that the moment she returned, Tawny would blow through like a blizzard, blanketing the place with brand-new clothes and scarves and boots, half of which she'd end up donating unworn in a few months to make room for her next round of "retail therapy."

But whether or not Tawny would notice the condition of her room on her return, Trip had other reasons to seek out evidence of laziness, incompetence or petty theft, evidence he wouldn't hesitate to turn to his advantage—especially when it came to the younger and more attractive female housemaids. In the past, he'd used such proof to his considerable pleasure, learning in the process that he preferred his sexual encounters with a side order of coercion. Once a man had a woman sufficiently desperate—whether it was to keep the job that allowed her to support her children or to keep herself out of jail—he could do almost anything he could imagine, without the fuss and bother of having to leave the comfort of the mansion to hire a prostitute.

Tonight, however, as his flashlight's beam skated one gleaming surface after the other, he found himself disappointed. Not only was the room perfectly clean and orderly, the maids who had come up after Hope Woods's accident—as most seemed to believe it had indeed been—had even remembered to close the windows after leaving them open overnight to air out the last traces of the toxic fumes...

The fumes that had left Hope's sweet and shapely body helpless, lying right here on the bedroom floor, where he might've stumbled upon her all alone. Might have put her into his debt by rescuing her himself, carrying her to the safety of, say, his own room, and his own bed, if that two-bit wrangler hadn't shown up and ruined everything.

But what real fun would it be anyway, taking an unconscious woman? Not his style, Trip decided, thinking how much better it would be to have a beauty like Hope healthy and awake, tears gleaming in her eyes as she realized that her only way out was submission to his lust.

Recalling the proprietary look in Frick's eyes when he'd barged upstairs to demand to know where the new maid was, Trip grinned. Because there was nothing he liked better than the thought of taking one of the smug, self-righteous cowboy's toys and breaking it before he'd even had the chance to play.

With that in mind, Trip's gaze found Tawny's laptop, lying forgotten on the nightstand. What if it were to disappear, and he were to mention to the police how he remembered seeing Hope slip out of the room an hour or so before her accident, hiding something, only to return later, clearly nervous? Perhaps she'd been so nervous, so stricken with guilt and worry, she hadn't paid much attention to the cleansers she was mixing.

Provided she survived, it could work, he decided, unplugging the laptop and tucking it beneath his arm. Better yet, it would give him the perfect opportunity to snoop through the computer's search history and check on his dear sister's recent online activities…because Tawny might be his greatest ally, but with their billionaire stepfather's illness making their future so uncertain, he would never be so foolish as to consider her a friend.

As he started toward the hallway, something at floor level glittered in the flashlight's beam. Curious, Trip squatted down to check out the rug's thick pile and came up, only seconds later, with a shriveled and misshapen disk smaller than his thumbnail.

A contact lens, he realized, but it was not until the next morning, with the daylight streaming through his bedroom window, that he noticed that this particular lens was ringed in dark brown…meant to be worn by someone out to hide the natural color of his or her own eyes.

Her, in this case, he was certain, remembering the clear glasses Hope Woods had been wearing. So he'd been right that she was hiding something…some secret he was more determined than ever to unearth.

One meal arrived and then another, but it didn't matter because Hope wouldn't eat them, no matter how often Dr. Colton lectured about keeping up her strength. He was more insistent about the breathing treatments, even waking her at night and sitting with her to ensure her compliance.

Mostly, though, she slept, a deep, drugged refuge from the grim reality she faced. But at some point—between her bound eyes and her drugged sleep, she had lost track of the time completely—she heard the background murmur of conversation, followed by the sound of one food tray being set aside and replaced with another.

Someone—she thought it was the doctor—said, "All right. I'll be back to check in another hour."

"No hurry. I'll sit with her," said another male voice, and an instant later, there was a scent, an outdoor aroma she associated with hay and fresh air, male strength and the memory of the kiss so searing it was a wonder the stable hadn't gone up in flames.

A kiss she couldn't risk repeating, no matter how lonely she was.

"Dylan," she rasped out, the first word she had spoken in many hours. Her mouth was parched, but the tightness in her chest had loosened its grip and the pain in her throat was far more bearable. "Why didn't you come tell me about—tell me what you found out about the elec—electri—"

"Shh," he said, "don't try to talk. Not until you've had some water."

There was a low hum as he raised the head of her bed, and moments later, she felt a straw touching her dry lips. Dr. Colton had made the same effort several times before, but this time, Hope sucked in a sip of water. It felt so cool and tasted so sweet, she kept drinking until he took it from her.

"Not so much, so fast," he said. "You don't want to make yourself sick. Speaking of which, do you mind telling me why you've refused every bite of food and drop of water for the past two days now?"

"Two—" She choked on the water. "I've been lying here for *two days?*"

"The longest two days of my life," he said, taking a seat in the chair at her bedside. "Every time I came to sit with you, you were out cold, but Levi—Dr. Colton—told me you weren't cooperating even when you were fully conscious. Why not?"

"What did you find out? Are my ex-husband's people still nearby? Have they been back to search some more?" she asked, pushing the straw away from her mouth and reaching for the bandages that kept her from seeing the truth or the lie in his expression.

As if she were anyone to judge...

He caught her hand. "Hold on just a minute," he said. "I have to lock this door."

By the time she heard the door latch, she was already unwrapping the strips of linen, emerging from the depths of a depression that had robbed her of her energy, of her will to fight, for too long. A moment later, she was groaning and covering her face with her hands against the blinding light.

"Here, let me turn off this overhead." With a click, the room grew dimmer. "Electricians got all the power back on line this morning. And before you ask, not *those* two. Those men are long gone."

She blinked and squinted, struggling to make her eyes work. "You're sure?"

"Sure as anybody can be," he said before explaining his theory about how someone had been bribed to tamper with the panel in the basement, allowing the assassins a chance to get inside.

"Who was it?" she asked, her voice still raspy. "Who did they bribe?"

"The electrician's son, most likely. And someone with easy access to the mansion, too."

"The same person who poisoned me?"

"I'm not sure," he said, and she noticed he looked exhausted, with worry shadowing his blue eyes as if he'd been carrying the weight of her problems while she slept. Had he and the doctor taken turns watching over her the whole time she'd been sleeping, making certain that no one returned to harm her?

"I can't say for certain you were poisoned, at least not intentionally. Can't prove it, anyway. But I'll admit, the timing has me worried."

"You, too? What a coincidence," she said drily.

"Worried enough," he told her, "that Amanda and I both think it would be best to get you out of town for a few days."

Hope tensed. "She's changed her mind, then? Decided I'm too dangerous to keep around here?"

It was true; she knew it. But it hurt anyway, to think of abandoning her last link with her old life. Her last chance to bury Renzo so deep she'd never have to be afraid again.

"Just for a few days," he repeated, "just for your own safety, until we can be certain they aren't coming back."

"But where?" she asked, throat tightening. "How?"

"I'll explain everything," he said, removing the cover from the tray on the bedside table, "as soon as you have something to eat."

"Just tell me," she said impatiently. The smell of the food turned her stomach. "I'm not hungry."

"You are," he assured her. "It's just that your body's forgotten how to pay attention to the signals. And you'll like Agnes's chicken and dumplings—promise. You're lucky I didn't steal your helping on the way here."

She winced, the thought of eating anything so heavy an unimaginable hurdle. "I can't, Dylan. I'll be sick."

"Listen, Hope. You're going to have to have something. And it'll be one heck of a lot more pleasant if you cooperate."

She glared at him. "My ex-husband used to pull stuff like this. Ordering me around and pretending it was for my own good."

He shrugged off her anger. "Yeah, well, the difference is, this *is* for your own good. And I won't send hit men out to find you if you don't do as I ask, though I have to admit, your stubbornness makes it kind of tempting."

"I can't believe you'd joke about that."

He held out a small plate containing a buttered roll. "And I can't believe you'd fight me over one of the rolls that launched a thousand cowboys. Now eat, and I can tell you all about our road trip."

She snatched the roll from the plate, then winced at the pinch of the IV needle in her right arm.

"It's just saline solution," he said when she turned her head to look at the clear bag that hung beside her, "since you weren't drinking. Last chance to eat your roll before we get to find out where the one for the food goes."

She tore off a piece of the bread and popped it angrily into her mouth, wondering why on earth she'd ever kissed him. Temporary insanity was the only explanation she could come up with. She'd been out of her mind, after learning of her father's—

She shoved both the thought and the wave of pain that followed out of her head. In the back of her mind, she knew she was being difficult, and unreasonable as well, but she wasn't going to cry again, especially not after this bossy cowboy…

Warm and featherlight, the bread began to melt in her mouth. And it was wonderful, so delicious that her first, insane thought was to get the recipe to share it with her cook at home. As if she'd ever have a cook, or her own home, to return to. She couldn't even make her own decisions.

She forced herself to swallow. "So where is it you're taking me?"

"I'm driving out to Jackson, Wyoming, for a few days. Have some questions that need answering."

"About your mother, you mean?"

He nodded, his expression a grim reminder that not everything was about her.

"I thought—" He cleared his throat. "I thought you might as well come with me. It's a good seven-hour drive from here—and then some, since I've planned a route that'll help us avoid the bigger towns. But first, I'll put the word out that I'm dropping you off at the bus station in Cheyenne. With your lungs the way they are, you can't be cleaning for a while, so we'll tell people you're going to visit with your sister in Nebraska. The brown-eyed you, I'm glad to say. Amanda got in your new contacts this morning."

"Sounds like you and Amanda have everything all worked out."

She tried to imagine endless hours riding across the empty state. Hours with nothing to do but think about what Renzo had taken from her and whether, in some fashion, she deserved it. She was tired, so very tired, of running. She wanted to stand, to fight, though it still hurt to breathe.

But as frustrated and upset as she felt about her situation, she realized that taking it out on Dylan wasn't going to change things. Especially since he was clearly making it his business to look after her welfare.

Then again, she realized, maybe looking after her really *was* his job. "Amanda asked you to look after me, didn't she? Right after that first morning, when we met in the stable."

"She did," he admitted.

"So when you came to find me in the stable that first night, you were only there because Amanda, your boss, assigned me as one of your duties."

"I wouldn't put it like that," he said.

"How would you put it?"

He shrugged. "She was worried about you, so she asked me a favor. A favor from a friend, not an employee."

Hope wondered, when he'd kissed her, had that been as a favor to his boss, too? But in her heart, she knew better, for she'd been in that stall with him. She had felt it, just as he had, had been drawn to the combination of rugged strength and real compassion, all wrapped up in one gorgeous package.

She reminded herself to forget his package—and the rest of that hard-muscled body—and focus on the business of survival these next few days.

Because if she did nothing else with the remainder of her wrecked life, she swore that she was putting her ex-husband behind bars for life.

Levi insisted that Hope stay and rest another night, which gave Dylan time to run to a medical-supply store in Cheyenne that afternoon to pick up a portable nebulizer and several prescriptions she would need. It gave him time, too, when he returned for the evening meal, to "confide" in any number of people that he was heading out to Jackson to ask questions about his mother's background and the fate of the infant the murdered Desiree Beal had been seen with.

He took care choosing his confidants, speaking first to Mr. Black, who looked relieved now that his wife had insisted on returning to work, completely recovered except for her still-missing memory of the incident the night of the basement fire. Next, Dylan talked to Agnes, Mathilda, one of the ranch hands—the quiet, intensely private Stewie Runyon—and finally to Misty Mayhew, who practically quivered with excitement to be let in on his secrets as they spoke in the stairwell.

Though he had no doubt that her recent interest was purely mercenary, he tried not to mind all the unnecessary touches. Tried to act halfway friendly, though he wanted nothing more than to get her out of his personal space before his crawling skin gave him away.

"Just be careful out there," she said, batting her dark lashes. "I don't know what I'd *do* if something happened to you."

Probably start sucking up to Trip again, he figured, but what he said was, "I'll be just fine—don't worry. As soon as I've dropped off Hope at the bus station in Cheyenne tomorrow morning, it'll be just me and the open road."

Misty made a face. "*Her* again. I suppose it's nice of you, befriending the new girl, but don't get too attached to that one. She won't be around much longer."

He took a step back. "What's that supposed to mean? Have you heard something?"

Misty shook her head, an escaped curl from her chignon bobbing merrily by her face. "No, not really. It's just…she clearly doesn't have a head for this work. Anyone can see it. Even Hilda's been complaining, telling Mrs. Perkins she should fire anyone stupid enough to poison herself."

"Hilda said that?"

Misty shrugged. "Well, maybe not *exactly,* but her point was clear enough. She's old-school like Mathilda, takes a lot of pride in working on a grand estate and doesn't want anybody here to blight its reputation."

"Regardless of what Hilda did or didn't say," he said, not entirely believing her, "Hope's not a stupid woman. She's—well, like you said, she's new to cleaning." *And set up to poison herself...*

He might never be able to prove it, considering that he hadn't yet located the missing spray bottle. But its absence in and of itself was evidence enough for him. Still, he kept his suspicion to himself, not wanting to give away more than he had to.

"I'm certain Mathilda will let her go as soon as she can. Especially now that we're all left scrambling to cover for a woman who's only been on the ranch for a week." She shot him a sly look. "Not that we've ever gotten a single day's real work out of her."

It took everything he had not to jump in to defend Hope, but instead he picked up the duffel bag that he'd been carrying downstairs and pulled a flashlight from his pocket. "I'll catch you when I'm home again."

"That would be wonderful," she answered eagerly. "I'd love a chance to really talk...to get to know you better."

He faked a smile and went outside, to pack his pickup to get an early start come morning. Although the ranch provided several big four-wheel-drive vehicles for the hands' use, he'd never liked asking the foreman's permission to go places on his own time, so he'd picked up the two-door, dark gray Ford a few years back.

Opening a door, he slung the duffel into the space behind the front seat. Though the truck was fairly Spartan and just a little beat-up, it ran like a champ and represented freedom, along with an opportunity to pick up extra money working with animals on neighboring ranches whenever his schedule allowed it. Because he didn't want to spend his whole life working on other people's outfits, he'd been saving all he could for a down payment on his own land.

His own land, with his own stock on it...maybe with a training facility where he could rehabilitate troubled animals and teach others to do the same. It would be hard work, he was certain, and he'd most likely never be a rich man, but the joy of building something lasting with his own hands was all he asked for in this world.

Though he never spoke of it to others, he had carried the idea of it with him for years, nurtured the tiny flame of it as if his life depended on its warmth. But what would happen if he were forced to face the fact that he had begun life as Cole Colton? Would the new reality— and all that came with it—snuff out the cherished dream?

Or maybe the question ought to be, did he mean to let it?

As he stooped to check the air in the truck's tires, he heard boots coming up behind him—someone in a hurry. Instinct—and the news he'd been circulating— had him reaching inside his jacket pocket, where he'd tucked Hope's snub-nosed revolver.

Just before he reached it, he recognized Amanda, looking as angry as he had ever seen her.

"What are you trying to do," she demanded, "get yourself killed?"

Letting go of the gun, he huffed out a relieved sigh. "Me? With everything that's been going on around here, you should know better than to come stomping up on a person like that, especially after dark. I could've— You might've been hurt."

He decided there was no need to alarm her by mentioning the gun.

Still too wound up to notice, she said, "Yes, you. What on earth are you doing, spreading it around that you're heading out to Jackson to do your own investigating?"

Pleased his plan had worked so quickly, he couldn't help but grin. "That sure got around fast. Mind telling me where it was you heard it?"

"Tom Brooks," she said, naming Cheyenne's ex-cop "babysitter." "He said he'd overheard it in the employee dining area after dinner. But why on earth would you be happy about it getting around? Don't you understand? The mastermind could hear about it, could follow you out there and—"

"Give herself away, assuming that it really is a woman."

"Give herself away?" Amanda echoed. "So that's your plan? To lure her out of hiding?"

"Something like that," he admitted.

She shook her head. "That's crazy, Dylan. Whoever this person is, she's already gotten away with murdering or arranging the murders of three women."

"I can take care of myself," he assured her, "*and* my mother's killer."

"Why? Because you're a man, Mr. Macho? I hate to

break it to you, but even the biggest, baddest Y chromosome out there is no protection from a bullet."

"I'll be watching out for trouble," he said, then decided that, in this case, admitting to the gun wasn't such a bad idea. "Besides, I'm not going unarmed. I have Hope's revolver, for one thing, and Mr. Black's promised to loan me an old shotgun."

"You're not invincible," she said, sounding unimpressed. "You know that? And you're not expendable around here, either—no matter how that DNA test finally turns out."

"Thanks," he said, forcing himself not to react this time to her mention of the looming results. "I'll be just fine. I promise. And I'll just be gone a couple of days, tops."

"And you'll watch out for Hope, too?"

"I won't let her out of my sight," he assured her.

"I only hope that she's up to keeping an eye on you, as well."

In the dirty gray light of this morning's false dawn, Joey Santorini remembered slivers of another dream, interspersed between the nightmares about being knocked off for his failures. Or not another dream, quite, only a repeated image—the memory of a woman's face.

It took him a long time to remember where it was he'd seen it. Longer still to figure out why that particular little nobody would have stuck in his mind, considering how much time he'd spent easing his tensions with fantasies centering around the hot, rich blonde Tawny Lowden, in the sweater that clung to her perky young breasts like a second skin.

But it was that maid with the dark hair and ugly

glasses, the one who'd practically huddled into a ball of misery when they'd had a little fun at her expense, that continued to nag at him over the next few minutes. The more he thought about it, the more familiar she seemed.

Could it be? Could he have actually spoken to the bitch he was pursuing and not even known her?

Finally, he felt his lips pull back in the peculiar expression that had frightened off all too many women. A leering smile, he had been told, a look that hinted he was anticipating either a very personal encounter or the possibility of bloodshed.

Or both, as in this case, he thought as he abruptly tabled his plans to leave the country for a safer climate, for it seemed he still had business right here in Wyoming.

Business he could scarcely wait to begin.

Dr. Levi Colton handed Hope back the small plastic device and asked her to blow into the mouthpiece one more time.

"Again?" she asked, feeling too restless and cranky to endlessly repeat the same test.

"Again, please," he said, without a trace of the impatience she was feeling. "Do a good job, and this'll be the last time."

Exasperated, she made an extra effort, blowing until she was dizzy.

"*That's* what I was looking for," he said, smiling as he checked the measurement. "Your lung capacity's improved immensely."

"And all it took was badgering me until I finally did it right."

He shrugged and said, "Comes with the territory. That and a lot of sleepless nights."

"Sorry you've been missing sleep on my account. And for the grumpy mood, too."

"Trust me, after tending to Mrs. Black and my father lately, you're a model patient. And Dylan's insisted on being the one to stay here with you at night."

It warmed her, the idea of Dylan sitting in the chair beside her in the darkness, guarding her sleep as he listened to her breathing. But that didn't mean she wanted to be treated like an invalid forever, nor deprive him of his rest on the night before their long drive.

"Could I maybe go back and sleep in my own room tonight?" she asked him. "Not that I'm not enjoying your lovely accommodations, but a girl likes a little space of her own now and then."

Even if that space was as cramped as it was Spartan, it was clean and tidy and hers alone.

The young doctor shook his head. "If there were only your lungs to worry about, I'd say go ahead and just stop back for one last breathing treatment in the morning. But Dylan's convinced—and he's nearly convinced me, as well—that you could be in danger in the mansion."

"In my locked room on the third story? I can't see how that would be an issue."

"Listen, Hope, when Dylan checked, he couldn't find that white container that you mentioned anywhere. Meaning it could only have been taken—and tampered with, most likely—by someone who belongs here."

"But why would anyone here want to hurt me? It makes no sense. It's not as if I know anything about this so-called mastermind. I've only been here for a few—"

They were interrupted by a knock, which Dr. Colton excused himself to answer. Though a screen blocked her sight of the infirmary door, Hope could easily hear a woman she thought might be Amanda's sister Gabby saying, "Hurry, Levi. Grab your bag. It's Dad. He's coughing something fierce, and he can't catch his breath."

He uttered a curse, then added, "I've been warning him that cough could be the start of pneumonia."

A moment later, Levi stuck his head around the screen. "I'm leaving for a while. May have to bring my father back down here for treatment, since there's no way he'll let me take him to the hospital. If you head straight up to your room and promise me you'll keep your door locked—"

"Of course," she said. "Don't worry about me another moment."

Once he was gone, she scouted around to find fresh linens and changed the hospital bed she had been using in case it would be needed for the ailing Mr. Colton. As she worked, she realized that for all her past efforts on behalf of the causes she had once supported, making up a bed was the kind of humble, useful effort she would never have thought of personally doing in the past. But of late, she'd come to realize that the simplest of gestures—the delicate, handmade spiced cookies the pastry chef had added to her tray this evening, the compassion Dr. Colton had shown her, or the sleep Dylan had sacrificed so she could rest in safety—meant more than all the money she had helped raise at formal galas.

Besides, with nothing else to give now, a few minutes' effort was the least she could offer to show her appreciation.

Afterward, she dressed and followed Levi's instructions to the letter, relieved to encounter no one on her way upstairs to her room. *Let's hope that means that no one sees me, either,* she thought, unable to muster the energy to deal with either curiosity or kindness, much less the suspicion that anyone she spoke with might be the very person who had poisoned her.

Trip paced the confines of his suite, cursing with frustration over Levi Colton and the wrangler, neither of whom had bought his repeated claims that he only wanted to see for himself how the poor maid was recovering. Even if they had allowed him to see Hope, Trip suspected any attempts at conversation would be strictly monitored.

So much for his plans to question her about the brown contact lens, much less threaten to use the missing laptop to have her dismissed. He'd have to wait, to bide his time until she'd recovered and returned to her normal duties.

But Trip had never been known for his patience, and tonight was no exception. Too restless to sleep, he sat down on a richly upholstered sofa near the fireplace in his suite and took another crack at gleaning something useful from his sister's computer.

Once again, he tried the names of Tawny's childhood pets, her favorite shoe designers, even such obvious choices as his sister's birthday, but no matter what he typed into the password field, he couldn't open Tawny's email. She'd been less careful with her web browser's history, which led him to searches mostly related to "designer handbags," "luxury spa resorts" and "hot fashion trends." He'd already clicked through to dozens of sites the first night he'd liberated the laptop, but this time he went back further into the browser's history.

Soon, he found himself visiting one of the gossipy news sites his sister seemed to favor. He skimmed one article after the next, with topics ranging from which Hollywood stars had undergone breast augmentation to the sexiest celebrities of the year. Sprinkled among these were a handful of stories featuring the kinds of crimes the media loved to dwell on, namely, those involving the lurid murders of attractive blonde victims.

If one of those victims happened to have connections, however obscure, to the rich and famous, so much the better…which was how he found himself looking at a photo of a stunning pageant queen with a rack that made him salivate. When he stared into her face, he started, but was what he was seeing real or only wishful thinking?

He squinted at the photo, trying to imagine the sleek, wheat-blond hair darker, the vibrant blue eyes brown. Still not completely certain, he began to read the details of the story, a story speculating about a possible connection to a mysterious fire death in Florida and the victim's missing daughter….

A daughter whose secrets, Trip soon realized, would provide him all the ammunition he would need to make her his.

"As soon as I catch you alone," he whispered, the lit fuse of his desire burning even hotter.

Hope didn't look at the digital clock at her bedside until just after 5:00 a.m.

Dark as it still was, she jolted awake, remembering that she and Dylan were to leave by daybreak, and there was no way she was going anywhere with her grubby clothes and unwashed hair. Sitting up and stretching, she psyched herself for the short walk to the communal shower most of the women on the floor used. After donning a fuzzy, white robe and shower shoes from the wardrobe where she stored her clothing, she made her way to the end of the hall.

With the lights low and the hall empty, it was quiet—the lull between the kitchen staff, the earliest risers, and the maids, who started their day somewhat later to avoid disturbing the family while working. Hope did hear a few noises, from the groan of a water pipe to the quiet thump of a dresser drawer closing, reminders that both this floor and this mansion had no shortage of inhabitants.

One of whom had deliberately tried to do her harm. Or at least that was what Dylan and Levi were both thinking. But what if they were wrong? If, instead of harming her, the mastermind had meant to kill another of the maids?

The more Hope thought about it, the more likely the idea seemed. For one thing, she'd seen nothing that stuck out as suspicious during her short tenure. Besides, the carts were stored together in an unlocked utility room when not in use, and no one would recognize her name.

Yes, it was true that each maid had her favorite, with cleaning tools and solutions arranged according to her preferences. One of the first things Mathilda had warned her about was to take care never to touch another woman's cart, as the maids could get a little territorial about them. But the mastermind wouldn't necessarily know that, she decided, warming to the idea as she stepped inside the shower stall and latched the door behind her.

It was never really about me at all.

After hanging her robe and towel out of range of the stream, she turned on the water and let the warm steam loosen her lungs. She lingered longer than she should have, imagining the water sluicing through her hair and body washing away her worries about poisoners who were masterminds and electricians who were killers. Washing away the nightmares she'd been having about her father's death, along with half-remembered dreams featuring a certain handsome wrangler.

As the tension drained from her, she began to think she might melt away, too, chasing both the swirling water and her problems down the shower drain....

Until the showers' outer door creaked and the lights abruptly went out, leaving her standing, frozen, heart jumping and teeth chattering as if she'd been turned out naked in the cold.

For what seemed like an eternity, she stood in silence, her mind trying to convince her that the mansion's power had not been repaired correctly, or maybe someone had turned the lights out not realizing she was in here.

But she'd heard the hallway door squeak, she was certain, and whoever had opened it would have surely heard the shower's hiss.

"Hello?" she ventured, shutting off the water and fumbling in the darkness for her robe. "Is someone in here?"

The only answer was the pounding of her own pulse in her ears.

"If this is some kind of prank," she called, her voice thin and shaky, "it isn't funny."

Could it be as simple as that? Was this merely one facet of some sort of initiation played out on the new staff? But try as she might, she couldn't imagine any sort of hazing taking place on Mathilda Perkins's strict watch, or involving cleaning chemicals, either, for that matter.

No, whoever was doing this was out to either hurt her or drive her away. But who would want to...?

"Misty?" she wondered aloud.

It made perfect sense, she realized, remembering the younger woman's jealousy when she'd seen her wearing Dylan's jacket. Though Hope had seen no sign of a real relationship between the two, Misty clearly had ideas of staking an early claim on Jethro Colton's missing heir—and, ridiculous as it seemed, she clearly saw Hope as the competition.

"If this is about Dylan," she called, her words echoing in the darkness, "I promise you, I'll back off. Besides, I won't be here much longer. You can ask Mathilda. I'm going back to… I'm just going. Very soon."

To testify, provided she lived long enough.

But aside from the drip, drip of the draining water, she sensed only emptiness around her. Whoever had turned off the lights must have reached inside the room, then fled, leaving her alone to cower in the darkness. If it truly was someone's idea of a joke, she wasn't laughing.

Drawing a deep breath and her courage, Hope slung her towel over her shoulder and unlatched the stall door. With her hands outstretched to avoid bumping the hard sinks or tiled walls, she groped her way toward the rim of light around the hallway door, telling herself in her calmest voice, "Just a few more steps."

But in that place, at that time, Hope didn't have a few steps.

Only one, before the first blow landed, slamming her down hard.

Chapter 10

Dylan was heading down for breakfast when he heard a woman's voice, high-pitched with hysteria, above him in the stairwell.

"Wait, please!" Her panic echoed in the stairwell. "Someone—someone's tried to— I'm hurt."

Wheeling around, he looked up at Hope, his gaze catching on the starkness of a white robe splattered with bright red. But she was moving, stumbling downstairs, her face streaked with the blood dripping from a small cut above her right eye. "Please. Help me."

He met her halfway, too afraid of hurting her to do more than grab her by the shoulders and scan her for other injuries. "Hope—what happened?"

She was shaking uncontrollably. "I was alone, in the shower. The lights went out and then—before I could get out of there, something hit me, hard. Knocked me right off my feet. My head slammed against the floor and—"

"Who? Who did this?" he asked, pulling back to look into her wild eyes. As painful as the bloody lump looked, it was the purpling line across her throat that sent his stomach plunging. "Your neck. Is that— That looks like—"

"I was knocked facedown, and then there was this

heavy weight on my chest. Someone's knee, I think, and then a sharp pain. I reached up, clawing at what felt like a strap or a cord, maybe, across my throat. I couldn't move it, couldn't breathe."

As her eyes welled with remembered horror, he took her into his arms and pulled her close, heedless of the blood. "Thank God you were able to escape, but how?"

"Something from a self-defense class I took switched on in my brain, and I pushed up with my arms and threw my head back. I smacked into something hard—his face, I imagine, and when he jerked back, I broke his hold and rolled free."

"*He,* you said. It was a man?"

She shook her head. "I can't be certain. I only know that when I fought back, whoever it was backed off. I heard the door creak. I caught a glimpse, a silhouette, and then I was alone."

"Then your attacker could still be up there." Dylan glanced toward the stairs, wanting to destroy the monster who would do this, needing to put a stop to the terrifying attacks once and for all.

But Hope was shaking her head. "I—I don't know. *Could* be. But it took me a few minutes before I dared to leave the bathroom. I was so afraid someone would be waiting for me in the hallway. Waiting to finish—" Her hand floated above her bruised throat. "To finish me."

Galvanized by necessity, he scooped her up into his arms and carried her into the men's hall, where he shouted for help. Two of the younger hands came boiling out of nearby rooms. The sandy-haired Stewie Runyon was bare-chested, his shirt still in his clenched fist, and the darker-haired Cal Clark hadn't yet put on his boots, but neither hesitated when Dylan told them what had happened and asked them to head upstairs to check on all the women.

"I don't care how shocked Mathilda and Agnes are to see men on the women's floor," Dylan added. "Make sure they leave the floor for their own safety—and keep a sharp eye out for any of the ladies who might look a little extra breathless or disheveled."

"You aren't thinking one of them would have done something like this?" Cal asked, his worried gaze flicking toward Hope, who had insisted she could stand on her own two feet.

"I don't know what to think at this point," said Dylan, but as both hands headed upstairs, he realized that Cal was right, that such a physical attack didn't sound like the sort of thing most females would attempt, especially against a young and healthy woman like Hope. But that didn't rule out another male accomplice, paid off just as young Duke Johnson had been before he'd killed Dylan's mother. If only the mercenary little punk had been able to name the person who had hired him, so much bloodshed could have been averted.

Hope shook her head, telling him, "I wish I could be more helpful. Wish I'd seen or heard something, anything at all."

"You got away," he said, hugging her to him again and stroking the back of her damp hair. "That's the most important thing. If things had gone the other way..."

She squeezed him back, her voice only a little shaky as she told him, "What did I tell you about us Jersey girls? We're tougher than we look."

Relieved to see her looking stronger, he pulled a clean bandanna from his pocket, along with the new cell phone he'd picked up to replace the one he'd broken.

"You might want to blot that forehead until we can get you checked out in the infirmary," he said, passing her the folded square. "First, I'm calling the police."

"Do you really have to?" Hope looked more worried about their involvement than the fact that someone had tried to kill her. "Is there any way we can leave them out of this?"

"Absolutely not," he said. "Because unless I miss my guess, these attacks have nothing to do with your ex-husband and everything to do with the mastermind who's already killed three people in this mansion."

"But why?"

"There's only one explanation I can think of. You had to have seen something without realizing it—something so incriminating that the mastermind feels she has no choice but to kill you. Or have you killed by another of her henchmen."

"Then I'm not safe here at all. Not until this person's caught."

"That's why it's more important than ever that I get you out of here as soon as Levi clears you."

Several hours later, Hope walked beside Dylan as he carried her bag to the pickup, his boots crunching on the gravel. Every few steps, he looked back toward her, tension written in his clenched jaw and troubled gaze.

"If you have any doubts at all about this," he told her, "we can still go to the medical center to get you checked out like Levi advised."

"He said himself my injuries look superficial."

"Not from where I'm standing, they don't. And I'm betting they don't feel it, either."

"Those painkillers he gave me are helping." Glancing

back toward the huge hulk of the mansion, she shivered. "And I'll feel even better once we put some distance between me and whoever did this. Even police chief Peters said he thought it was a good idea."

He'd been disappointed that she'd been unable to provide more details of the attack and even more disappointed that the hands' search of the third story turned up nothing.

Opening the passenger door, he put her bag behind her front seat, then offered her a hand up. Her first impulse was to tell him not to treat her like an invalid, but she was feeling a little shaky, queasy with the idea that someone had actually jumped on her and tried to choke the life out of her. She could still feel the knee jammed into her back, the pressure against her neck, the darkness spilling over her, like an oily slick of evil.

"Thanks," she managed, grateful for the warm strength of his hand as it squeezed hers. His chivalry might be old-fashioned, but it made her—*he* made her—feel safe, and right now there was nothing in the world she needed more.

Once they were both inside and buckled in, he slid another look her way and shook his head. "People are going to take one look at you and think I'm the kind of scum who gets off on beating women."

"Nobody who knows you, that's for certain." She smiled and adjusted her scarf to better hide her bruised neck. "There you are. That better?"

"Nice try," he said, his gaze zeroing in on the bandaged square stuck to her forehead, which didn't begin to cover the bruise she'd gotten from her earlier fall in Tawny's room. Shaking his head, he added, "But it won't be better until police chief Peters makes an arrest."

"You really think he will?"

"Not until we find him some better leads to go on. He seemed to agree that it couldn't have been one of your ex's goons, or you would be dead, but the idea that someone in the mansion, someone we all know and trust, could do something like—"

"Three women have been killed here, right? And there've been other attacks, too."

"But why you now? Why you in particular."

She sighed, knowing it was a question with no answer. Not one of the possible motives she'd discussed with the police chief had sounded anything but laughable, from the late delivery of a load of laundry to poor housekeeping skills to a borrowed jacket on a cold night.

Only a mile or two after leaving the ranch gate, he crested a small hill and Dylan pulled over to the shoulder, to a spot that overlooked a herd of white-faced cattle grazing on the range.

"Forget something?" she asked, then nodded toward the animals, some of whom had looked up at them, still chewing. "Or did you stop to say goodbye to all your buddies?"

"I stopped to make sure we aren't being followed," he said, peering steadily into the rearview mirror.

"Of course." She hugged herself, pulling her jacket tighter around her.

"Are you all right?" he asked. "Need me to turn up the heat?"

"I'm warm enough. It's not that. It's—you'd think I'd be used to it. For over a year, now, I've been looking over my shoulder, waiting for Renzo's men to show up. But somehow, having this mastermind in the picture, too…" She threw up her hands and shook her head. "And to think, I was once the popular girl around town. You know, popular with *other* people besides killers."

His gaze was somber as it drilled into hers. "You know, you took ten years off my life when I saw you in that stairwell."

The memory slithered up her spine, making her skin erupt with goose bumps. "I was so relieved that the first person I ran into was someone I could trust. I was afraid, just terrified that I'd meet up with…"

She swallowed hard, her hand drifting reflexively toward her throat.

"It's all right now," he assured her.

"But you're worried someone might be right behind us, aren't you?"

He shook his head. "I don't know. But it's possible you aren't the only target."

"What do you mean?"

She listened intently as he explained how—and why—he had made it known that he'd be traveling on his own to Jackson.

"It's only fair that you should know," he said, "that while I might be getting you clear of both the ranch and your ex-husband's assassins, you might still be at risk as long as you're with me."

"Then I'll have to help you, won't I?" She straightened her back, suddenly infused with purpose. "With your investigation, I mean."

His eyes met hers in the mirror, those deep blue eyes she couldn't help but want to fall into, to drown in, no matter how hard she fought the attraction. But how much of what she felt was real, and how much because she saw him as a safe place, the one thing that was keeping her alive?

Either way, she could never risk pursuing a relationship with this man. Soon, she'd have to leave here, and she refused to consider ruining or risking his life, too.

But that didn't mean she couldn't repay his concern and kindness in some other coin.

"You'll see," she said, cheering with the idea of helping him to find his mother's killer. "I'm not always such a burden."

"I never said that."

"You didn't have to. Since you've met me, I've been nothing but a headache to you and Amanda. I should have never come here in the first place."

"You're not a headache, Hope. You're Amanda's good friend, and you're in a horrendous situation. A situation you had nothing to do with."

A pang of conscience made her stiffen, a reminder of a truth she would far rather forget. Unable to face his sympathy, she looked away from him, toward rolling hills bathed in the silvery light of a cool morning.

"Did I say something wrong?" he asked.

Hope shook her head, then changed her mind and nodded. Because it *was* wrong, to let him and Amanda go on thinking she was innocent. "Not you. *Me,* if I've left anyone with the impression that I'm a purely blameless victim."

"I don't follow. You turned your ex in when you found out, right? Divorced him and agreed to testify against him, at great personal risk to yourself—"

"Not right away, I didn't," she admitted, wondering what it was about Dylan that made her want to talk. She'd heard he was an animal whisperer, that he connected with even the most troubled horses and cattle in a way others found mystifying. Did he have the same skill with people, or was she simply so desperate, after a year of isolation, that she was primed to spill her guts to the first attentive stranger she met?

"I imagine it was tough making that decision," he said carefully. "It must've been hell, giving up everyone you knew and loved, your home and your possessions."

"It wasn't things, or even people, as much as I hated leaving my father and all my good friends that held me back. It was a dream."

"A dream?" he asked.

She nodded, a lump forming in her throat. "You see, we'd been...trying for several years."

"Trying? You mean—for a child?"

Her eyes squeezed closed, but there was no stopping the flood of memory. "For a baby, yes. I wanted..."

Wanted. Such a tame word for the monstrous need that had taken root, only to give way to an increasing sense of desperation as she marked each monthly cycle as another failure. She'd blamed herself, though her testing had come back normal and her doctor had repeatedly reminded her that her husband was nearly twenty years her senior and had no children from his previous marriage, either. In his stiff-necked pride, Renzo had flatly refused to submit a sperm sample for analysis, no matter how she'd begged him. But whoever was to blame, it eventually grew impossible for her to watch mothers with their children, to attend one more friend's baby shower, to shop for yet another gift—tiny, precious outfits that blurred with her own tears.

She'd so hated being jealous, hated reducing her success or failure to her obsession with this one goal, which had been blown out of all proportion with the loss of her own mother. But no matter how she'd chided herself, she could think of little else.

"That terrible day," she confessed, "the day I showed up at Renzo's office and heard his side of that awful phone call, I'd just taken a home pregnancy test—I swear I should've bought those things by the case, I'd used so many. But that morning, that one time, it was positive. I couldn't believe it was finally happening for us."

Dylan stared at her, looking as stricken as she felt, remembering all the doomed dreams dancing through her head.

"I was so excited, I was beside myself. I couldn't wait to tell him," she went on. "So even though I knew how much he hated interruptions while he was on the phone, I cracked open the door, hoping to catch his attention. But his back was to me, and he sounded so angry.... Still, when I heard him order someone to 'take out' the man I knew was my husband's business rival, I convinced myself I *must* have misunderstood."

"You were in shock," he said, "blindsided."

"I *deliberately* refused to acknowledge the truth. Now when I look back, I realize there were other signs, so many clues about the nature of the family business. I just didn't want to see them. Didn't want to believe the man I loved didn't exist."

Dylan blinked at her, his expression contemplative. "Sometimes, it's tough, wrapping your head around the one thing that changes everything."

"But people *died* because I couldn't—not only the man Renzo wanted dead, but his wife, too," she blurted. "That's what finally snapped me out of it, when I heard about their 'accident,' their two little ones, both orphaned—I could've stopped it if only I'd gone to the Feds right away."

"I'm sure you would have, if you'd known for certain. You're a good person…Aurora. Anyone can see it."

She answered with a shake of her head. "Please don't call me that. And don't make excuses for what I did. It was murder, nothing less."

"You're no killer. You were just scared."

"Killer, coward, fool—one's as awful as the other. I still can't believe I was so stupid that I would pretend away the words I'd heard with my own ears."

"You were listening with your heart, that's all. Because you loved your husband."

"Loved the *idea* of him maybe. I never knew the real man."

A silence stretched between them, like the fragile new ice of a first frost. Too delicate to support much weight, but too solid to deny.

"You said—you said you were pregnant," he asked quietly. "What happened? Where's the— Did you have the—"

"Please," she said, her voice breaking. "Let's talk about the weather, Dylan, or you can tell me about what you do with the cows and horses. Or maybe, do you follow sports? What do you think about the Giants—or whatever team you watch—this season?"

The raspiness of her voice gave way to a squeak, but it didn't matter—nothing mattered except finding some way to change the subject. Because having come this far, opened herself up to more of the truth than she had ever before admitted, she couldn't lie to him now.

But she knew instinctively that sharing the remainder of her story would shatter her completely. And she couldn't let that happen, couldn't stop until she'd made sure her ex-husband's ruthlessness would never break another heart....

Even if the effort stopped hers in the end.

In a single glance, Dylan read the light flush in her face, the gleam of moisture in her eyes. Whatever had happened to Hope, and to the child she had so desperately wanted, she couldn't speak of it now....

And anyway, he warned himself, *it's none of your damned business.* But try as he might not to care about this woman, the sight of her bandaged forehead and her bruised neck, along with the emotion in her still-raw voice, all conspired against him.

"If you'd rather not," he told her, "we don't have to talk at all."

It didn't take empathic abilities to hear her exhalation or see the tension flowing from her body when she nodded. Still, he felt her pain, her grief and her fear as keenly as he did his own.

And heaven help him if he didn't want to find a way to ease it, want it as badly as he'd ever wanted anything, no matter that she still loved the bastard who had hurt her. No matter that, in the end, a woman born to the life she'd known would only break his heart.

"I think it's safe to go," he said before chancing to look up at the rearview mirror. There, he saw a flash of red that drove every other thought from his mind.

"Get down, now," he said, pulling Hope's revolver from his pocket and giving her a light shove to push her down.

"Who is it?" came her frightened voice as she ducked beneath the level of the dashboard.

Too focused on the approaching SUV to respond,

Dylan cranked down the driver's-side window. Gravel crunched beneath the tires of the shiny new Land Rover as it stopped beside them and a tinted window lowered with a soft, electric hum.

"Everything okay there?" Trip Lowden asked, his eyes hidden by dark glasses. "That piece of junk finally break down on you?"

"I'm fine, thanks," Dylan answered, irritated as ever that this spoiled man-child, who traded in his ride for a new car every year on Jethro's dime, would disparage the perfectly serviceable vehicle he'd worked so hard to buy in cash. "Just stopped to take a call."

"Really? 'Cause I heard that you were taking Hope Woods to the bus station. Did I hear wrong? 'Cause I wanted to check on her, make sure she's okay. You know how concerned I've been about her."

Whatever Trip had wanted with Hope these past few days, it was inconceivable to think he only meant to offer his sympathies. Just as Dylan was about to tell him an old friend of hers had shown up earlier to give her a ride, she popped up beside him, her cheeks flaming.

"I'm right here," she said. "There's no need to worry about me, Mr. Lowden."

"Whoa." From inside the gleaming red SUV, Trip leered. "And here I thought you were a lesbian. Sorry if I, um…interrupted."

As his passenger-side window closed, he saluted Dylan and drove off smirking.

"Ugh." Hope sounded as disgusted as she did embarrassed. "He actually thinks that I was down there—that we were…"

Dylan couldn't help but burst out laughing. "He thought you were a *lesbian*? What's up with that?"

She shot him a withering look, clearly furious that he would find the situation funny. "He's just an idiot, that's all, and you know as well as I do, he'll never keep his mouth shut. I don't want people thinking…"

Sobering, he promised, "I'll tell them you were resting, that's all. You were nearly killed just hours ago, for crying out loud."

She shook her head and shot him a look. "Yeah, right. Like anybody'll believe the truth when they can have a nice, hot helping of nasty gossip instead."

He put the truck in gear and pulled back onto the road. "Listen, Hope, I know he's been harassing you. It's why you told him you like women, right?"

"I didn't! All I wanted was for him to stop bugging me while I was working."

"Don't you worry about him anymore. I'll be more than happy to have a talk with Trip. Or more, if that's what it takes to make him lay off." Dylan almost hoped the jerk would give him an excuse to deck him, even if it cost his job.

"Forget about him. He's nothing I can't handle."

"I wish I could believe that," Dylan said, gesturing toward Trip's flashing brake lights as he turned right far ahead. "But that's the road toward Cheyenne he took, where I'm guessing he'll just so happen to show up at the bus station looking for you. Probably plans to offer you a chance to ride in style," Dylan added with a grimace.

She shuddered visibly. "Sounds *exactly* like something that piece of slime would do. Only he'd be thinking of ways I could repay his 'kindness' before we made it a half mile down the road."

"Fortunately—" Dylan slowed, then waited until Trip's vehicle was well out of sight before driving past the turnoff "—we're not heading anywhere near Cheyenne. If anybody asks about it later, I'll say they must've misunderstood. I dropped you off at the bus station in Dead, the closest town."

"Good," she said before adding, "I still can't believe I came to a place called Dead for my own safety. What a gruesome name."

Glad that she had hit upon a safer topic of conversation, he said, "Pretty sure it wasn't chosen for its tourist appeal."

"Why was it, then? Do you know?"

"Local legend has it that one of the original ranchers in this area was found floating facedown and full of arrows in what came to be called Dead River—that's what the ranch is named for."

"Tough history."

"It's a tough land, but rumor has it, those arrows were all for show, shot through him as a distraction after the bullet that struck him down."

"Whose bullet?" she asked.

He shrugged. "Some say it was a neighboring rancher whose pretty wife was receiving overnight visits whenever he went out of town on business. Others figure it was a man he'd crossed in business or maybe even one of his own sons, who were tired of waiting to inherit."

She shook her head. "People never really change, do they? Whether you're looking in the history books or all around you, they're sneaky and self-centered."

"Not all of them, Hope."

"You're right, of course," she answered. "I wouldn't want you to think for a moment I don't appreciate Amanda, and you, too, especially considering everything else you have going on in your life right now."

"There's no need to thank me. That's not what I was after."

"Then what is it, Dylan?" she asked. "Why'd you really bring me?"

He thought for a minute before pointing out some elk ahead off in the distance. A herd of about thirty, grazing on a hillside beneath a crisp, blue sky.

"Beautiful," she murmured, her voice filled with awe.

In answer to her question, he admitted, "Maybe I brought you along for company. It's going to be a tough thing for me, talking to a woman who knew my mom when she was young. Who maybe knew me, too, back before I *was* me, if it really turns out I'm…him. You know, Cole Colton."

Around Hope, it was easier admitting his fears, maybe because she understood how it took a person time to admit he'd been living a lie for the better part of his life. Because she understood how high the cost was of giving up cherished illusion.

"I know, Dylan," she said, reaching out to cover his free hand with hers.

As he turned his wrist to squeeze her fingers, he made out the huge bull elk raising his shaggy head, his rack silhouetted against the clearing sky. Watching over his herd, even if it put him in a hunter's sights…

Watching over those his instincts claimed.

Chapter 11

As the truck bounced over a rut sometime later, Hope jerked fully awake, tensing with the memory of the attack that began her day.

"Sorry about that last pothole," Dylan told her, his familiar voice easing the knot of nerves in her throat. "I'm afraid the bumps are part of these back roads."

She looked around, taking in the hills on either side of them, clothed in tawny grasses with a few bare trees here and there. In the distance, a purplish ridge of mountains held up an endless sky, but nowhere beneath them did she spot a single sign of human habitation: not a car or house or building, not even a fence or power line.

The last of her tension gusted away on an exhalation. Out here, there was no need to fear lurking assassins or murderous masterminds. With Dylan, she could let down her hair as well as her guard, could let go of the strain of pretending she was someone she was not.

"How's the head?" he asked.

"It's fine. I'm fine. Sorry if I haven't been very good company these last few minutes."

He shot her an easy grin. "These last few *hours,* you mean, but it's okay. We still have plenty more to go."

Her stomach rumbled loudly, reminding her she'd been too upset to eat anything this morning.

"How 'bout a little break?" he suggested. "I need to stretch my legs, and you're sounding like you're ready for a little lunch."

"You know of a café or something not too far ahead?"

He laughed. "Not unless it's run by pronghorn antelopes or mule deer. But it's warmed up enough that I thought maybe we could enjoy a little picnic on the tailgate."

"You brought along food?"

"My friend Kate insisted on packing us a gourmet lunch."

"The pastry chef, right?" Hope asked, remembering a young woman with long, brown curls and big, kind eyes.

He nodded. "Sure is. And Levi Colton's girlfriend, too."

"Dr. Colton's girlfriend? Really?"

Smiling, Dylan nodded. "It's so great to see her happy again. They seem really great together."

"I'll never get all these people straight." Hope laughed before a pang of realization struck her. "But then, I'll never really have to. I'm leaving, Dylan. Leaving soon. I've decided I'm going back to testify after all. I have to, to finally put an end to it, provided I make it that long."

"You'll make it," he vowed, heat sparking in his blue eyes. "We're going to find this mastermind, and until we do, Amanda says she's hiring another bodyguard, one specifically assigned to you. And I'll be watching, too."

Hope sighed. "Maybe I should just contact my WITSEC liaison again as soon as we get back to the ranch."

"I thought you said you couldn't trust them."

"It's tough admitting this, but I doubt it was ever really

them," she said, the grief of it a throbbing wound in her chest. "*I* was the one who dared to use a public-access computer at the town library to let my father know I was all right. I thought I was being so smart, funneling my email through a proxy server, but more than likely, I led them straight to me in Iowa—and sealed my father's fate, too."

"Oh, Hope. I'm so sorry." He laid his big hand on her shoulder.

"And *I* was the one who sought shelter at the Colton ranch, knowing full well that anyone who dug too deeply into my background might find my connection with Amanda." She shook her head, setting it to aching. "How could I have been so damned stupid, so self-centered, to forget that no one on the planet's more motivated to track me down than a criminal organization with everything to lose?"

Releasing her seat belt, she climbed down out of the truck, her energy too wild to be contained another moment. She slammed the door behind her, then paced along the roadside and stared out across the burnished, frost-dried grasses to the mountains far beyond.

Gradually, she became aware that it was still cool enough for her to be glad she'd worn a jacket with her jeans and boots and a light sweater. Still, the sunshine felt good on her face, and it was a relief to stretch her legs.

In her peripheral vision, she caught glimpses of Dylan pulling out a plaid blanket and an ice chest, then lowering the truck's tailgate and covering it with a folded layer of warm wool for them to sit on. He popped the top on a can of cola and took a leisurely drink while leaning against the gate's lip, but he didn't try to rush her. He didn't try to talk.

Instead, he eventually opened the cooler and started

taking things out, allowing her however long it took to settle before she came to him.

When she finally approached, she said, "I'm beginning to see why you're so good with the animals. Although I'm not sure I'm flattered, knowing you're applying the same principles to me."

He patted the tailgate beside him and waited for her to plant her hands and swing her rear onto the blanket. Once she had, he smiled at her. "If it makes you feel any better, I think of you more as a filly than a heifer."

She laughed, admitting, "I guess I walked right into that one, didn't I? And thanks. I think."

He flashed a row of even, white teeth. "How 'bout something to drink, then?"

"Any water?" she asked. "I don't do bubbles, unless it's champagne."

"What a diva," he teased before handing her bottled water and a wrapped sandwich.

They turned their attention to the food next, beginning with sliced roast turkey, Brie and some kind of cranberry-nut relish with baby greens, all on a thick, dark multigrain bread. Kate had also included raw, cut veggies with a tangy dip, along with iced pumpkin cookies for dessert.

"Wow," said Hope when she had eaten far more than she'd meant to, "your friend should open her own restaurant. This is all amazing."

"She's a great cook, though it probably doesn't hurt that it's the first real meal you've eaten since you came here, either," he said. "Now that you know what you've been missing, aren't you sorry?"

"Kinda. Except the turkey and cranberry and the pumpkin remind me way too much that Thanksgiving's coming."

He slanted a look her way. "You have something against Thanksgiving?"

"It's not like that. It's just—it was always my favorite holiday, that's all. My mother used to…"

"Used to what?" he asked, an invitation in the curve of his lips.

She took a deep breath. "She always invited every 'stray' she met—friends, neighbors, anyone who didn't have a family to share the day with. It always started small, then blew up into this huge feast. Took almost a week of preparation, and she insisted on doing every bit of it herself. At least until that last year… That year, we cooked together. We laughed so much that week. It was crazy—we even had a flour fight. You should've seen the kitchen afterward. But it was so worth it."

"Sounds like some great memories."

"They're very special," she said, though her eyes were welling. "I didn't know it at the time, you see, but she was finally letting me help, making sure I copied down the recipes to make everybody's favorites, because she knew it would be her last Thanksgiving, and she wanted me—wanted the whole tradition—to go on in the years to come."

"Did it?" he asked carefully.

She shook her head, thinking of how much had changed, how swiftly. How her little family had shattered like dropped crystal, leaving nothing but the shards embedded in her heart.

"I'm sorry," he said, reaching toward her.

With a shake of her head, she turned away, pretending that she didn't see him. As she snatched up another of the pumpkin cookies, she tried to joke. "Might as well quit moping and enjoy my dessert. On the bright side, with the trial coming up, there's no point in worrying over all those nasty calories."

Normally, he moved so carefully around her that she was shocked by his speed when his hand shot out to grasp her wrist. "If you're talking about suicide, you need to put it out of your mind."

Reflexively, she let go of the cookie, then watched it bounce off of the tailgate's rim and break into pieces on the hard ground. "Oh, relax," she told him. "I'm pretty sure it won't be suicide, just murder."

Though she'd meant to sound lighthearted, she knew Dylan was right. There was nothing remotely funny about her situation.

Releasing her, he snarled, "The hell it will. You're not going back East. Not to be killed. You're not sacrificing yourself out of guilt about your father."

"I'm not *sacrificing* myself. Not willingly, at any rate. I intend to listen this time, to do everything the U.S. Marshals tell me. And if I do survive my testimony, no one from my old life will ever hear from me again."

Their gazes locked, the gazes of two people realizing on which side of the dividing line Dylan would stand from her. And in his eyes, she saw the pain, the same pain she felt at the thought of their fragile, new connection being severed.

A connection that, for all its immediacy, felt more real and right and natural than any she had known before.

"What if I told you," he asked, "that I didn't want you to leave? That I believe your life is worth more than it would cost to stop him?"

"How can you," she asked, her still-raspy voice strained to the point of breaking, "when people have died because

I stuck my head in the sand instead of going to the authorities? When two babies were orphaned because I—"

"Because you were thinking of your own child?"

She shuddered, looking away, the words *your own child* sparking off bitter memories. Pushing off the tailgate, she stalked a few feet farther. Her stomach pitched so violently she was afraid she might be sick.

Dylan's boot heels crunched the gravel as he strode up behind her. "And once you realized what your husband had done, you gathered up your courage and you went to the authorities."

She wheeled around to face him, her vision blurred with tears. "And people *still* died—others who came forward, that poor young grocery manager. M-my own father, too, because no matter what I do, people won't stop dying!"

"Your husband and his thugs are the killers, not you." He took another step before reaching out to cup her cheek in his hand. "Never you."

When his rough thumb stroked her flesh, her eyes slid closed. Because she didn't want to feel what she was feeling, didn't deserve the waves of pleasure sparking through her at his touch. Not a woman who had chosen a monster for a husband. A woman who no longer knew who she was anymore.

His fingers touched her eyelids. "Open them for me," he whispered, his voice rough as his hands were gentle. "I want you to look into my face, Aurora. This time, I want you watching when I kiss you."

Before Dylan could lean in closer, her eyes flashed open, those deep brown contacts that made him miss the hidden light beneath. But there was no hiding her resistance, especially when she planted her splayed fingers in the center of his chest.

"Please don't," she told him. "Just don't, Dylan. There's nothing you can say that's going to change my mind, and it's already going to be hard enough, doing what I have to."

"But that's just it. You *don't* have to. We can find another way," he said, "a way to keep you safe."

He knew how ludicrous it must sound, when she'd been attacked and nearly killed this very morning. He knew, too, that even if the mastermind were apprehended and her ex-husband's men never again came calling, a gorgeous, cultivated woman like her would never be content living out her life stuck in some remote corner of Wyoming masquerading as a housemaid.

No more than she'd be content with a man who wrangled livestock for a living. For a moment, he wondered if he would stand a chance with her if he really turned out to be the missing Colton heir, with all the money and the prestige that would certainly come with that discovery. But the thought brought with it a rush of shame, not only the idea that he'd wish away his blood connection to the mother who had loved him, but the knowledge that Hope was certainly no Misty Mayhew, out looking for the chance to enrich herself.

"If *you* get half a chance to put away your mother's killer," she said, "you and I both know you'll never let cowardice—or anything else—stop you from doing it. Especially not after everything you've done to paint a target on your own back with this trip."

"These are professional hit men you're talking about going up against," he insisted, ignoring the similarities in what both of them were doing. Because this was different; *she* was different, and he didn't give a damn if that made him some kind of chauvinist or not. "Hit men who won't give up until you're dead."

"If I go back, I'll have the support of the U.S. Marshals, who assured me early on that they've never lost a single witness who followed their instructions to the letter. And trust me, I've learned one heck of a harsh lesson about bending the rules for any reason." She sighed, her expression so weighed down by grief, so vulnerable that all he wanted to do was wrap his arms around her and keep her safe forever.

But she'd made it clear she couldn't bear it, so he swallowed back the desire and said, "Guess we'd better pack up and get going. At this rate, we'll be lucky to make Jackson by eight."

She nodded, and very soon, they were on the road again. But other than a few words exchanged during a fuel and restroom pit stop in a small town along the way, there was little conversation, each of them too tormented by his or her own thoughts to reach out to the other.

By the time they reached the town of Jackson it was too dark to point out the nearby mountains the town was perched against—craggy, snowcapped peaks whose beauty stuck out in Dylan's memory from a visit years before. Since his appointment with Marnie Sayers, the former waitress who had bought his mother's diner, wasn't scheduled until morning, he headed toward the room he had reserved.

"Getting hungry?" he asked Hope, who was looking out the window at the businesses and restaurants along the town's main drag. "As soon as we're checked in, we can head out to grab something."

"Something light, I hope. I'm still pretty full from that

delicious lu— Wait. You made a motel reservation here in town? Under your real name, after telling everyone where you were going?"

"I've already told you—I'm not hiding."

"Not hiding at all." Her look was pointed. "You're *hoping*. Hoping that this mastermind will show up to try to stop you. And you accused *me* of being the suicidal person in this outfit?"

"Don't worry," he assured her. "If this killer comes for me, I'll be ready."

"And what exactly am *I* doing, in this O.K. Corral scenario you've dreamed up?"

"Staying in another room—as far from mine as I can swing. And crawling under the bed if you hear any gunfire."

"You *have* to be kidding. No."

"What do you mean, *no?*" In his mind, her refusal wasn't an option.

"I mean, you're giving me my gun back—you brought it, didn't you?"

"There's no need for you to—"

"*Didn't* you?" she repeated, sounding surprisingly stubborn for a woman as battered as she looked.

"Yes, I brought it," he admitted, irritated and impressed at the same time with the way she'd dug in her heels. "And a shotgun, too."

"Well, I'm more familiar with my pistol, so I'll take that one, and we'll take turns sleeping. Both of us, in your room. Unless you're scared to be alone with me," she added with a wink.

"The only thing I'm scared about is how I'd ever explain it to Amanda if anything happened to you— Hell,

Hope. You know it's more than that. I'd never be able to forgive myself."

"Same here," she assured him. "I've already got too many corpses on my conscience to handle even a cock-sure cowboy like you."

Snorting, he flashed a grin in her direction. "*Cocksure,* huh? I think I like the sound of that."

"You're incorrigible," she said, lips quirking as she fought the impulse to smile back. "You know that?"

"I like the sound of that, too," he said, relieved that they had finally found their way past the awkwardness that had plagued them throughout the afternoon. Or maybe it was the promise of spending the night alone with a partner watching his back that cheered him.

Or a night alone with the beautiful, brave woman who was distracting his thoughts—and invading his dreams—far too often.

He had chosen a small locally run lodge not far outside of town rather than one of the chains that catered to the annual flood of visitors that descended on both Grand Teton and Yellowstone national parks and the surrounding ski resorts. Known for its scrupulously clean but rustic side-by-side log-cabin-style rooms as much as the staff's hospitality, the Mountain View was the perfect spot, dark and quiet enough that the mastermind might well feel safe approaching.

After referring a time or two to the directions he had printed using a Dead River Ranch computer that was accessible to all employees, he pulled up to the lodge's office.

"You'd better wait out in the truck while I check in," he told Hope. "Otherwise, I'm betting I won't get a friendly reception."

"Why not?" she started before answering her own question. "My bruises, right. I get it. I saw that death-laser look the clerk gave you when I went into the gas station to get the restroom key."

Dylan winced. "The moment you left, she gave me a piece of her mind to go with it. Told me I ought to get down on my knees and beg forgiveness to the Lord and you both for leaving a pretty thing like you in that condition."

"Ouch," Hope said.

Reluctantly, Dylan returned her revolver. "I'm not expecting any trouble yet, but just in case, you keep this. Just try not to wave it around and scare any random guest that walks by."

"Or moose, maybe, from the looks of this place," she said, peering into a darkness broken only by a few security lights.

"You shoot one of those," he joked, "you be sure to field dress it for our dinner before I get back. Driving makes me hungry."

"I'm beginning to think that *everything* makes you hungry."

"Guilty," he allowed, then went inside to take care of the registration, a part of him braced for the sharp crack of a gunshot just outside.

Nervous as Hope felt about Dylan setting himself up as a target, she grew at least as worried about the prospect of spending the night together in the same room. Because no matter how she warned herself against growing too attached, she was finding it more and more difficult to resist his strength, his kindness, even the protectiveness that she found so maddening.

She told herself it was all wrong, that she was only lonely. And that if she didn't learn to stand on her own, she would never survive the coming months. With this in mind, she did her best to keep her distance over dinner at a candlelit corner table in a little café where Dylan ordered a massive rib eye while she dived into the crispest, most delicious salad she'd eaten in months. Before the meal was halfway over, though, he lured her from her quiet mood with stories of his life on the rodeo circuit that soon had them laughing and teasing as if they'd known each other for years.

When the meal was finished, he did his best to coax her into dessert. "Be a shame to pass up this cherry pie. Says right here on the menu it's 'world famous.'"

"Really, Dylan, I'm full."

"You aren't one of those women who're scared of food, now, are you?"

"You funny, funny man," she said. "You're talking to a person who threw an ice-cream-sundae party the day she retired from the pageant circuit. When I'm feeling more like myself, I could eat you under the table any day."

His gaze deepened, locking onto hers with an intensity that made her mouth go dry and her heartbeat speed up. For there was no mistaking the raw sexual attraction. "So who are you feeling like now?" he asked quietly.

She shivered, imagining him peeling back the layers, layers that would lead from Hope Woods back to Dena Miller, the name she'd used in Iowa, and straight past Aurora Worthington-Calabretta. Would lead him finally to the innocent girl she'd been so long ago she'd lost touch with that self.

She only knew it was the part of her that ached for him, that young girl who had loved her weekly riding les-

sons so much, she had dreamed of running away aboard
the old schooling mount she favored and heading to the
wide-open spaces of the West. There, of course, she'd
imagined she would meet a handsome cowboy who would
win her heart.

But Dylan was more than the embodiment of a child-
ish fantasy, and he deserved more than a woman who
could only bring him pain.

"I don't know who I am anymore," she answered. "I
only know I want to be a better person."

"I'm beginning to realize," he told her, "that I don't
know a better person. Not a braver one, at any rate."

"If that's what you're thinking," she said, her voice
strained to the point of breaking, "I'm afraid that I've
misled you. Because you don't really know anything
about me. You don't know the worst."

After Hope's admission, Dylan didn't bring up dessert again or even after-dinner coffee. Instead, he called
for the check, which he insisted on paying in spite of her
offer, and they returned to the room.

On check-in, he'd requested a room change, moving
the two of them to a unit with a pair of double beds so
she would feel more comfortable and he would be less
tempted. Because whether she felt he knew her or not,
there was no way he would be able to hide what she did
to him if they tried to sleep in the same bed...or keep his
hands from exploring that lush body.

He watched her all too intently as she sat on the edge
of the bed she'd claimed and checked the load on the revolver, a stark reminder that they weren't here to act out
his fantasies.

"So you really know about guns?" he asked, still holding the shotgun he had brought in from the truck.

The cylinder clicked shut, and she tucked the weapon into the waist of her jeans. "Don't be so surprised. My father wouldn't have had it any other way."

"Why's that?"

"My grandfather patented some kind of industrial fastener that was a huge breakthrough at the time. Made him a fortune...nothing like Jethro Colton's, but let's say he was more than comfortable. Then someone—a couple of disgruntled employees, it turned out—kidnapped his son."

"Your uncle?" he asked, reminded once again that the rich had no immunity from grief.

She nodded. "My father's older brother. A ransom was paid, but...the body was found a few weeks later, in The Meadowlands. My grandparents never got over it, and neither did my father."

"So he did his best to keep you safe."

"Always." She blinked hard and looked away. "Until my problems got so big, they swallowed him up, too."

Before he could think how to respond, she changed the subject.

"I slept half the way here," she said, "so why don't you go to bed first while I stand guard?"

"But I didn't start my day out being attacked. You go ahead."

"Really. I'm not tired." She went to dig something out of the carry-on-sized black suitcase she had brought. "I'll just prop myself up in bed with these pillows and relax for a while."

He peeked at the garish black-and-red cover of the book she'd pulled out. "With a murder mystery?"

She smiled at him. "Occupational hazard. I had a job shelving books in Iowa, and one of the librarians got me totally hooked on this series."

He was a little self-conscious as he turned in, fresh from the shower and wearing a dark T-shirt over boxers, but true to her word, Hope was sitting in the soft, yellow light of her bedside lamp with her shapely, jean-clad legs crossed at the ankles. Engrossed as she was in her reading, he could have probably come out naked without eliciting any response—a thought he found more irritating than he would ever admit.

But maybe not, he realized, as he caught her peeking over the book's cover. Caught in the act, she swiftly returned her gaze to her mystery, but he couldn't help but notice that it was a long, long time before she turned another page.

Good, he thought, rolling over onto his side, happy to imagine he wasn't the only one suffering from distraction. Because the more he thought of her, so lovely in the soft light and so close at hand, the less he focused on his meeting with Marnie Sayers come morning.

Eventually, he must have drifted off, for the next time he looked at the glowing numbers of the LED clock on his nightstand, it was after 5:00 a.m. Sitting up abruptly, he was about to demand to know why she hadn't awakened him sometime around two-thirty as he'd asked her to. But the head behind the book propped on her chest had nodded, and her eyes had fallen closed.

At some point while he slept, she must have showered, for she smelled of some softly floral shampoo and wore a pair of cotton pajamas in a fuzzy, turquoise-and-white print. Everything else about her position looked uncomfortable, from the way she'd kicked off the covers to the awkward angle of her neck, which had slid down off the pillow.

Getting up from his bed, he crept to her bedside, then removed the book from her hands and tucked in the bookmark. He dropped the hardcover next to the revolver on the nightstand, then moved to pull the blanket over her before abruptly stopping…and sucking in and holding a sharp breath.

For in moving her book, he'd exposed the soft swell of her generous breasts beneath the thin material—the first time he'd seen them unbound. His hands tingled, burning with the need to undo those tiny pearled buttons down her front, to expose every bit of her completely.

Instantly hard, he looked away, reminding himself that he wasn't the kind of man to take advantage of a sleeping woman, that even if she was interested, he couldn't afford the distraction. Still, he ached to touch her, to bury his nose in sweetly scented hair and taste the fullness of her lips.

She murmured something, maybe the word *cold,* and hugged herself, inadvertently pushing her breasts higher. Gritting his teeth against temptation, he pulled the blankets to the level of her shoulders, but couldn't stop himself from bestowing a soft kiss in the center of her forehead, next to the butterfly bandage she still wore.

She reached out and caught his hand in hers, her eyes sliding open. They were blue this morning, he saw, blue as the bottom of the crispest autumn sky.

"Some guard I turned out to be," she said, her voice soft and sleepy. "Sorry. It's just—my eyes were burning. So I took out my contacts and then closed my eyes a moment."

"No harm done," he said, his mouth dry as one of

the Chinook winds that sometimes came down from the mountains. "Unless the mastermind's hiding under the bed or in the closet."

"Mmm," she said, pulling him closer. "Could you— Would it be too weird to ask if you could hold me, just hold me for a little while?"

He groaned and said, "You don't know what you're asking, Hope. But if I come close enough, you're sure to find out."

"Oh," she said, her drooping eyelids flaring. A troubled expression rippled across her beautiful, bruised face, and she pushed herself up on her elbows and confessed, "I, ah— Last night, I was having so much trouble concentrating on my book. I kept finding myself watching you while you were sleeping. Watching you and wishing there were some way things could be different. Some way we could run away from here and leave our problems all behind."

"I'm pretty sure those problems would follow us," he told her gently. "Even if they didn't literally, the guilt would be sure to eat us both ali—"

"My pregnancy was all wrong," she startled him by blurting. "I only thought I— My delay cost those little kids their parents, cost that couple their lives, and what good did it do anyone?"

"You miscarried?" he guessed.

Beads of moisture trembled on her lashes, falling only when she shook her head. "A week later, I felt sharp pain, pain like nothing I'd ever felt in my life. I tried to pretend everything was all right, that it was only a stomach bug I'd picked up. But Renzo finally noticed how pale and quiet I was and insisted on taking me to the E.R. Just in time, it turned out. My fallopian tube had ruptured, and

I was bleeding inside. Bleeding to death, if it weren't for the surgery."

"Oh, Hope. I'm sorry."

"The doctor called it an ectopic pregnancy. The egg had implanted in the wrong spot—it never stood a chance. And I'd put off calling the authorities for nothing, nothing but a fantasy."

He let her admission sink in, let the reddening of eyes and the bobbing of her throat speak to her misery. "So that was your big secret, huh? That you loved your husband and the idea of having a family of your own too deeply to take what you heard at face value. Well, I hate to break it to you, Hope, but it's no sin, what you did. Yes, it did turn out to be a tragic mistake, but the blame's all on your ex and his cronies."

"Then you don't—"

"I don't blame you. I won't judge you. The question is...will there ever come a time when you stop judging yourself?"

Chapter 12

"I don't know what I can say that I haven't already told you and your friend on the phone," Marnie Sayers said as she lit a new cigarette off of the old one, then stubbed out the latter in a nearly overflowing ashtray in the booth where she sat across from Dylan. A thin woman with a short mix of sandy-gray hair, she was twitchy, with darting brown eyes that followed the waitresses bustling about the pleasantly homey and old-fashioned little diner once owned by his mother.

He imagined he could feel her presence here, in the well-polished surfaces and the small vases of brightly colored flowers that graced every table, the handwritten "specials" chalkboard that boasted about today's Denver omelet and a hearty harvest stew made with venison and root vegetables. But Marnie herself couldn't be more different than the warm and welcoming woman he remembered. From the moment they'd arrived, she'd acted so nervous that Hope had quickly whispered that she was going to walk to the pharmacy next door to pick up a few things. Since their earlier talk had ended so abruptly, Dylan wondered if she'd volunteered more out of eagerness to escape his presence than to be helpful, or if it was safe to let her out of his sight.

But she had her gun and they had passed a peaceful night, so he told himself it would be okay, then returned his attention to the questions that had haunted him.

"I'm just trying to fill in a few gaps," he told Marnie, trying to sound as casual as possible. "Trying to find out a little more about my mother."

Smoke streamed from her nostrils, and she sucked in another drag. "I'm sure Faye was a good mother to you," she said thoughtfully. "She always loved kids, to a fault."

"What do you mean, *to a fault?*"

Marnie shrugged, gaze dancing away. "Just an expression, that's all. Making conversation. 'Cause it's not really a fault, is it, loving children, wanting some of your own? That's what makes the world go 'round, after all, right?"

"It's no fault," he said, waving away smoke from his eyes to better see her reaction, "unless it turns into an obsession."

He glanced toward the front windows, which overlooked the sunlit mountains, thinking of how much Hope's desire for a child of her own had cost her. And how much more, still, it might, if she refused to see the sense of staying as far as possible from her ex-husband's trial.

Worry gnawing at him, he wished she would hurry with her shopping and get back to have some coffee, as she'd promised.

"I wouldn't call Faye obsessed, exactly," Marnie told him, a tic playing at the corner of her mouth. "It's just…a person couldn't help but worry about that Desiree Beal's baby."

They both looked over when the door jingled, but it wasn't Hope, only a couple of older men coming in to be seated.

"Getting a little crowded," Marnie said. "This won't take much longer, will it?" She fumbled an attempt to relight her cigarette.

"Here, let me." Dylan took the lighter from her shaking hand and produced a flame on his first try. Though what she'd said had him tensing with anticipation, he kept his voice and movements slow and steady, as if she were a skittish horse that might be frightened into bolting. "There you go."

Setting the lighter back down on the table between them, he asked, "Did you mean that you were worried about what happened to Desiree's baby after she was killed out in the parking lot?" Shot during a robbery, the police report of the time had concluded, since the diner's cash pouch had been taken. Not for the first time, Dylan prayed that it was true.

"It was tragic, what-all happened to that young woman," she said, her bony fingers fiddling with the various sweetener packets in their holder. "And far be it from me to badmouth the dead...."

"But," he supplied, looking at her expectantly.

Twin streamers of cigarette smoke rose from her nostrils before the words exploded from her. "You've never seen a less maternal woman in your life. No instinct at all for mothering. He might've been a stranger's child, for all the connection she had with that poor, sweet little babe. A real piece of work, that one."

His heartbeat picked up steam. "Is that when my moth—when Faye started to suspect that Desiree wasn't what she claimed?"

Marnie pursed her lips, her brown eyes darting toward the antique cash register's merry jingle. "I've said too much already. No sense dredging up old—"

"This is a great location you have here," he said, abruptly shifting his approach. "Seems to do a good business."

Marnie smiled, pride warming her thin face and smoothing out a little of the nervousness. "This place is a local landmark. We have regulars who've been coming here for over thirty-five years, generations of 'em."

"Makes me wonder why my mother'd give it up so abruptly, the way you said. She must've put a lot of time and effort into it."

"Superstition, that's all," Marnie said without a moment's hesitation. "After Desiree was killed, Faye couldn't be shed of the place fast enough. Sold it to me for a song."

"Because she thought it was bad luck?" Dylan perked up, remembering how foolish his mother had always found the head cook, Agnes, with her crazy kitchen superstitions. A practical woman to her bones, his mother wasn't the sort to make a fire-sale offer, either—unless she'd had something to hide.

Ignoring the growing column of ash on her current smoke, Marnie fastened her gaze to the tabletop, but not before Dylan noted her sudden pallor.

"You know why she was really in such a hurry to leave town," he asked, "don't you?"

"I never really *knew,* exactly," she shot back, her voice so loud that several customers at nearby tables looked their way. Scowling to ward off the attention, Marnie dropped her voice to a whisper. "Guessed, maybe, that's all."

Dylan didn't buy it, but he decided to play along. "Guessed *what,* exactly. I need you to tell me."

Her eyes narrowed. "And I need you to leave now. I have a business to run."

"A business you all but *stole*," he accused, certain she knew something, "as the price of keeping quiet about Desiree's murder. *And* what really happened to her baby."

She slapped the table hard enough that the column of ash spilled to its surface. "It wasn't like that at all! Faye came to me with the offer. Buying this place wasn't my idea!"

"Maybe I should have my lawyers look into whether a sale under those circumstances was really legal. Bet I could tie you up for years in lawsuits, long enough to put you out of business."

"But you can't. I've sunk more than thirty years into this place. Never took a sick day, or a vacation, either," she blurted, her face a mask of horror. "I've revamped the menu, borrowed to add on, completely remodeled after a kitchen fire ten years back. You can't take it from me."

He hated being the kind of man who would threaten a woman her age, but he reminded himself that there were more important things at stake here than her feelings. "I could talk to the D.A. Ask him what the average sentence around here is for someone charged as an accessory to murder and kidnapping."

"I never helped her! Never!"

"Then tell me every detail. Do it, and I swear to you, I'll never trouble you again."

Marnie glared at him through damp eyes, shaking with rage, and Dylan reminded himself that she was far from innocent. That if his suspicions were correct, she had profited immensely from the pain of others.

After a tense silence, she asked, "How do I know you won't be back, or that you won't send others?"

"You'll have to take me at my word as Faye Frick's—

Faye Donner's—son. She raised me to believe a man's no real man unless he keeps his word, and I give you mine that I'll do everything in my power to make sure it's the last time you'll have to talk about it."

She considered for several moments before asking, "What about the police? Will you be sharing what you learn with them?"

"If I have to share anything, I won't name the source. Even if it means going to jail myself to keep the secret." He put out his hand, offering to shake hers.

Ignoring it, she scowled and puffed her cigarette before relenting. "Fine," she said. "Faye *was* suspicious about Desiree, who took advantage of her offers to babysit, then would disappear for hours—sometimes days. When she did come back, she never asked how the baby had been, and she didn't seem to know even the most basic things about how to care for him. But that night, the night Desiree was killed, Faye came out of the kitchen and overheard her on the diner phone. Overheard her threatening to tell everyone the details of 'this so-called kidnapping' if she wasn't paid off."

"So was it blackmail she was after or a ransom?"

Marnie shrugged. "Faye was so upset when she told me, I didn't ask too many questions. I suspected but—I knew that whatever she'd done, that innocent child was better off."

"Faye killed her, didn't she?" It sickened him to have to ask, but he had to know, no matter what. "She shot Desiree and tried to make it look like robbery."

Instead of answering, Marnie sucked on her cigarette, the look in her eyes as hard as flint.

"What happened to him, Marnie?" Dylan pressed.

"What happened to that baby? Did my mother take him with her?"

"You'd have to ask the police," she said, waving away smoke. "Most likely, they returned him to his rightful family."

"Or maybe your old boss took him, took him for her own."

Marnie's thin chin thrust a challenge toward him. "If it's true, who's to say that poor kid wasn't better off? If it was really a 'supposed kidnapping' and not a real one, who's to say his real family deserved him?"

He let the words sink in, then slowly shook his head. "You knew, then. Knew it and kept it to yourself all this time that my mother murdered—"

"It was self-defense, not murder!" The harsh whisper was as heated as steam escaping a teakettle. "When Faye confronted her, Desiree went for a gun in her purse. Your mother grabbed it, and they struggled. It was only by the grace of God that when it went off, the muzzle was pointing in the right direction."

"And you've known all along that I'm not Faye Frick's— Faye Donner's—natural child, didn't you?" he accused. "You kept it hushed up all these years for no better reason than to keep hold of a restaurant my mother sold you under duress."

He didn't accuse her a second time of blackmailing his mother into selling in the first place, but the suspicion hung between them in a haze of hostility and smoke and in the angry defensiveness in Marnie's dark-eyed silence.

"So she wasn't pregnant when she left here, and my birth date's just as big a lie as all the rest," he said.

A fleeting look of sympathy passed over her thin face as she stubbed out her half-smoked cigarette. Crossing

her thin arms over her chest, she said, "You want to believe in what your mother told you, you go right on and
believe it. But I promised to tell you what I know about
it. And I do know—I found Faye back in the kitchen, crying her eyes out the day her doctor told her that there'd
be no babies for her. Big as her heart was, she was a barren woman, barren as the moon."

After picking up a few snacks for the road and de-
flecting the clerk's stares with a story about a recent
skiing accident, Hope took a seat on the bench just outside the pharmacy. She knew Dylan would be watching
for her, but she figured she had a little time before he
began to worry.

Pulling his cell phone from her pocket, she stared down
at the screen. Temptation prickled in her fingertips—or
was it conscience, not temptation, urging her to make
the phone call?

Not just conscience. Duty, she told herself, pressing
*67—the code that would block the outgoing caller ID—
before tapping in the number she had committed to memory months before. Her mind flashed to a memory of
her WITSEC liaison, Inspector Ryan Kinney of the U.S.
Marshals Service, drilling her on it, along with details
about her "background," his hard gray eyes and gruff
efficiency refusing to allow her to give in to emotion.

When he answered on the first ring, she said, "Hi. It's
me. Your problem child."

She heard the sharp intake of breath before he all but
shouted, "Where on earth have you been? Do you have any
idea how many man-hours have been wasted looking—
But never mind that right now. Let me have you picked up.

We need to get you back in protective custody, right away, before the judge throws out the FBI's case."

"Throws it *out?*" she echoed, her heart pounding. "I thought they had enough evidence to dismantle the organization on the racketeering charges alone."

"Let's just say you weren't the only witness to go missing, and without their help corroborating the forensic-accounting evidence we've gathered, it's touch-and-go. Which is why it's imperative to make the murder charges stick—and to bring you in as soon as possible. Today, if I have anything to say about it."

"I'm fine, thanks for asking," she spat out. "Other than the shell shock from watching my car go up in—"

"There's no need to get sarcastic. We can talk later about why you ran off instead of going straight to the police, then calling this number. We must've gone over the protocol at least a dozen times."

She'd been braced for his anger but hadn't expected the answering lash of her own. Did he really think she'd run for no other reason than to inconvenience him? "I know. Believe me, I do, but at that moment, all I could think to do was run and hide before I ended up dead, too."

"At least you must've picked a good spot," he conceded, "seeing as how you're still breathing. Now give me your address, and I'll get in a car, a plane, whatever it takes to get you to an FBI safe house with round-the-clock security. The WITSEC pretrial placement experiment is over. You won't be left on your own again until your husband's trial."

Glancing toward the mountains, she breathed in air so crisp and pure, so dazzling in the brilliant wash of morning sunshine that she wanted nothing so much as to leave Dylan's cell phone in the truck and head into the wilds, forgetting she had ever met Renzo Calabretta. Within hours of telling Inspector Kinney her location, she knew she would be whisked off to some airless compound, as fortified as a prison—and as inescapable.

"I'll come in on my own. I swear it," she told him.

"How do I know you won't flake out again?"

"I didn't *flake out*," she said irritably. "I was running for my life."

"You have no idea what's at stake here, how many years of hard work, how many lives—"

"You think I don't know?" she said, rising from the bench to pace along the walkway. "I watched a man die, for no other reason than offering to pull my car up in the rain. And my poor father, too..."

When her voice broke, he said somberly, "So you heard about him, did you? Heard that they got to him, too?"

A cold queasiness gripped her stomach. "So it *was* murder, wasn't it? The arson was just there as a cover-up."

"I'm sorry," Kinney said. "The way I figure it, they must have tried to extract your location from him when they couldn't find you. He was—"

"*Tortured?* Is that what you're saying?" Her strained voice shook through the questions. How could the husband who'd once sworn he would always love her, the man who'd gotten along so well with her parents, who'd generously supported all of her pet charities, have ordered such a thing? "They tortured him to death because I—"

"Blaming yourself won't bring him back. Or put any of those responsible in prison."

Barely noticing the tone that indicated another incoming call, she said, "But he didn't know! He never knew where I was! I only—only wanted him to know I was all right. So he wouldn't be so worried."

"We'd already done that for you," Kinney quietly informed her. "You see, your father had an inkling. He contacted us and begged us to let him know if you were alive."

Because he loved me...

She ignored the passing cars and the white panel van with darkened windows crawling through the parking lot, her glazed eyes registering next to nothing. "It was all my fault. My fault."

"There's nothing you can do about it now—except start listening to me, okay? That's what he would want," Kinney said, his gruffness giving way to unexpected sympathy. "We'll make this right. I swear it. We'll get you through this. You'll see."

"I can't talk any more right now," she said, undone by his kindness. "I'll call you back and tell you when I'm heading your way."

"You can't!" he said, the words so sharp with urgency she imagined her ears bleeding. "This is no game. If you're really serious about surviving, give me your location. Because Joey Santorini's out there hunting—him and heaven knows how many others."

"I'll have to call you back," she said, her head throbbing.

"Please. Don't hang up."

But Hope disconnected, her attention drawn to a flash of sunlight reflected off the restaurant's door as it swung open. Dylan stepped outside, putting his hat back as he scanned the area. Tall, intense and impossibly handsome as he looked for her.

Wiping away tears, she raised a hand to catch his attention.

An instant later, the white panel van she'd noticed earlier made a U-turn to pull up in front of her, blocking her sight of him. When the unmarked side door slid open, adrenaline blasted through her body....

A split second later, the phone clattered to the concrete as she dropped it, her free hand darting for her gun.

Chapter 13

The sight of Hope across the parking lot kicked Dylan's instincts into overdrive. Reeling as he was from his conversation with Marnie Sayers, he immediately noticed that Hope's face was red and blotchy, her skin shining with tears.

Hurrying his steps, he started toward her, only to have an unmarked white van with tinted windows turn to block his path. Adrenaline blasted through him and he broke into a run. He rounded the rear of the van just in time to see Hope braced in a shooter's stance, staring down the barrel of her revolver.

At the other end, two slightly built, dark-haired men in coveralls jabbered excitedly in what sounded like Spanish. Though he didn't speak the language, there was no mistaking their pleading tone or the terror in their eyes.

"I'm so sorry," Hope told the two of them, as she stepped back and raised the muzzle. "I thought— It was a mistake, that's all. An honest mis—"

Before she could finish, the van sped away, tires squealing and the side door slamming shut.

"Oh, my—oh, no." Trembling from head to toe, Hope cast a pleading look toward Dylan.

"Better let me take that," he said, peeling her fingers

from the gun to claim it and swallowing back his own shock. "Now let's get out of here, before somebody calls the cops."

After stooping to retrieve his cell phone from the walkway, he led her to his pickup and helped her inside. With her gaze wide and unfocused, he took an extra moment to pull the seat-belt harness across her, then snap her in securely.

Though his heart was pounding, he forced himself to slow down, to drive with extra care as they pulled out of the lot. As they turned, he checked his mirrors, looking for bystanders checking out his license plate too carefully or phoning 9-1-1.

Spotting no one, he headed for the highway that would lead them back to the ranch. When no pursuit materialized over the next ten minutes, he eased his death grip on the wheel.

"I think we're in the clear," he told Hope, "but I'm glad we packed up our things and checked out of the lodge this morning."

"I'm such an idiot," she murmured. "I thought those guys were— I'd been talking to—"

"When I saw that van, I thought the same thing you did. And I'm still not entirely sure that they weren't up to no good. It's possible they weren't expecting to find you armed and ready for them."

"I know fear when I see it. They were definitely afraid, not angling for a way to grab me."

Still unconvinced, Dylan let the subject drop to ask, "Who were you talking to?"

"I called my WITSEC liaison, to let him know I'd be returning for the trial. And he—he said…" She trailed off, then wiped at her face.

Passing her a bandanna, he asked, "You told him where you were?"

"Not yet. And I blocked the caller ID so he wouldn't be able to track your number."

"Does that even work with law enforcement?"

She nodded and then frowned. "I thought it did, but who knows? I hung up on him when I saw you coming, and then that van pulled up. They'd been circling the parking lot, and I—I'm so sorry. I think I dropped your cell phone."

"No problem. I've got it," he said, pulling it from his pocket and seeing it was no worse for wear, thanks to the protective case. He noticed it showed a couple of missed calls and a voice mail—both from Amanda Colton.

A ripple of unease gripped him. Had something else gone wrong at the ranch? Noticing Hope's shivering, he put the phone down on the seat between them. "Are you cold? I can turn the heat up."

"I'm fine."

"You don't look it. I don't mean— You know what I mean."

"My heart's still pounding. I could've killed two innocent people."

"You stopped yourself in time," he reminded her. "You didn't pull the trigger."

"I'm sure that comes as an incredible relief to the two men who are probably on their way home right now to change their boxers." Shaking her head, she added, "I thought for sure it was The Jawbreaker—that's the guy who came to the ranch disguised as an electrician. My WITSEC inspector's warned me he's still out looking…."

He hesitated for a moment before saying, "So that's why you were crying?"

She shook her head, eyes closing.

"What is it?" he asked quietly. "Tell me."

"He said if I don't come back, they'll get away with what they did. T-to my father. They t-tortured him, Dylan, tortured my poor dad to give up information I'd never even shared."

After that, he could get no more from her as she drew into herself, pulling up her knees and hugging them as she turned her beautiful, bruised face toward the window.

"I'm sorry," he found himself telling her, again and again. As if that would change a damned thing, any more than all his friends' words had consoled him after the shooting that took his mother's life.

My mother, he thought, painfully reminded of what Marnie had told him. Was it true? Had his mother been unable to bear children? Could the doctor have been mistaken?

He'd heard of such things before, heard of couples who, long after giving up on ever having a child of their own, had found themselves expecting. Had it been that way for his mother, in the wake of some brief affair? Or had she, as Hope had suggested before, adopted someone's unwanted infant?

Or stolen a kidnapped child, one she'd meant to return to his parents?

For the first time, he let the thought lie, rather than shoving it aside. He already knew that his mother had lied to him about his father, that she'd withheld the truth for decades about killing another woman in self-defense.

Why, then, was it so impossible to accept the idea she was not his biological mother, either? To imagine the possibility that he was the son of a man who, at their last meeting, had treated him like dirt to be scraped off the bottom of his boot? Plenty of people survived having jackasses for fathers—along with drunken mothers who'd abandoned them.

But not me, he prayed. *Not me.*

The sight of a cell-phone tower reminded him that they would soon be out of range. Unwilling to spend the next eight hours wondering what Amanda had wanted, he said, "I'm pulling over for just a minute. Need to check a voice mail."

She didn't respond, and he didn't try to force it, his mind on the recorded message as it played.

"I hope everything's okay there," Amanda said, the strain in her voice unmistakable. *"But that's not why I called. I wanted to let you know I signed for a piece of mail for you this morning...."*

His heart bumped and his breath hitched, for he knew there was only one piece of mail she would have called about.

"I haven't opened it," the voice mail went on. *"I wouldn't, without your permission. But it's—it's from Rapidsure Labs. It's the results, Dylan. The results from your testing...."*

He forced himself to breathe, his finger poised over the "call back" button. But Amanda's message didn't end there.

"I know you agreed to all this, Dylan," she went on, *"but if it's what you want, we can forget this. I'll burn the envelope or shred it, or I'll leave it for you to do. Just let me know."*

He thought about it for a moment, tempted by the idea of letting things go back to the way they'd always been. Letting himself pretend he was the miraculous sole son of a barren woman so he could go back to the life that he'd had planned.

Instead of calling her back, he put the truck back into gear and headed over a hill. Headed out of phone range, his heart too heavy to bear more.

"I told that idiot of an electrician's helper I'd only get involved if you never knew my name, never had my number," said the woman who had been only too happy to take Joey Santorini's money in exchange for rigging the explosion in the basement.

"Well, I've got both now." Feeding on her fear, Joey leered as he spoke into the telephone. "And unless you want everybody else to know, too, you're gonna answer my damned questions."

A brittle silence crackled in the static of a bad connection. But finally, she broke it with a wheedling: "So what's in it for me—if I decide to help you again?"

"Depends on the results. But if I get what I'm after, you can rest assured there'll be something in it for you. Something very valuable." *Such as your ability to continue breathing.* In reality, he wasn't certain he could allow a loose end such as her—especially one so amenable to bribery—to live under any circumstances. Or the electrician, either.

"As it happens," she said with a slyness that reminded him it could be dangerous to underestimate her, "I do have information. Information I'm sure you'll be glad to hear. But first, you're going to have to name a figure."

He did, making it a generous amount, but not so extravagant that she would realize that the only payoff he intended to deliver was a bullet.

She had the guts to dicker with him, to try bargaining for more. He argued for a while before conceding a few thousand dollars—grumbling just enough to let her think she'd pulled something over on him.

"All right, then," she agreed, dropping the question and telling him that she had overheard Amanda Colton telling her half brother that Hope was coming back this very evening—coming back with the wrangler, Dylan Frick.

"He imagined we're all idiots, believing they'd gone their separate ways. But I heard from a very reliable source that they were seen together…in a very compromising situation."

He nearly told her to shut up, that he didn't give a damn about her stupid gossip. But he listened anyway, telling himself he couldn't care less about the salacious nature of the details, only whatever advantage they might offer.

And reasoning that if he couldn't get to little Miss New Jersey, he could always grab her boy toy and use him for leverage. For if there was one thing he knew about Aurora, it was that the do-gooder in her would never long stay hidden while he methodically dismembered someone she cared about.

About an hour into their drive, Hope couldn't take the silence any longer. It gave her too much time to think of what had happened and what might have, and far too much to worry over what came next.

Desperate for distraction, she asked, "So what happened at the restaurant? Did the waitress have any new information about your mother?"

His forehead creasing, he shared what Marnie Sayers

had told him about Desiree Beal's death and the events that followed.

"Do you believe it?" Hope asked.

"Considering the way I had to drag it out of her, I do," he said. "She had no reason to lie to me and every reason to want to keep it to herself. So it seems, my mother really was a murderer."

"Self-defense isn't murder."

"And Faye might not've been my mother. At least not if her doctor was right about her being barren."

She hesitated, uncertain what to say that might make him feel better. Or if trying to give him another ticket to denial was even the right thing to do.

"Whatever the truth is," he said, "I'll find out soon enough. Amanda left a message saying there's a letter waiting for me at the mansion. A letter that'll tell me the DNA results."

"It's time for you to find out once and for all," she said, "so you can move on with your life. But meanwhile, what could it hurt to talk about the good memories? They're part of what you had with your mom, too, and no one—not this mastermind and not whatever secrets your mom kept to protect you—has the power to take them from you."

"Is that what you do?" he asked. "Remember the good times you had with your parents?"

"It's a process, but I'm trying. Trying not to wall off the good memories along with the bad," she told him, wondering if there would ever be a time she could think about the past without pain jabbing at her stomach and tears coming to her eyes.

"From what you've told me about your mom," she managed, "I'm sure she wouldn't want you to forget the special times you had together, all the things that she did just to make you smile."

The hint of a smile warmed his handsome face. "Every year, for Thanksgiving, she had us do the decorations. They weren't grand enough for the Colton dining room, of course, but the staff never minded letting us 'fancy up' their table. There were gourds and cornucopias, little turkeys made with pinecones, and the centerpiece was always a big pumpkin, hollowed out."

"Like a jack-o'-lantern?"

"Better," he said. "She lined the hollow with a little plastic basket, and every kid dropped in a handmade card with a list of what they were thankful for that year, but no one was allowed to sign it. After a while, the staff started joining in, too, and after the meal, before the pumpkin pie was served, we'd take turns drawing out the cards and reading them aloud. Then everyone would try to guess which card belonged to which person."

"Sounds sweet."

"It was. And fun, too. Whenever someone read a really gushy card, some smart aleck would always call out, 'Is it Mrs. Black?'"

Hope laughed. "I have to wonder what she was thankful for, other than laundry starch and the fluff cycle on the dryers."

He snorted. "She always just wrote her husband's name. No muss, no fuss, no gushy explanations."

"That's sweet. It's a shame that Amanda and her sisters had to miss out."

He smiled, that strong, white smile that always made her heart beat just a little faster. "They weren't supposed to come down to the staff dining hall—the family always ate early on Thanksgiving and then left us alone to have our dinner. But everyone looked the other way when they sneaked in to join us, before the pumpkin pie."

"Sounds like a wonderful tradition."

"A memory, you mean. Because the only kids here now are still babies, and without my mother to keep everything going…"

"You never know. Maybe someone will take up the reins."

"Maybe," he said and afterward fell silent, each of them drifting on a raft of memories, the bitter with the sweet.

But all too soon, Hope's thoughts circled back to the duty she had too long put off, a duty from which nothing, not even pleasant memories, could protect her.

The darkness stole upon them sooner than it had any right to, or so it seemed to Hope until she noticed that the skies had clouded over, and it was nearly 5:00 p.m. "Where are we?" she asked him, seeing far more buildings ahead off the highway, gas stations and fast-food places that she didn't recognize from their trip the day before.

"We're coming into Laramie," he told her, the first words he had spoken in hours. "Took the more direct route this time. We'll reach the ranch in about an hour."

"Pull off," she said abruptly. "We have to take this exit."

Grimacing, he braked and did so. "Next time," he complained, "how about a little more warning?"

"Sorry."

"So what is it you need that can't wait? Restroom? Food?" he asked as they slowed in advance of a stop sign.

Her voice came out shaky as she answered, "I think

you'd better drop me off at a motel. I've decided I'm not—It'll be easier if I don't go back to the ranch with you, if I don't have to argue with Amanda about what I'm doing. But please, Dylan, let her know how very grateful I am, how I'll never forget—"

"WITSEC's failed you once already."

She shook her head. "I failed them—and my father, too. Besides, there's no way the FBI will ever let me out of their sight again, not until I testify."

"You're sure about this?" he asked, before taking the turn that would lead them into town. "Sure there's nothing I can say to change your—"

"Dead sure." At her own choice of words, she felt her face heat. "As sure as I've been of anything for a long time."

For a while, they drove around in silence, with Dylan carefully studying each motel they encountered. Finally settling on what he grumbled looked like "the best of the lot," he pulled into the parking lot, just beneath a security light, and climbed out of the truck before coming around to open the door for her.

"You don't have to come in," she said, feeling something tear loose inside her chest. Hope, maybe, the same desperate hope she had chosen for her name. Hope for more than mere survival. Hope of finding some connection. But what use was it to feel it when she only had to leave? "So let's just say our goodbyes now."

He looked into her eyes, his expression brimming with determination. "The hell I will. There's no way I'm letting you wait here on your own."

"I'm sure they'll have someone here to pick me up by morning, so if you'll just give me back my gun—"

"Absolutely not, Hope. I'm not having it on my conscience if you shoot some innocent hotel maid. *Or* if you're so hesitant to fire because of what happened in Jackson that you can't pull the trigger if you need to."

One look at the cold steel in his eyes convinced her that all the arguing in the world would not help. Still, as he grabbed their bags, she couldn't help but protest, "Didn't you tell me earlier you needed to get back to the ranch this evening?"

Pain shifted through his gaze, a dread so sharp it made her stomach spasm.

"Could be I'd just as soon put off going back, too."

"Oh," Hope said, remembering the letter that would almost assuredly change his life. "Of course."

With no reservation and none available with two beds, he accepted the one nonsmoking king room the motel had available. "Unless you'd rather we check around?" he turned to ask her.

But she saw another question in his eyes—not simply a question, but a wild hope, a need that matched her own. A yearning to wrest whatever desperate comfort they could out of these last hours.

"No," she told him. "Take it." Thinking one room and one bed would be enough. Enough to delay the moment she knew would break her heart.

Enough to get her through the hours and the minutes until they had to say goodbye.

As he carried the bags to the empty elevator, he said nothing, but when the twin doors closed behind them and she pressed the button for the third floor, his gaze locked onto hers again.

"I don't want to get this wrong, Hope. Don't want to make assumptions that I have no business—"

"No more words, no overthinking." She took a step,

one short step that had her heart pounding, and laid two fingers across his lips. Two fingers that she moved an instant later as she leaned in to offer the gentlest and most tentative of kisses.

There was one *thunk,* then a second, as he dropped the bags and wrapped strong arms around her, deepening the kiss and pressing her back against the elevator wall.

His body crushed to hers. The hard length jamming into her hip sent a thrill up her backbone, a need exploding through her brain with a force that cast away every other thought but the desire to have as much of him as he would give her. She was so wrapped up in sensation, in the dance of tongues and the feverish movement of their hands over one another, that she never felt the elevator shudder to a stop or heard the doors roll open.

It was Dylan who stepped away to whisper hoarsely, "To the room. And hurry. Before we scare any small children."

Too inflamed to return his smile, she hurried down the hallway while he gathered their bags. He caught up just as she had found the room and handed her the key card with a shaking hand.

It took her three swipes to get the green light. Three tries until the lock disengaged and they tumbled into the room on a wave of nervous laughter.

Once inside, she flipped on a light to orient herself, looking past the tiny closet and the bath to the big, inviting bed and heavy curtains just beyond it. Then she turned it off again, casting them back into darkness— and causing Dylan to growl, "Don't do that. I want to see you. Want you to see what you do to me."

But when he moved to hit the lights again, her hand

clapped over his. "No. Please. I—I'm nervous enough, being here."

His callused finger feathered the lightest of caresses along the side of her face, caresses that found her neck and drew sweet shivers. "What are you afraid of?"

"You," she breathed.

"You should be," he said, "because I want you, Aurora. I want *everything*."

His mouth claimed hers, igniting a host of glittering sparks behind her closed eyes. Wave after burning wave of sensation rippled through her, swirling through her body to pool in places far too long untouched.

As her head tipped back and her lips parted, she let the purse slide off her shoulder and shrugged off her jacket, too. She had to hurry, to rid herself of the barrier that kept her from feeling his hands on her, from feeling the heat of his bare skin against hers, the sharpness of desire.

She felt his balance shift and heard the clunk of each of his boots as it hit the carpet, of his jacket as he made short work of it, as well. For a while, they were content to kiss, to hold each other for dear life.

When he pulled away, she felt bereft, until he wiped her cheek.

"I thought your face was wet. What is it? Is this too much, too fast, after everything that's happened? Because if it is, you tell me. Tell me now and I swear I'll stop."

She knew he meant what he said, no matter how much his voice hinted it would cost him.

"Don't you dare stop, Dylan," she murmured. "Don't you stop for anything, or believe me, I'll be crying harder."

"Then you're all right?"

"For the first time in a long, long time, I'm much

more than all right. Because whatever happens, wherever I end up, *whoever* both of us end up, we have this moment. We have *now*."

Dylan, Cole—here in the darkness, it didn't matter whether he was a poor widow's only son or a billionaire's lost heir, no more than it mattered whether the woman in his arms was a runaway socialite or the mansion's newest housemaid. All that mattered was the liquid warmth of her mouth beneath his, the heat of her flesh as his day's growth of whiskers trailed down the length of her neck, at least as far as her clothing would allow him.

Frustrated by the roadblock, he abruptly scooped her into his arms, eliciting a gasp that sent a jolt of pure lust streaking through him. He took the woman he had wanted from the first day he had met her to the bed. Once there, he helped her pull free of first one sleeve and then the other before carefully removing the turtleneck sweater she'd chosen to hide as much bruising as she might. Remembering that lurid trail, he laid her back against the pillows and kissed his way across her neck with all the gentleness that he could muster.

"I wish I could take it from you," he whispered. "All your pain, your bruises. I'd take it on myself."

"You would, wouldn't you?"

"I would," he said, and when she arched her back, he slid his hand behind to find the closure to her bra.

He hesitated, loving the way her breathing quickened, but before he could release her breasts—those breasts that had cost him so much sleep the night before—she caught his hand and whispered, "I'm cold."

"I'll warm you up. I promise."

"Meet me under the covers, cowboy," she suggested. "And I'd better not be the only one there naked."

She wasn't, and he made good use of what he knew would be his only opportunity, touching, suckling—driving every memory of the past, every fear about the future from both of their minds. Finding that sweet spot, the source of pleasure between her thighs, he parted inner folds to stroke and tease and torment, bringing her to the precipice before backing off.

"Don't. You. Dare. Stop," she panted, with a whimper of frustration that had him trailing kisses down her belly, tasting damp curls before making love to her hot center with his lips and tongue. As she wriggled against him, a fierce need raged inside him, but her muscles were already tensing, her breathing building toward a shattering crescendo.

As she began to cry out, he plunged a finger into her to feel her come apart around him. To feel the power he had over her as she arched and threw her head back, crying out his name.

The only name he knew or needed; the only name he cared to claim.

Before he could take her over the edge again, she was pulling at him, whispering, "No, not that. Not now. Come up here. I want to have you in me. I need you, Dylan, now."

She didn't have to ask twice, for almost before the words were out, he was over her, his entire focus arrowing down to this one moment. But first, he forced himself to lean forward, to reach above her for the switch of the headboard reading lamp.

"Hurry," she whimpered.

"Watch your eyes," he warned before he turned on the

light to look down at her, her hair tumbled wildly across the pillows, her lips moist and pink and swollen…and her face filled with such desire, so much emotion that he knew the image would be seared into his memory for all time.

"I had to see you. To see this," he explained. "And to let you see me take you."

"Yes," she said, breath hitching as she turned her long-lashed gaze to meet his. "Oh, yes."

Unable to restrain himself an instant longer, he plunged, deep and hard, inside her, releasing every ounce of stress into the thrusts she met as she moved with him. Trying to slow down, to take his time and savor the tension building in her slender arms, her strong thighs, in the sweet, wet heat that gripped him. But there was no help for his struggle, no mental trick capable of driving back awareness of the joy of claiming this woman he had come to love so very quickly. As their rhythm built, all sensation in him coiled, winding tighter, until she began to pulse and throb around him, moaning her release.

No longer able to hold back, he spilled himself inside her, her true name torn from him like a war cry, every ounce of energy wrung from him, as well.

Afterward, as he spooned her body, Dylan nuzzled her neck and tried to stop himself from whispering the promises that neither one could keep. It was only when the touching and the kissing began to progress that realization struck him.

A realization that stopped him, cold as the coming winter winds.

Chapter 14

"What's wrong? Where are you going?" Hope turned her head to ask.

Seeing the stricken expression on his handsome face, she rolled to face him, pulling up a sheet to hide her breasts. For as much as she longed to stall reality a while longer, it had clearly reasserted itself.

Regret shadowing his blue eyes, he shook his head as he sat on the bed's edge. "I'm so sorry, Aurora. I don't know what I was thinking."

Heart bumping, she tried a smile. "I thought it was kind of obvious...thank goodness."

"It's not that. Don't you get it? It's that I didn't—couldn't—stop for a moment."

"If you had, I might've slugged you—or maybe even shot you, if I could reach my gun." Her toes curled as she imagined losing control again, losing herself as she watched him do the same. Only this time, she wouldn't be too shy to leave the lights on throughout the whole encounter. This time, she would memorize the hard glint of lust—or maybe something more—in his eyes.

It would be little enough to carry with her, little enough to warm the lonely nights to come.

"Stop to think about a condom, I mean," he said. "Of all the irresponsible—"

Realizing what he meant, she straightened, the implications squeezing her beating heart into her throat. But surely, it was ludicrous to imagine that a single encounter, when she was on the verge of leaving, would result in the consequence that troubled him....

A consequence she would welcome, if she were allowed such a miracle. She knew, though, she was wrong to hope, that she had no right to wish the danger she faced on another innocent life. And no right to wish fatherhood on a man who could never know about, much less meet, his child. A man who had most likely been stolen from his natural father, too.

"There's no need to worry," she assured him, the words bitter as ash on her tongue. "It took me forever and a day to get pregnant in the first place, and that was before the surgeons had to remove the ruptured tube—"

"Maybe it's unlikely," he conceded, the stubbornness in his face telling her he'd never let his child go willingly, that he'd throw away everything, up to and including his life, to save his son or daughter from growing up inside a lie as he had. "But it's not impossible, is it? Not quite."

It took her a long time to shake her head again, to tell him, "You need to understand. To save my life, they had to rush me into surgery. When they do it that way—no, there's no chance. The surgeon said I'll never have a child of my own."

She dropped her gaze, face heating, fearing he would hear the lie in her voice or see it written in her eyes. Instead, he gathered her into his arms and kissed the top of her head.

"I'm sorry, Aurora," he told her.

She snorted. "Sorry but relieved, I'll bet."

"If only things were different, I can't think of anything I'd love more than the chance to get to know you a whole lot better, and maybe someday, if everything fell into place…" The warmth of his sigh stirred her hair. "But that won't happen, will it? You're about to get dressed and then call back your WITSEC contact. And as soon as I know you're safe, I'm about to face my future."

She looked up at him and ventured, "But maybe that phone call could wait until the morning?"

"I wish to hell it could," he said. "But if I spend another night with you, I know damned well I'll never let you go."

Several hours later, Dylan was on his way back to the ranch alone, his throat clogged and his chest tight with the memory of the moment Hope climbed into the backseat of an unmarked SUV driven by two deputy U.S. marshals. The younger of the pair had eyed him suspiciously, especially after she'd burst from the backseat and run back to him, then threw her arms around his neck.

"If only things were different," she'd whispered into his ear, echoing his own words as she clung to him. But instead of telling the waiting men to go on—to go to hell and leave them—she'd only given him one last, lingering kiss before climbing back inside the vehicle.

Thanks to its tinted windows, he'd been unable to see if she'd looked back when the deputies drove her away. He only knew that she carried a bleeding chunk of his soul with her.

He swallowed hard, then told himself there was no point in dwelling on it since he'd never see her again. Yet as he drove through the ranch's main gate, he still tasted her on his lips. Still felt the moisture of her tears on his face, even though they'd long since dried.

By the time he parked the truck and came inside, it was after eleven, too late to go looking for Amanda. An early riser with an infant to look after, she was most likely sound asleep, but she must have had someone watching for his return, for he'd barely gotten back up to his room with his duffel when her text came to his cell phone: Meet me in my solarium, five minutes.

It's waited this long, he replied, wishing he had told her to rip that damned letter into a million pieces. It can wait till morning.

You sure? she asked.

I'll come by to see you first thing, he responded. Because with his emotions so close to the surface—and the memory of Aurora's blue, blue eyes cutting through him like a laser—he couldn't handle dealing with the outcome of the DNA test, too.

As good as his word, he got there early, feeling as if he hadn't slept at all. And maybe he hadn't, for he kept worrying about Aurora—whether there was anything he could have done to stop her, how and where she was, and if she'd already put their interlude behind her.

If she'd already written off a one-night stand with a Wyoming cowboy.

"Are you all right? You look pale," Amanda asked when she let him inside her solarium. Dressed for the day in jeans and a sweatshirt, she waved him toward a wicker sofa, where her tailless cat was curled up sleeping.

He remained standing to answer, his mug of coffee cupped in callused hands. "Didn't sleep well last night. Every time I dropped off, another nightmare woke me."

He didn't remember all of them, but the last involved

her stepbrother, howling with laughter as he handed him a silver spoon. "To muck out the stalls, of course," Trip had said, grinning at his sister and their mother, Darla, both of whom glared murderously at Dylan.

"You should have called me," Amanda said, her golden-brown eyes brimming with compassion. Shaking her head, she added, "I didn't sleep well, either. I kept wondering how you and Hope made out in Jackson."

"I need to tell you that she's left. She's back in WITSEC. She wanted to thank you, but she couldn't stay—"

"I shouldn't be surprised she didn't feel safe here after she was nearly strangled."

"Horrible as it was, it wasn't that. She had to testify, especially after she found out her father was definitely murdered. And tortured, too, for information on her whereabouts."

Amanda's eyes widened. "Oh, no. Do they think— Do the authorities believe he told the killers anything?"

Dylan shook his head. "She said he never knew—and they never would have killed him if she hadn't tried to get him a message saying she was alive."

"Poor Aurora. She must be devastated."

"She is, but she's determined, too, to make her ex pay. And to stop the killing, no matter what it costs her. I tried to talk her out of it, but—but she was right about one thing. I'd do the same if it could put away my mother's killer."

Amanda sank down to the cushions of the wicker sofa and stroked the cat's long, orange fur. Looking up at him, she said, "We'll never hear from her again, then, will we?"

"Not if all goes well, we won't. She'll be living a new life, with another new name."

"It's funny…before she showed up, I hadn't heard from her in years, but now, I'm really going to miss her."

He found a chair and sat on its edge. "Wish I could say you were the only one."

She studied him carefully, letting his admission sink in before saying, "I'm sorry you were hurt. When I told you to watch out for her, I never meant for the two of you to—"

"I never meant to care about her, either, but she's—Aurora's—" He blew out a long breath, then shrugged, needing to change the subject. And knowing he would continue to grieve the loss for years. "She's gone now. And whoever tried to hurt her, whoever killed my mother, is still on the loose."

"You really think it's the same person? That the mastermind would go after Aurora twice?"

"I can't say for certain, but I think it's likely. We've had household staff targeted before."

"What if her ex-husband's men—"

"Someone would've spotted strangers. And if they'd really recognized her, she would have never escaped."

"I suppose you're right about that," Amanda said, absently scratching the cat's ear as she rolled over, purring loudly enough that Dylan heard the rumbling. "Did you get anything helpful from that waitress you went to speak to? Anything that could help us to connect the dots?"

"I'm not sure how, or even if, it's all related to the mastermind," he said before sharing the details of his conversation with Marnie Sayers. Hard as it was, he left out nothing—including what she'd said about his mother's inability to bear children.

"Mind you," he cautioned, "all this is coming from a

woman with her own agenda. But I can't imagine what she'd have to gain from lying about that part. I just wonder—"

"You don't have to wonder anymore," Amanda told him, moving aside the cat to rise and open the drawer of a small table. "I have your letter right here. Why don't you just get it over with and open it? Then one way or another, we'll at least know."

"No matter what, I'll always be Faye's son," he managed, the coffee shaking in his hands when she withdrew the envelope, still sealed. Just an ordinary envelope, like any other, though its contents had the power to change his life. To change him, if he let it. "She raised me, taught me—"

"And she loved you with her whole heart. Everybody knows that. Loved you enough that she'd hate seeing what all this wondering is doing to you." She held it out to him.

"You open it," he told her. "He's *your* father."

The hurt in her eyes told him he'd done it again, had said the wrong thing to her, but he couldn't find the right words to apologize or to tell her that if it were possible, he'd do anything within his power to save the old man's life.

"If you're not ready," she said nervously, "we don't have to do this now."

"Putting it off won't change anything. And on my way here, someone mentioned that your father's come down with pneumonia."

"He has," she admitted. "Levi's treating him, but it's very serious, in Dad's condition."

"Then we'd better stop the stalling and read the letter now."

She shook her head. "You don't have to do it ever if

you don't want. I promise you, Dylan, I won't hold it against you."

He considered it once more, tempted by this final offer to let things go back to the way they'd always been. But he thought about the high price Aurora had paid for pretending that nothing had changed that day she'd overheard her husband's phone call. Thought about the guilt she carried for the people who had died because of her decision.

If he chose to have Amanda destroy the DNA test, she would lose her final chance—the chance she and her sisters had all prayed for—to save their father's life with a marrow transplant. Regardless of Dylan's feelings for their old man, he wasn't about to break the Colton daughters' hearts, certainly not out of fear for the effects on his own life.

"Open it," he managed, the dry gravel of his voice betraying his emotions. "Open it right now, before I change my mind."

"All right. Just know that no matter what it says—" Amanda sounded as nervous as he felt as she tore into the envelope. "I'm on your side, Dylan. Catherine, Gabby, Levi and I all are."

He strained his ears, hearing the faint rustling of paper over the drumming of his heartbeat. In the moment, he imagined he felt a ghostly hand—Aurora's warm hand—covering his, and illusory or not, he would later swear it was the only thing that anchored him to earth.

He heard a choked sound in the room, a sound that— Wait. Was that the stoic and sensible Amanda, weeping?

"What is it?" he managed. "Are you all right?" *Has this all been as big a joke as I imagined from the start? The idea that a governess's brat—most likely some un-*

wanted bastard she'd informally adopted—could be a high-and-mighty Colton?

"Please don't cry," he told her. "Even if it had been me, there's no guarantee the marrow would've been a match—"

"That's just it," said Amanda. "The marrow *does* match. Because you're him, Dylan. You're Cole Colton. You've been him all along."

Chapter 15

Her eyes gritty and her nose sore, Aurora did not want to get up and start the day. Comfortable as the bed was in a secure Denver hotel room where the deputy U.S. marshals had tucked her away for the night before their flight east this morning, she wanted to melt back into a dreamless sleep, to forget she'd ever been so foolishly optimistic as to call herself "Hope" these past few weeks.

But with the silvery light of early morning rimming the edges of the heavy curtains, sleep refused her call, and she couldn't help but wonder what new identity she'd be given and how long this one might last. Or if she'd ever again live in a place as magical, for all its hidden dangers, as the ranch she had been forced to flee.

One thing was for certain. She'd never meet another man like Dylan—the only man she'd been able to trust with both her secrets and her heart. She realized now how foolish she had been, how she'd risked her life as well as any chance of contentment for something that could never last.

But for all the pain it cost her, she knew she would have done the same thing if she'd had it to do over. Because even the briefest flare of love—struck like a match against her despair—had helped to light her way.

As quickly as it had ignited, she trusted that the feeling had been real, far more real than what she'd felt for a man who'd been more a father figure than a husband, a man whose evil had taken more from her than she'd ever believed she had to lose. Or was she merely being foolish, confusing the first flush of attraction with something that might last?

A tapping interrupted her thoughts: a knock at the connecting door between her room and the one shared by the two deputy U.S. marshals, a door the men had insisted on keeping open after putting some kind of locking device on her own door. The older of the deputies, a veteran named Smithfield, had claimed it was for her protection, but the look he exchanged with his younger partner told her it had just as much to do with the possibility that she might get cold feet and disappear in the night.

It was only then that it sank in that she was truly in custody, both protected and imprisoned, in a sense, for the duration. The thought was like a lead weight inside her chest, a burden as cold as it was heavy.

"Awake yet? I've got coffee, good and hot," came a voice she recognized as that of the senior officer, a good-natured sort whose slight paunch, blue eyes and short, silvery haircut reminded her painfully of her father. "Sent out my partner for the real stuff, and he came back with pastries, too. Which is a damned good thing, considering the way he snored last night."

She could hear the deputy in question—Mr. All Business—in the room, too, talking on the phone to someone. No surprise there, as he'd been glued to the thing most of last night, talking with Inspector Kinney on the East Coast.

"Thanks. I'd love coffee," she said, then forced herself to add, "and a pastry would be nice, too."

Nervous as she was about returning to meet with her liaison, she wasn't certain she could eat it. But she'd try, or tuck it in her purse for later, since she had no idea when she'd get another meal.

"Soon as you finish," he said, "you'll want to go ahead and start getting ready. We'll be leaving for the airport in about an hour."

"Can I shut the connecting door, at least?" she asked, the old Aurora flaring to life.

His blue eyes were apologetic. "The bathroom door, yes, but not this one. Sorry, miss, but it's for your own safety."

"Or for *yours,* since your boss might kill you if I Mac-Gyvered my way past that lock somehow." Did he know she'd thought about it, her resolve wavering ever since she'd said goodbye to Dylan?

At the thought of him, she wondered, had he already learned the results of his DNA test? Was he celebrating, hurting—and did he have anyone to talk to who would understand?

Smithfield shrugged. "Orders are orders, miss."

"Miss *Who?*" she asked, her mouth tightening in a grimace. "Do you have a new name for me?"

He nodded. "For this trip only, you're going to be Yasmin Ahmed. Think you can remember it?"

"Remember it? Maybe. But if there's a spelling test, I'm toast."

"Kinney tells us you're a real quick study. I'll help you with that part and with the outfit we've brought for your disguise."

Alarms went off in her head. "What outfit?"

He smiled. "Guess you didn't notice the bag I put in your closet after we checked in last night. It's a hijab and abaya."

When she raised a brow in question, he explained, "An Islamic head scarf and cloak. About as far as you can get from the swimsuit competition."

Wincing, she said, "That's offensive on so many levels, I don't know where to start."

"How about with keeping you alive?" he asked, the mask of friendliness slipping to reveal the tough professionalism beneath. "Because I'm a hell of a lot more worried about getting you back East in one piece than political correctness. You got that?"

"Yeah, I've got it. But I don't like it. At all."

"Duly noted," he said, resuming to his amiable persona before turning to get her the promised breakfast.

She drank most of the coffee, then nibbled on a pumpkin scone, which reminded her of her picnic with Dylan, surrounded by nothing but open sky and endless space. Sweet as it was, the memory spoiled the taste of the coffeehouse confection, making her ache with grief for that lost taste of happiness.

Or the possibility of it, anyway, for as she showered and attempted to figure out how to put on the unfamiliar dark blue garb, she told herself that what she'd felt for Dylan couldn't possibly be real. Both of them in crisis, it made sense they'd come together, that they'd fall into each other's arms for what amounted to, at worst, a one-night stand. Or maybe it had been more of an oasis in the desert, a necessity for their short-term survival but no long-term solution.

Confusing it with love had been a terrible idea. But as she arranged the scarflike hijab to hide her hair and neckline, all she could think about was ducking out on her two keepers and going back to slake her thirst.

Cole Colton. I'm Cole Colton, Jethro's missing son.

But the fact of it lay like an oozing puddle on the surface of Dylan's shell-shocked brain, where the knowledge stubbornly refused to sink in.

"Are you all right?" asked Amanda, peering into his face. "Maybe you should sit back down before you fall down. You're white as milk."

"I'd better—uh— I've got things to do," he told her. "Outside stuff, with the cattle." He hoped she didn't press for details, because he wasn't capable of thought, let alone coherent speech.

"The animals can wait for a few minutes," she said.

He was certain she was right, but *he* couldn't wait, not for an instant, so he turned and left, doing what he always did when emotion overwhelmed him. Shutting down, murmuring that she could tell whomever needed telling and make whatever arrangements would be needed to start the ball rolling for the transplant, then stalking down the hallway in his haste to get outside where he belonged.

Wanting to avoid the busy kitchen and any of the staff who were already up and around, he made a beeline for a little-used back door behind the great room. Or at least, that was his intent before Trip Lowden came down the back wing staircase and called to him, "Hey there, wrangler. Hold up. I need a word with you."

Dylan stopped in his tracks, his gaze swinging to Trip, who wore tousled blond hair and a smug expression over a plush velvet robe. Normally, he wouldn't ooze out of bed for hours, but Dylan was too unraveled to care why—or put up with any of Lowden's usual abuse.

Mistaking Dylan's hesitation for agreement, Trip headed his way, dropping his voice to a rough whisper. "You tell your little friend Hope I'm done playing games now. She can quit avoiding me if she doesn't want it spread all over that she's really—"

"Really *what?*" Dylan said, the words in an ominous growl. "Really *sick* of your harassment, maybe? Because I'm sick—everybody's sick—of the way you throw your weight around here. Especially Hope."

Trip snorted, seemingly amused—and clearly oblivious to the way Dylan's hands fisted the moment he brought up Hope.

"You just tell her that I *know*...and if she doesn't want anybody else to find out about her past, she'd better come and see me the moment she's— *Agh!*"

Moving in on him in two strides, Dylan grabbed the front of Trip's robe and balled it up so tightly in his hand that the weasel's face reddened and his eyes popped as he struggled to backpedal.

"You listen to me, Low-Down. Listen like your worthless life depends on it," Dylan told him, not giving a damn who overheard him. "Hope's gone, and if you ever try to find her—or I ever in my life hear the slightest suggestion that you're bothering any of the women on this ranch—I will make it my personal business to stomp your ass so flat, we'll be using it to wipe the muck off just outside the servants' quarters."

Trip was gaping like a fish as he tried to mouth words. When his purpling face gave away the fact that he was strangling, Dylan relaxed his grip but didn't let him go.

Coughing and choking and grabbing at his throat, Trip stammered, "Y-you won't get away with this! With *at-*

tacking a member of the Colton family! As soon as I tell my stepfather, you'll be sent packing—"

Maybe it was his threat to Hope, or the way he held up the name Colton—a name that Dylan refused to have forced on him—like a shield, or maybe it was only the result of years of contempt finally coming to a head, but this time, at long last, Dylan could hold back no longer. Drawing back his right arm, he threw one punch, a single punch that struck Trip—already squealing in terror— right beneath the eye and sent him flying backward and crashing to the floor.

Dylan heard footsteps behind him, followed by the gasps of those drawn by the sound of Lowden's cry. Shaking with fury, Dylan didn't turn to see who had come. Instead, he kept his gaze locked on Trip, who was sitting up, holding his hand over his injured eye and bleating, "You're finished, Frick! You're done here! You may as well go pack your bags!"

Finished. Done here. The words sliced through the remnants of Dylan's rage, leaving a blast of cold reality in their wake as he realized that for the first time in his worthless life, Lowden might be right.

After warning Trip one last time, "I damned well meant what I said. Bother the women here again, and I'll blacken the other eye—or worse," Dylan stormed away and out the back door, into the chill morning.

Relieved when no one tried to follow, he started toward the stable first, where he thought he might run the mare, Chica, through her paces before her owner came to pick her up this afternoon. But in his current mood, he would set back the sensitive horse's progress, and neither his own buckskin nor even Jethro's stallion—a powerful black beast he'd been exercising since the old man fell ill—was up for the kind of gallop Dylan needed to get this out of his system. Instead, he headed out for his personal pickup, since that key was the only one that he had on him.

Revving the engine, he backed away from the trees, then peeled out in a spray of flying gravel. First, he headed out to check on the cowboys he'd sent to repair fence line during the quiet weeks when the cattle required little handling. Sure enough, he caught a couple of the hands loafing, but rather than stopping to lecture them about it, he drove straight past, barely registering the way they hustled back to their assigned task when they spotted him. Instead, he kept on going, jouncing over the rutted dirt road toward the pasture where they had been adding supplemental feed to the hay and forage given to the new weanlings, telling himself it made sense to make notes on estimated weights for his report to Jethro, who had always cared deeply about the cattle and the horses even though they comprised only a tiny percentage of his income.

Guess my father really did pass down his love of large livestock, just the way my mother—my true mother—always claimed....

Had Amanda given the old man the news yet? Assuming he was coherent enough to understand it, how had he reacted? Was there shock, regret, fury, to learn that the governess he'd entrusted with his daughters had duped him on such a grand scale?

Or was Jethro disgusted, imagining, as he'd implied before, that now some half-assed cowboy was going to bear his name and claim his fortune, or as big a chunk of it as he could wheedle?

"The hell I will," Dylan murmured, peppering the air with curses as he realized that in all these years, Jethro hadn't put in the money or the effort to find his missing firstborn. Oh, he might have made a few lame attempts during those first harrowing days or hired a private investigator to make things look good, but surely, he could have found a kid parked under his damned nose for thirty years.

Instead, the old SOB had clearly written off the lost child of his desperately unhappy first wife and gotten busy working on breeding some replacements. Had he been disappointed to have gotten three girls and no legitimate sons? Knowing Jethro, it was possible, just as it was possible he'd made those daughters pay.

Even so, Dylan seriously doubted the old man had lost much sleep over his firstborn's absence during the past three decades. Certainly, he was never known to speak of what had happened. Which was why Dylan wouldn't lose much sleep over what he planned to do.

Because leaving was his only chance to be the man he wanted. Not the prodigal heir, to be prodded and examined and squeezed into the mold of what was expected of a firstborn Colton. Not the eternal "victim" of a decades-old crime or a man to be envied or resented for his new-found fortune.

As he slowed in front of the gate, he climbed out of the vehicle. Chilly as he was without the jacket he'd forgotten in Amanda's sunroom, he was nonetheless glad of the fresh air and the wide expanse around him. The weanlings hurried his way, mooing eagerly in the hope he'd brought more of the supplemental grain, which he sometimes sweetened with a little molasses. They were looking more like healthy yearlings than calves these days, their bodies filling out with the rations that replaced their mother's rich milk and their red-and-white hair growing wooly in advance of the winter's cold.

In spite of all the turmoil crashing through his brain, he found himself smiling at their approach, at the eager swish of their tails, thinking that everything made sense out here among the animals, who didn't give a damn about name or social status, who had always known who he was nonetheless. But instead of coming all the way to the gate, the herd veered suddenly, bawling in distress.

Turning to see what had spooked them, he heard an engine's roar and saw a blur of motion—a white F-250 pickup with a huge brush guard on the front end speeding directly toward him. Dylan recognized it as one of the ranch vehicles—but whoever was behind the wheel was moving way too fast.

For a split second, he thought it might be one of the hands, or Amanda, coming to insist that he return to face the truth. But an instant later, he realized the well-maintained vehicle careening toward him must have somehow lost its brakes.

Either that, or the driver was mashing down on the accelerator, aiming straight at him on purpose.

As quickly as the thoughts ran through his mind, his body was moving behind the bulk of his own pickup, then placing a palm atop a fence post and vaulting the top string so he wouldn't be caught between the truck and enough barbed wire to slice himself to pieces.

Strong and agile as he was, Dylan's earlier distraction had cost him valuable seconds—only this time Betsy and Bingo weren't around to bark him a reprieve. As he jumped, the heel of his boot caught the top wire, and he pitched forward, falling so hard on his chest that the blow knocked the air from his lungs and he felt something on the left side—maybe ribs—crack.

Before he could draw breath, a tremendous crash echoed with the shock waves of twisting, ripping metal. Metal sliding toward him all too fast.

T-boned by the brush guard on the big Ford, Dylan's pickup snapped fence posts like matchsticks as it was shoved sideways. With no way to escape, Dylan flattened himself as best he could, covered his head with his arms and scrunched his eyes shut, thinking, *This is it.*

The sound was all consuming, a thunderclap that enveloped him before it shuddered to a stop. It took him several stunned moments—and a shallow breath that sent pain flaring through his injured ribs—to realize that his heart still galloped in his chest.

Opening his eyes, he looked up at the twisted undercarriage of his pickup only inches from his face and breathed the words "Ho-lee hell."

An eerie silence followed, broken only by the ticking of a cooling engine, the dripping of some liquid. Water from the radiator and not gas, he hoped, before hearing the *clunk* of a truck door closing, then the sound of footsteps crunching over gravel. Crunching closer.

Tilting his head, he saw a pair of feet, not wearing cowboy boots but work boots: scuffed, dark brown and enormous—at least a size thirteen. The same boots Hope had described the assassins/electricians wearing.

Before he could think of what to do, someone grabbed his legs and roughly hauled him out.

Dylan had broken bones before. More than once, on the rodeo circuit and in his work with livestock. But this pain went far deeper, setting off fireworks as agony exploded in his ribs and his right forearm—which, in protecting his face, had been painfully scraped by part of his truck. His mouth opened but no scream would come; however, the fireworks kept exploding…

Until one of those huge boots came flying toward his head.

Chapter 16

Though the two men both wore sport jackets that covered their badges and kept their weapons concealed, their short haircuts and watchful gazes marked them as law enforcement as surely as a uniform. With one walking on either side of Aurora in her hijab and abaya, the trio attracted far too much attention.

Shivering beneath the dark robe, she thought at first their plan had backfired. She was attracting glares, along with murmured insults that included words like *terrorist* as some of her fellow passengers jumped to the wrong conclusion. Anyone who ventured too close was warned by one of the deputies, politely but firmly, "Back off and give us some space," but that only underscored the impression that she was in their custody.

The majority of those in the terminal, however, were content to avert their eyes, and even the rudest seemed focused on the "foreign" garb rather than her face. As uncomfortable as she felt, she realized the deputies might have been right about this being safer. Still, she didn't want to board their flight to Newark, didn't ever want to set foot back in New Jersey again, where she was half-convinced that Joey Santorini and his cohorts would be waiting for her.

As they cleared security and headed for her gate, her feeling of foreboding grew more and more intense. She pictured herself ducking between the two big men and running...running back to Dylan, who she imagined must need her now as badly as she needed him.

Or was that only panic talking?

Leaning her head toward the friendlier Deputy Smithfield, she murmured, "I think this is a really bad idea. My stomach's flipping around, and I think I might be—"

"You'll be fine. We're seeing to it," he assured her, just as his partner, a fit, young red-haired guy named Vanak, reached for his buzzing phone again.

"Yes, sir?" he asked. He listened for several minutes before saying gravely, "I'll inform her and my partner right away, sir."

Aurora stopped short, her feet freezing at his tone. Something had gone wrong; she knew it. She saw it in his pained expression as he looked from her to his partner and gestured toward an unoccupied bank of chairs.

Smithfield glanced down at his watch, then nodded, and the three of them sat down, the two deputies flanking Aurora.

"What is it?" she blurted as he slipped the cell phone into his pocket.

"It's your husband," Vanak told her.

"Ex-husband," she automatically corrected.

"Well, now he's your *late* husband," Vanak said irritably. "Renzo Calabretta's dead, murdered in the federal holding facility. Apparently, he knew too much about too many people, and they somehow found a way to—"

"He's *gone?*" she blurted. "He's— He *can't* be." Tough and virile, despite his graying hair, Renzo was a purveyor of death, not its victim.

Anger pulsed over Smithfield's amiable features. "How'd they get to him?"

"I don't know how they pulled it off, but Inspector Kinney said the Feds are mad as hell about it. Found Calabretta hanged with a homemade noose. Pretty sure it was meant to look like suicide, but there were too many signs of a struggle for anybody to buy it."

Shock drained the strength from her body. She could not believe her ears. "It has to be a trick," she said, "to bring me out of hiding."

"No trick," Smithfield said more gently. "We wouldn't lie to you about this."

She blinked back tears, remembering the man she'd married. The man she'd thought so kind and noble, so handsome with his dark brows and lightly silvered hair. A man mourned and feared and hated.

"Do I still have to go back?" she asked the deputies. For without Renzo, who was there for her to testify *against,* since she had no direct knowledge of anyone else's crimes?

"Obviously, this changes things," said Vanak, "but I'd strongly advise you to come with us. We'll put together a new relocation packet for you. For your safety."

"I—I appreciate it, but I can't go," she said, her mind flashing to Dylan.

"You're in shock," Smithfield interjected. "You can't possibly think they'll let you go back to your own life. To any life."

"I'm no threat any longer. Why would they bother to hunt me down if I can't hurt them?"

"You already have. Badly. Trust me, whoever's in charge would like nothing more than seeing you killed— as painfully, as horribly as possible. Sends a message to the other wives and family about how disloyalty's 're-warded.'"

The world tilted drunkenly, and she covered her face with her hands. "I—I need to use the restroom. Need to splash some water on my face and pull myself together. Please."

"We don't have time for this," Vanak complained. "She needs to get on the damned plane and let us do our job."

"There's a little time," Smithfield insisted, glancing at his watch again, "as long as you don't take long. We'll walk you to the ladies' and wait outside for you."

She was still shaky as she went inside, her vision hazed by a shimmering cloud of disbelief. The restroom was busy, packed with female travelers moving at what seemed like warp speed, none of them seeming to pay her any heed in spite of her attire. Some juggled purses, laptop bags and rolling carry-ons while others herded children or tried to navigate while checking their phones.

So it shouldn't have come as a shock to her, as she bent her face to the sink, when she spotted the corner of a sparkly pink case peeping out from beneath a wad of paper towels. A forgotten cell phone, she quickly real-ized, palming it without thinking.

She should run back out after that last woman, the harried-looking young blonde who'd been struggling to wash two squirmy toddlers' hands here moments ear-lier. But after a moment's hesitation, temptation over-whelmed her, and Aurora retreated to a relatively quiet corner instead.

Promising herself she'd turn in the phone to the lost and found once she was finished, she started punching numbers before she could overthink the impulse. Be-cause this minor miracle was the chance she had been looking for, the one chance she would ever get to hear Dylan's voice again.

And how she needed to hear him now, to listen to him tell her, in his strong and caring tones, that leaving was the right thing, the only thing she could do. That, rich or poor, he would be just fine without her. Would bring the mastermind to justice and then move on with his life.

She heard a slight click as the call connected, but not a single word of greeting. "Dylan?" she blurted, turning her back to a woman who was looking at her strangely. "It's me. I had to tell you—"

"You're one lucky bitch." Waves of lethal menace rode on every word, a menace far too cold to be Dylan's. "Or I should say your boy toy here is."

Aurora's stomach plunged at the remembered voice, shock loosening her knees. "J-Joey?" she asked, her heart pounding so hard, she thought it might explode. "Where's Dylan? What've you done with him?"

He answered with cruel laughter, then: "More than I meant to, maybe. Got a little carried away, thinking you might be sitting in that truck."

Cupping her hand over the receiver, she whispered, "Please don't hurt him! It's me you're after, not him!"

"Too late," he chuckled. "He's already hurting plenty, or will be, once he comes to. But I'll tell you what. You get back here by one o'clock, and I won't mess him up any worse. Probably."

"You have to let me talk to him! I have to know that he's alive."

"If you think you're in any position to tell me what I *have* to do, you're even dumber than I thought. *And* you're wasting time."

"Listen, Joey. I'll come. I'll come, and we can talk this

thing through. Did you know Renzo's dead, murdered in the federal holding facility this morning?"

On the other end, she heard the big thug breathing. But nothing more.

"So there's no more reason for you to do this, Joey," she pleaded. "One of your own guys took him out."

"You're lying."

"I swear I'm not. You can look it up."

After another hesitation, his voice vibrated in a low growl. "So you went and got him killed, too, did you? Of all the— What d'ya think? That Renzo's death absolves you? That we'll turn our back on a traitor to the family just because he's gone?"

"No, but that doesn't mean you have to hurt innocents. Let Dylan go, please. He has nothing to do with this. I haven't told him anything—haven't told a soul."

"Won't be the first innocent whose blood's on your hands, will it? That idiot at the grocery store, your own daddy—you can stop it here today, if I don't get too impatient waiting. Or too pissed off, rememberin' how I lost somebody, too. You remember my cousin Luca, don'tcha? We practically grew up together, and then we were partners for a lot of years—before we blew up the wrong guy in Iowa."

"I'm sorry for your loss," she forced herself to tell him. Because she would say anything, do anything to stop this. "But I'm coming back. I swear it. Just don't hurt Dylan anymore."

A scoffing sound came back to her. "You're cuttin' it awful close, sweetheart. If you want to make it here before I do to him what got done to your father."

Panic zinging through her, she looked around wildly for a clock to check the time. 10:45 a.m., which left her barely enough time to get away from the detectives and find her way back to…where, exactly?

"Are you on the ranch itself?" she asked. "Where is it I'll be heading?"

"Make for Dead, and I'll call you back at this number—"

"No, Aurora!" shouted someone in the background. Dylan, she was certain, his voice strained as it was resolute. "Don't come here! He'll kill—"

There was a muffled grunt, followed by the sound of a struggle. And then the crack of gunfire before the line went dead.

Moments later, she walked out of the restroom, shrouding her panic in an icy calm as she insisted to the waiting men she was revoking her participation in the WITSEC program. And there wasn't a damned thing they could tell her that would change her mind.

Chapter 17

Injured as he was, Dylan found strength enough to try to get up. But with his aching head spinning and what felt like several left ribs and his right wrist throbbing, his plan to pop to his feet and launch himself at the armed monster looming over him was hopeless from the start.

He told himself it didn't matter, that if Aurora had heard him being shot, she'd have sense enough to call the sheriff in Dead—who might be able to use his cell phone to track his location—then run in the opposite direction, disappearing with the deputy marshals as she'd planned. As she *must,* if she were to live.

Because there was no way he was going to. Easy to see that, with the grinning Goliath bearing down on him as if he were going to particularly enjoy finishing what he'd started with the stolen pickup. But first, the son of a bitch swung at the side of Dylan's head, his ham-sized fist wrapped around the gun.

Dylan lurched sideways to avoid the lethal blow and grunted with an explosion of agony when he slammed back down to earth, landing on a rock. With bursts of color cascading across his vision, he kicked out with both legs, his boots striking the larger man's ankles and knocking him off his feet.

As the gun bounced from the big man's hand, the weapon discharged, and before Dylan could wonder if he'd been hit, air hissed from the front tire of his already-wrecked truck. He lurched for the fallen pistol—which had landed closer to him than his attacker—but the effort sent another shock of agony through his torso, pain that would have had him screaming if he could have only drawn the breath to do it.

Then the big brute was scrambling on his hands and knees, lunging for the gun, bellowing like a bull moose in his fury. In that single, shattered moment Dylan knew that hurt as he was, there wasn't a damned thing he could do to stop the maniac from finishing what he'd started. But that wasn't going to stop him from fighting like hell.

Using his clumsier left hand, Dylan pulled the rock he'd fallen on from beneath him…and flung it at his attacker like the desperate hope it was.

By the time the car got up to fifty, it was shaking, but Aurora only pushed it harder, praying that the engine wouldn't blow.

A glance down at the odometer she'd been too panicked to look at earlier gave her even worse news. The former police cruiser she had purchased from a fly-by-night "dealer" recommended by a sketchy-looking cabbie had over two hundred thousand miles. Though the tires were nearly bald, the fenders rusty and the former department markings hidden by primer gray patches, she'd had no choice and the grubby little woman knew it. After all, no reputable person would offer a four-carat diamond ring in trade for any running vehicle, as long as the deal came with no paperwork or questions.

So Aurora had said goodbye to her last illusion of

security, exchanging a piece of jewelry easily worth a hundred times the cost of the old beater she'd been sold. Using nearly all the cash she had left from the airport taxi ride to fill the gas tank, she started racing, hell-for-leather, north toward the Wyoming state line.

She knew there was no way she was going to make Joey's one-o'clock deadline without speeding, just as she knew that pushing the vehicle—which apparently had no heat—was likely to blow its rattled, lurching engine. And if she broke down now, dressed as she was in the clingy blue T-shirt and dark slacks she'd been wearing under the religious garb she'd stripped off in the taxi's backseat, she'd probably freeze.

To her relief, the sedan's shimmy settled once she pushed it beyond the posted speed. "A car after my own heart," she murmured, eyeing the shoulders for any sign of a real police cruiser.

Seeing none, she nudged the accelerator just a bit more but held short of taking it to a level likely to attract unwanted attention or cause an accident. Reminding herself that either could cost Dylan his life, she leaned forward, her cold hands cramped around the colder wheel, her back aching with the tension in her muscles.

Dylan might be dead already. Hadn't Joey said that he was hurt, unconscious? So if Dylan had roused enough to try something, as his shouted warning indicated, it was likely Joey would have shot him. Finished him, so his hostage wouldn't cause more trouble.

At the thought, her stomach contents turned to ice water. Then she began to shiver, harder than the car had shaken, as she struggled to tell herself her fears could not be true.

She thought of the powerful arms that had held her,

the muscled thighs and ripped abs of the cowboy she had taken for a lover. Dylan was not only tall, he was imposing, in peak condition from years of working with large livestock. In the prime of his life, he was probably close to a decade younger than Joey Santorini, too. But would any of that matter against The Jawbreaker, who was even bigger and more powerfully built? Besides, Joey was a stone-cold killer, nothing like the man who gentled wild or mistreated animals with his hands and voice....

The man she'd been so foolish as to endanger with her love.

How was it, she wondered, blinking back tears, that Joey had found out about him? Who could have told him that she and Dylan had grown close enough to make him a tempting hostage?

Trip Lowden, she suspected, remembering his vile assumptions when he'd pulled up beside them on the road. For if Joey had himself spotted her with Dylan, he would have grabbed and killed her on the spot. As it was, it was only pure, dumb luck that had her calling in time to keep him from finishing off his captive, just as another of her husband's men must have killed her father.

As she continued driving, Dylan's words kept coming back to her. *Don't come here! He'll kill—*

If they had been his last words, was she dishonoring him and what they'd had together by blindly racing back to her death? For surely, if she simply met Joey as directed, she would never have the chance to do anything but die. And even if Dylan had survived the gunshot she'd heard, there was no way Santorini would risk allowing him to walk away.

So both of them would be dead. And Renzo would have succeeded in destroying her, and destroying someone else she loved as well, from beyond the grave. Still, the idea of Dylan, being tortured for information on her whereabouts and then set ablaze, screamed inside her aching head, even louder than the voice of self-preservation.

Picking up the cell phone, she tried calling Joey back to beg him to be patient. Her stomach knotted as the line rang, and she prayed she wasn't already too late. When Dylan's voice-mail message started, she hung up and tried one more time, her heart thumping, but once again there was no answer, and all she could think to do was drive.

Or maybe… What if she called Amanda and explained to her what was happening? Would Amanda call the police—or mount a rescue effort on her own, possibly with some of the ranch hands? Aurora wanted to trust her friend, wanted to believe she wouldn't get Dylan or possibly herself and others killed, but in the end, the memory of Joey's threats, and his warnings to tell no one, kept her from calling Information for the ranch's number.

By the time she crossed the state line, her feet were numb and her teeth were chattering with cold, and maybe shock, as well. Cursing herself for not keeping the abaya for whatever warmth it might have offered, she made a quick stop in Cheyenne for a convenience-store coffee, telling herself she'd never stand a chance in Dead if she grew too cold to think.

Hurrying to the cash register, she offered an older man wearing a Denver Broncos sweatshirt some scrounged coins for her coffee.

"You have any other sweatshirts here?" she asked, still shivering, despite the store's warmth. "Anything for sale? My car's heater's broken, and I'm freezing."

"Sorry. We don't carry any clothing items—"

"What about that sweatshirt?" she said, nodding toward the one that he was wearing. "Would you sell it to me? Or trade, maybe? I don't have much, but—"

Realizing that, more correctly, she had *nothing,* nothing but the cell phone she needed to call Joey, she felt hot tears sliding down her freezing face.

"Oh, dear, please don't do that, miss," the clerk said, his blue eyes softening as he handed her some napkins. "No, I won't sell you the shirt off my back. But I can give you this jacket right here." He reached under the counter and then handed her a fleece-lined, denim jacket that had clearly seen better days. "Fella left it here one day when he stopped by for some smokes, but he never came back for it. You look like you could use it more, anyway."

"Thank you so much! You're a lifesaver." Gratefully, she pulled on the jacket, beyond caring that it smelled of old sweat and cigarette smoke. Sipping at the hot, black coffee, she waved goodbye and headed out.

But when she went back to the junker, the engine wouldn't start.

The hand that grasped the phone was bloody. The eyes that peered down at its face were too bleary to read.

Still, he somehow found the list of frequently called numbers. And somehow found the strength to push one of them—he wasn't sure which.

The phone rang twice, then three times before a woman's voice came through on the line.

"Dylan? Are you all right?" asked a female voice. "I've been so worried about you—especially after what I heard happened with Trip this morning."

His attempt to speak sent sharp pain arcing around his midsection. A pain that drenched his vision in swirling puddles of ink. Was he shot? Stabbed? There was no way to be certain of anything but the necessity of keeping absolutely still.

"Dylan? Dylan, speak up." This time, she sounded frightened. "I need to know you're okay. Do we have a bad connection?"

When he didn't, couldn't, answer, the woman begged, "Just tell me where you are, please. Tell me, and I'll come for you. I'll come for you right now."

But as he heard the truck start up behind him, the man lying by the wrecked gate forgot all about calling anyone for help. Dropping the phone, he laid down his head and prayed as his lifeblood turned the dust to mud.

Chapter 18

Aurora's gaze darted to the rearview mirror, her heart pounding so hard it felt as if it might explode in her chest. But the flashing red lights she was expecting hadn't yet come—and with any luck she'd reach the turnoff to the ranch before they did.

She still could not believe what she'd done, stripping off the jacket and thrusting out her breasts as she batted her baby blues—the contacts had come off, too—at the middle-aged man in a truck-stop gimme cap who'd pulled his pickup into the convenience store beside her. As his door swung open, he was stopped dead by her imitation of a porn-film damsel in distress—though she was still so cold, she felt more like a slut-sicle.

"I'm having a little trouble with my car," she said through pouty—and probably blue—lips. "You look like you might know your way around an engine. Think you might be able to take a look under my hood?"

He could, he vowed, and did, leaving his nearly new truck running to tinker with the junker's engine while doing his best to make conversation.

"Not sure if there's anything to be done here," he said, speaking mostly to her breasts, "but if you'll grab that tool kit out of the backseat of my truck, for me, I'll show you what I can do with my spanner—"

Feigning a ditzy giggle, Aurora bounced into the front seat, then put the truck in gear and took off in a flash, thanking her lucky stars that testosterone so often trumped men's good sense. If she survived, she swore she'd find a way to return the pickup unharmed and pay the poor guy for his trouble, but for now, her total focus must remain on saving Dylan.

Once more, she tried his cell phone, her pulse roaring in her ears as it began to ring. "Please answer me, please answer," she whispered, her eyes welling as the call once more rolled over to voice mail. This time, she left a message, crying, "I'm almost there! Please call me! Please don't hurt him, Joey. I have money hidden offshore, and I swear I'll give you every penny. It's enough for you to go somewhere and start a new life anywhere you want, for you to be the boss this time, with servants and a private island."

Exaggerated as the claim was, she cursed herself for not thinking of it sooner. Joey might be loyal to her husband's family—she was pretty sure, in fact, that he was somehow distantly related—but the thought of running off and living like royalty in some tropical wonderland was a lot of people's fantasy. If she'd only offered it to him sooner, maybe Dylan would still be alive.

No, she couldn't think it. Couldn't allow herself to give up hope. But as she sped toward the ranch, the sharp crack of the gunshot she'd heard echoed through her mind, and the dashboard clock glowed an accusation—12:58 p.m.

As fast as she'd been driving, she wasn't going to make it, but even if she had, what good would it do her, with no one answering the phone?

Since she had no other choice, she finally reached out for help, calling the ranch's main phone line. When a woman answered, she was too upset to recognize the voice, but it didn't matter. She was weeping, begging to be put through to Amanda.

"Who is this?" the woman demanded.

"Hope Woods," she had just enough presence of mind remaining to say. "I'm almost there, but I need to talk to Aman—to Miss Amanda now. Hurry, please! It's urgent."

The seconds passed with glacial slowness, but finally there was a click, followed by Amanda's worried voice. "Aurora? What is it? What's happened? I thought you were gone for good."

"He's taken Dylan!"

"Who has?" Alarm sliced through Amanda's voice, but somehow she managed to pull herself together. "Take a deep breath and explain."

"It's Joey Santorini, one of the men who was posing as an electrician. When I called Dylan's cell to see how he was doing this morning, Joey answered, and he said he had hurt Dylan, said he'd kill him if I didn't keep my mouth shut and get back by— It's after one already."

"I knew there must be something wrong! I just had a call from Dylan's number, but he didn't say a word, and finally, the call went dead. I radioed the hands and asked them to look for him, but— Do you have any idea where they are?"

"Only that they must be close by. But, Amanda, he might've— When I was on the line with him before, there was some kind of a struggle, and I heard a gunshot. So Dylan could be—"

"We'll find him. We have to."

Aurora blinked back tears, her voice shaking as she asked, "But will we find him alive?"

This close to achieving her goals, the mastermind saw red when she spotted that little bitch jumping out of a blue pickup near the stable. Back again, to cause more trouble—or at least to draw back the former partner and ruin everything.

Not for the first time, she regretted panicking when Aurora had struggled free of her grasp in the darkness of the women's showers. One moment, she'd been squeezing the maid's throat, the next, Aurora was kicking her away and fighting back.

Who would have guessed that such a pretty thing had so much strength to her? If she'd stayed and fought, the mastermind could have been injured, or even worse, caught. Caught and put away for all her crimes.

She wasn't about to take the risk, she impulsively decided. Only this time, she was going to take care of her problem the right way, with a gun.

Dylan passed out twice behind the wheel, the second time dropping the ranch truck down into a gully. When the pain of a splitting headache and his other injuries finally woke him, he stared into the brittle, brown-gold grasses surrounding the hood and, out of habit, reached for his phone.

That was when he remembered the rock striking his attacker's hand, making him drop the gun he was holding. Cursing, the huge man had grabbed for it, only Dylan reached it first.

Awkward, with his raw and bloody right arm, he had gotten off only a single shot at close range before his opponent wrenched it from him. But as he aimed the barrel at Dylan's chest, the man swayed once and dropped to his knees, his free hand clutching at his bloody gut.

Staggering out of range, Dylan had climbed into the still-running ranch truck. Thanks to the grille guard that had crushed the side of his own pickup, he found the big Ford undamaged and quickly drove away. Unfortunately, his escape had left him without a gun to defend himself or a phone to call help—and no way to know whether the assassin was lying dead or simply lying in wait, believing that Hope might still come.

Not Hope, Dylan remembered, but Aurora. What if he'd left the gunman still alive to reel her in with another threatening phone call?

No way was he about to sit here freezing in this truck cab and let that happen. He managed to restart the engine, which must have died at some point, but the truck remained stuck fast, and he knew there was no way he would be able to get it out without help.

So he would have to walk, then make his way back to the main ranch road and pray that he could flag down a passerby for help. *If* there was a passerby along this rarely traveled road.

Pain shot through his damaged ribs as he forced the passenger door open, then climbed with agonizing slowness from the gully. With a backward glance at the truck, he thought, *The old man'll be sure to give me hell about this,* before remembering with a shock that the old man in question was his father, a father far too sick to answer all the questions, or work out any of the emotions, that discovery dredged up.

As he walked, the deepening cold gnawed through his clothing, and the pain of his injuries reverberated through his body with each step. Only by focusing every ounce of effort was he able to continue trudging forward, step by step.

He was gritting his teeth, his attention funneled down to the few yards of gravel road before him—so much so that he was startled when an unfamiliar pickup pulled up beside him and the driver's-side door was suddenly flung open.

"Dylan! Dylan, you're alive! Thank God!"

Warm arms were flung around him, squeezing him so tightly that he grunted in pain.

"What did he *do* to you?" Aurora asked. "There's blood on your face and— Here, get in, where it's warm. You're freezing."

"You came back," he murmured, his voice shot through with disbelief.

The damp, blue eyes that peered into his shone like crystal in the sunlight. "Of course I had to come back. Joey had you. But what happened? How did you get away?"

"Sh-shot him, maybe killed him," he said as she walked him to the passenger-side door, "by the eastern gate, where we have the weanlings. I got away but then— wrecked the truck."

"Here," she said, opening the door for him. "Let's get you inside. Then you can tell me what happened on the way to the ranch."

Nodding, he managed to climb up, groaning as he did. Moments later, she was behind the wheel and shifting into Drive.

"Wait!" he said, pointing up at his face. "Your eyes."

"Forget about it," she said. "I'm a lot more worried about you."

"No, Aurora. You can't risk drawing any more attention to yourself than you already—"

"Oh, for heaven's sake," she said, sounding exasperated as she reached for the small purse she'd been carrying. "I'll put the contacts back in, if it makes you feel any better."

As she did so, the heater's blessed warmth soaked into his flesh, and he asked her, "Where'd you get this truck?"

"Trust me, cowboy," she said with a grimace. "You don't want to know."

He felt the flare of anger, along with his returning strength. "*What* did you do? And how'd you manage to ditch your shadows?"

"Seems to me I just showed up in time to save you from a very long walk—or more likely, dropping in your tracks and freezing to death. Now, enough about me. Tell me what happened to your head."

"Somebody kicked me in it with one mighty big boot." Just mentioning it made him want to be sick. "After he tried to run me down, that is."

"Is that what happened to your arm?"

He nodded. "Don't think it's broken, only scraped up. Ribs might be another story."

"I'm so, so sorry."

"Don't be."

"But you'll never be safe as long as anyone believes you mean anything to me."

"It's nobody's damned business how I feel about you."

"Someone's guessed. Somehow, word about us must've gotten out to Joey."

"There is no *us,*" he said stubbornly. "There can't be because you're going back to federal custody, if I have to handcuff you myself and take you back in."

"Things have changed. My ex-husband's dead now—murdered in custody. But we'll talk about our situation later," she murmured as the mansion came into view.

"There's nothing to talk about," he responded. "You're going back where you'll be safe from your ex's people, with WITSEC looking out for you. And as for me, I'll be working on some ranch as far from Colton influence—and the Colton name—as I can get."

Her gaze swung to meet his, her eyes filled with a compassion that assured him that she'd already guessed the results of the DNA test, that unburdened by the emotional blinders he'd been wearing, she must have realized from the start what he'd refused to see.

What he was refusing to accept, even now.

Chapter 19

It had to be Dylan's injuries, combined with the shock of learning that he was Jethro Colton's oldest son, making him look at her so coldly. Making him reject her as strongly as he had.

But as Aurora sat waiting for word from Levi, who had asked her to step outside while he examined Dylan, his words kept echoing through her mind, the finality in them unmistakable.

"You have to understand," Amanda told her, "he's just found out that everything he thought he knew about himself was a lie, a lie told to him by a woman he's grieving all over again.... I'm sure of it. With love and patience, he'll learn to accept that he's—"

"But he's right about me," Aurora answered, tears sliding down her face. "I nearly got him killed. If I stay, how long would it be till someone else comes by and this time kills him, like my father. Or *you* and your family, for that matter."

"No one's going to hurt me or you or Dylan, either," Amanda insisted. "First of all, the hands found the assassin dead by the gate, and he seemed to have been working alone. And until the mastermind's in custody, I'll hire enough additional security to keep you and Dylan and everyone on this—"

"If security were all it took, these attacks on the ranch would've ended months ago, right?"

Amanda pressed her lips together, her golden gaze betraying that, much as she would like to argue, the continuing incidents would not allow it.

"Which means Dylan was right. I have to leave again," Aurora told her. "If I can't patch things up with the WITSEC program now that my ex-husband's dead, I'll have to risk accessing my money so I can—"

"To do that, you'll have to get out of the country."

Sighing, Aurora said, "I don't have a passport, or enough credentials to get one." She felt exhausted thinking of it.

"We'll find a way. I'll help you."

Aurora stared at her, surprised to hear Amanda suggest doing anything illegal.

With a shrug, Amanda added, "Colton money and connections ought to be good for something. And we'll get that pickup you hijacked back to its rightful owner, too, along with a substantial compensation for his trouble."

Aurora threw her arms around her friend. "You're the best friend a Jersey girl could ever have. You know that?"

She only wished she could risk sticking around long enough to allow Amanda to give her the help she'd offered. But for everyone's sake, she needed to slip away as soon as she learned that Dylan would be all right.

For with her finally gone for good, maybe he would find a way to make peace with who he was now and embrace his newfound family. And maybe someday she would find some way to forgive herself for all the pain and the heartache she'd caused…even if she never forgot the man she left behind.

"I don't know why I bother advising people to go to the hospital," Levi grumbled as he taped up Dylan's ribs, hiding the ugly purple knot on his left side. "No one around here listens to me anyway."

"It's nothing that I won't get over," Dylan said, telling himself that he'd get over leaving the ranch behind, too. But not Aurora, not if he lived to be a hundred years old.

Still, letting her go was the right thing, the *only* thing he could do. He only prayed she hadn't blown her last chance by coming back to try to save him.

"If you start coughing up blood, I want you to promise me you'll tell me. And if you lose consciousness again, I'm calling an ambulance whether you like it or not."

"I won't pass out. Trust me, I've had worse on the rodeo circuit and the back pastures. I'll be sore for a few days, but—"

"Weeks," Levi corrected, "or months, most likely."

When Dylan didn't give an inch, the doctor shook his head and gave him a rueful smile. "You're as stubborn as my father. *Our* father, I understand."

Scowling, Dylan said, "So Amanda told you?"

Levi set down the roll of tape and nodded. "My condolences, man. And welcome to the family."

Awkward as it was with bandages and his right arm sore, Dylan grudgingly accepted the handshake Levi offered before conceding, "Guess you're about the only one who halfway understands."

Levi shrugged. "My situation was different. Rough in its own way, though. If I didn't have Kate here to help me through it—"

"I'm pretty sure she feels the same way about you," said Dylan, though the thought of their relationship only made him ache to have someone of his own to help him celebrate the good times and share the burden of the bad.

Not just someone, but Aurora—the one woman he could never have.

Just as he would never find his own way to fit into the Colton family. He'd meant what he'd said when he had told her it was high time he moved on. But first, there was one responsibility he couldn't shirk.

"So how long before I can do this marrow-transplant thing for Jethro?"

Levi frowned. "I'll tell you what I told Amanda earlier. There's not going to be a transplant. Not even if Jethro pulls out of this coma."

"He's in a coma?"

"Unfortunately, yes. And I'm hampered in how aggressively I treat him. You see, the stubborn old coot had a living will drawn up, forbidding me to give him anything but the most basic palliative treatment to relieve his suffering. He's done fighting, Dylan."

"But what if I could cure him? Or my marrow could, I mean?"

"First of all, you'd have to have further testing. There are other markers beyond blood type that would have to be checked out, and who knows if he'd live long enough for any of that to happen. More importantly, I'm telling you, he would refuse it, absolutely. Gabby, Cath and Amanda all imagine they could talk him into changing his mind, but he's been very adamant with me, and very specific about how he wants things to proceed. You know what he told me, last time that we talked?"

Dylan shook his head.

Levi dropped his voice in an approximation of Jethro's graveled tone. "He said, 'I've made enough money, done enough deals, loved enough women and lived enough life. Done enough wrong, too, for about a hundred lifetimes. You tell those girls of mine that. You tell 'em all that, if they ask you why, and tell 'em I'd rather go out on my own damned terms if I have to go at all.'"

Dylan snorted, a smile pulling at the corners of his mouth. "Sounds like the arrogant old coot, all right. I only hope it won't be too hard on his daughters."

"And his sons, too," Levi said, gently clapping a hand down on Dylan's shoulder. "Speaking of the devil, I'd better go back upstairs and check in on him. I imagine you could use a little rest now anyway, before the police chief comes by to interview you about the specifics on that dead assassin."

Nodding, Dylan thanked him, but he was far too keyed up to sleep. So instead, he hauled himself up from the exam table minutes later and dug through a desk drawer until he found a pen and pad of paper. Painful as it was to move, he was determined, knowing this might be his only chance for privacy before he left.

Dear Mr. Colton, he began, thinking it a surreal way to address the man who was—he was still reeling with the shock of it—his father. His *biological* father, anyway, with no more of a paternal bond with him than Jethro's stallion Midnight had with the many foals he'd sired.

But that didn't mean they had no history together, a history marred by Dylan's growing disgust with the ranch's caste system and three decades of dealing with Colton's casual contempt, not only for the employees he was only too happy to remind of "their place," but for the family he professed meant everything. A family that included three broken marriages, five children—unless his long history of adultery had resulted in other bastards besides Levi—and the kind of "friends" Dylan wouldn't trust at his back with anything sharper than a crayon. The kind of friends who hadn't come to visit once since hearing the Colton family patriarch was dying.

Sorry you aren't well enough to have this conversation man to man, Dylan wrote, wishing he were more at ease with words. But with Jethro now too sick to see him, he reminded himself this was his only shot at saying his piece. *If you hadn't refused to consider a marrow transplant point-blank, I want you to know, I would've done it. Not out of pity for you or for the money, either, but I'd help you for Amanda's sake, and Gabby's, and Cath's and Levi's, too. They're good people, daughters and a son you should be proud of.*

He left the rest unspoken, how Jethro's adult children had turned out well in spite of, rather than because of, his influence. Because he hadn't been raised to chase a sick man to his grave with accusations, especially not the employer who'd been his and his mother's bread and butter all these years. But he kept writing:

It's too late in the game for us now, too late to try to elbow my way in and claim a name I don't feel easy with, much less any of your money. Maybe I wasn't raised as your kid, but I've still got enough of you in me to want to make my own way—to build a business and maybe someday a family on my own steam instead of taking something that I haven't earned.

That's why I'm leaving Dead River Ranch—and the name I was born with. I'll have a lawyer draw up papers, and I'll sign them, giving up any inheritance. After what you said the morning after the fire, I imagine that might surprise you. It isn't meant to hurt you, though. I only wish you peace.

Peace and a little more time to get things straight with the kids you still have. To tell them that you love them, if you have half as much sense as you have money, and let them tell you back. 'Cause I can tell you, I'd give every dollar in that fat bank account of yours to tell my mother—and by that I mean Faye Frick, not that poor wreck of a drunk woman who ditched us both—that I love her and forgive her and to hold her one last time.

You might want to think on what it is that really matters while you still can. And you might want to do something about it before it's too late.

He signed the letter with the name that defined the man that he was, not the man he might have been if not for that kidnapping so many years before.

Thinking of that man, he jotted one last note...and passed it to the first person he saw when he stuck his head out into the hallway.

"Would you take this to Hope Woods, please?" he asked, needing to say something to blunt the harshness of his earlier words. Though it would change nothing, he didn't want her to leave regretting their few stolen hours together, or believing he would ever be sorry they had met.

As the sun dipped behind the mountains, Aurora's heart sank even lower. Because as dangerous a refuge as

Dead River Ranch had proved, she desperately wanted to cling to what little familiarity she'd found here.

Even more, she wished to hold on to the possibility of a real relationship with Dylan, or at least to interrupt his rest to see for herself how he was before her last goodbye. After what they'd shared in Laramie, she owed him that much, she knew, but earlier, Levi had gently told her and Amanda that Dylan needed rest now—and that he had been adamant that he preferred to rest alone.

"It's the DNA test, not you," Amanda had assured her. "I'm sure he'll come around soon."

But Levi had only shaken his head and countered, "I'm not so sure he will. But I'll remind him again you're waiting after he's spoken to police chief Peters."

Aurora had gone back to her room and waited. Waited for hours for an invitation that never came.

It's better this way anyway, better not to give me a chance to be talked out of doing what I have to. What's best for us both, in the long run.

Brave as the thought was, a bruised hollow of her heart still felt his silence as rejection. But if it was, so be it, especially if it made their parting easier for him.

It was after ten that night when she slipped downstairs with a small bag containing a few remaining items packed up from her room. There was little enough to account for her short life as Hope Woods, even less to help her get through whatever came next. But when a person was down to almost nothing, she grasped tightly to what was left.

Even if all that remained were memories—and the need to do right by those she'd come to care for.

With a new bodyguard on his way to the ranch the following morning, Aurora knew Amanda would be upset that she hadn't waited. Her good friend might even be angry, especially considering the expensive payout she'd negotiated to convince the owner of the stolen truck to call the police and tell them his initial report had been a big mistake.

As for Aurora, she'd find a way to safely pay Amanda back, once she'd made it safely beyond U.S. borders. And she swore that she would find a way to accomplish that goal, too, one way or another.

But first, she had to put some distance between herself and her friend's good intentions, along with the temptation to turn back to the man who'd nearly lost his life on her account. Closing her eyes, she sucked in a breath for focus, then dredged up the memory of what he'd looked like as he trudged along that cold road, staring blankly as ribbons of blood dripped down his face and arm.

Time to leave him to heal, she told herself, *whether it ends up being here or elsewhere.*

As she reached the ground floor, she noticed Hilda Zimmerman, pulling a set of car keys from her coat with a tired sigh.

"You're here awfully late tonight," Aurora told her. "I thought you usually left for home before dinnertime."

Hilda grimaced. "With Thanksgiving coming, Mrs. Perkins wants everything cleaned and polished to a shine."

"You mean the staff still plans to go ahead and have a formal dinner, even with Mr. Colton so ill?"

Hilda drew up with a shocked look. "Why, certainly. We wouldn't want it to be said that we're slipping, regardless of the circumstances. But it has been a challenge, especially considering how short we are on *qualified* staff. Why, even Mrs. Perkins has been scrubbing and rubbing right alongside the rest of us—as bad as her arthritis has been lately. Now, *that's* true dedication, unlike some employees I know."

At her sniff of disapproval, Aurora's temper got the better of her.

"I'll be the first to admit I had a lot to learn about housecleaning when I came here," she said sharply. "Still do, but I can tell you, my learning curve might've been a little shorter if *you* hadn't advised me to use two incompatible cleaners."

Aurora meant it as a bluff, for she'd never really imagined the older woman had purposely poisoned her. But she took a step back at the malevolent look that darkened Hilda's normally kind face.

"I told police chief Peters, and I'll tell you," the maid said hotly. "I've used those two products together dozens of times—hundreds, maybe. You're obviously confused about what you mixed. Or just a troublemaker out to distract Mrs. Perkins from your own incompetence by getting other employees—valued, capable employees—in trouble."

Forcing herself to take a deep breath, Aurora assured her, "I really wasn't trying to cause you or any of the others trouble. I was just trying to help the police catch whoever's been killing employees on this ranch—"

"I can't think why anyone would want to kill *you*. You haven't done enough honest work around here to see or hear anything that—"

Aurora pulled down her turtleneck to reveal the garish bruises she had been concealing, bruises that looked a lot worse than they felt. "Do you think I made this up, too? That I attacked myself in that dark bathroom?"

Hilda cringed, her eyes widening as she stared at the

damage. "I—I never said that, and I wouldn't. I just can't help but wonder."

"Neither can I," Aurora answered, "but fortunately, it's not my problem anymore."

Looking down at the bag in her hand, Hilda said, "You mean you're leaving the ranch."

Aurora nodded. "Yes, and for good this time. I hope you'll stay safe, Hilda, and that whoever's doing these things is finally caught and locked up."

"And I hope," Hilda told her, "that you'll find your next position something more…in keeping with your talents."

Aurora wondered exactly what the older woman had meant before figuring that Trip's ugly gossip—or maybe Misty Mayhew's—had undoubtedly beaten her back to the ranch. Telling herself she had enough to worry about without caring what reputation her latest alter ego left behind here, she waited a few minutes to give Hilda time to get into her car and drive off before slipping outdoors and heading in the direction of the stolen truck.

With the cloudless skies, the temperature had fallen. Shivering despite her coat, Aurora hesitated beside the pickup, staring up at the myriad stars. Brilliant stars, so far from the town's lights…even farther than she felt from any living soul.

Glancing back at lit windows of the Colton mansion, she reminded herself that there was only one that mattered. One who'd rejected her as firmly as he had his Colton name.

Steeling herself for what was sure to be a long drive, she grabbed the cold door handle with her bare hand—and sucked in a deep breath as what felt like the hard end of a metal pipe was jammed into her back. A pipe that instinct told her was not a pipe at all.

"You scream, I'll put a bullet through your lungs, bitch," the harsh whisper confirmed. "You try to fight, and you die faster."

"Who?" Aurora started, nearly certain the speaker was a woman. "What do you wan— *Unhh!*"

The word turned to a groan as what must have been the barrel struck the base of her neck, a blow that dropped her to her knees and brought tears of pain to her eyes.

"Any more questions?" rasped her attacker—an attacker whose brutality left no doubt in Aurora's mind that this was the same person who had jumped her in the women's showers, the same mastermind who had already killed at least three times before.

Swearing she wasn't going to be the fourth victim, Aurora shook her head and whimpered with the pain radiating between her shoulders.

"Get up," the woman ordered. "We're going to take a little walk now. Out into the woods."

Chapter 20

Sweat beaded on Dylan's brow as he went to Levi's desk, where the extension had been ringing on and off for the past ten minutes. With Levi upstairs tending to his father, Dylan had no other choice except to answer if he wanted to get any rest at all.

Not that he could sleep, for worrying about Aurora. Had she gotten the note he'd sent asking to see her, then decided it was better if they didn't speak again? Or had the woman he had trusted to deliver his words decided the errand didn't fit with her agenda? Dylan wouldn't put it past her, considering the resentful look she'd given him when he'd asked.

"Infirmary. Dylan Frick here," he said into the phone.

"Thank goodness I finally tracked you down, Mr. Frick."

"Who is this?" asked Dylan, unable to place the familiar male voice.

"This is Leon, Leon Nelson. You remember?"

"The electrician, sure." Dylan wasn't likely to forget his scuffle with the man's ne'er-do-well son, who had clearly known more than he'd admitted. "Did you find out anything more from Junior?"

"Acts scared spitless every time I ask him about the fella who contacted him in the first place—"

"That I can understand," Dylan said, remembering the giant bearing down on him, a giant who would never trouble Junior or anyone else again.

"But I did get one thing outta that boy—the name of the ranch employee who tampered with that deadman panel. A real quick study, he said, and real eager to make money, no matter what it took—"

"Who was it?" Dylan interrupted, reminded that, with Jethro dying, Trip's and his family's free ride was about to come to an abrupt halt.

But Leon surprised him, saying, "That little maid.... Can you believe it? That one with the curly black hair and blue eyes."

"Misty?" Dylan's gut twisted, and his pulse zoomed higher. "Misty Mayhew, you mean?"

"Yes, indeed. Seems she's in a heap of trouble. Owes a lot of money to the wrong people, on account of gambling over at the reservation."

Instincts blaring, Dylan thought once more of the note he'd given her, a note whose contents might have been enough to drive a desperate woman to an even more desperate act. After thanking Leon, Dylan told him, "Call police chief Peters, will you? Ask him to come out to the ranch right away."

"But what about my boy? I know he's done wrong and all, but he didn't hurt anybody. And I swear I'll straighten him up, if it's the last thing I—"

"I'll leave him out of this if there's any way that I can," Dylan promised, though he was far from sure that the older Nelson would be successful. "That's the best I can do for you."

Leon was still thanking him when Dylan hung up the extension and then phoned Amanda and asked to speak with Aurora.

"She's not here," Amanda told him, her voice shaky. "She told me she was going to pack up a few things in her room before she moved into the guest suite I had made ready in the family wing."

"You let her go up alone?"

"I know I shouldn't have. But she waited until I was distracted putting Cheyenne to bed, and—Dylan, I called the servants' wing to check on her just a couple of minutes ago. One of the kitchen helpers checked, but Aurora wasn't anywhere around. I thought she might be on her way back—or maybe she'd stopped by to see you."

"We need to find her right away. And Misty Mayhew, too." Quickly, he explained what the electrician had told him. "Nelson's calling police chief Peters, but meanwhile, I'll organize a search."

"But you're hurt. You should stay in bed while I call—"

Dylan dropped the phone into the cradle, then headed for the door just as Levi came in, greeting him with a look of disbelief.

"You promised me you'd rest."

"That's not an option right now."

As soon as Dylan briefed him, Levi's expression turned serious. "How can I help?"

Gritting his teeth against the pain of sudden movement, he grabbed his coat, which Amanda had draped over a chair earlier. "I'm heading outside to see if Hope's truck is still out there, or if she might've taken off on her own, since she's talked about it earlier. Meanwhile, if you could concentrate on finding Misty, that'd be great.

Don't try to confront her alone, though, not unless it's an emergency. For all we know, she's a murderer—maybe even the mastermind herself."

"I don't see how she could be," Levi said with a shake of his head. "She didn't even work here when Faye— when your mother—was killed."

"That's a good point, but we definitely know she's desperate enough to risk burning down the place for money. Desperate enough to try to kill Hope twice already, too, I'm betting, just to get rid of a threat to her plan to get close to me."

As Dylan hurried outside, he swore that this time, Misty would be no more successful. That no matter what it cost him, he would save Aurora's life.

Filled with panic at the thought that this walk would be one-way, Aurora reflexively looked back at her captor and immediately wished that she had not. For the figure standing behind her wore an oversize black parka with a hood, a muffler and a huge pair of ski goggles obscuring most of his or her face.

But it was the sight of the pistol in the gloved hand that had sent adrenaline spiking through Aurora. Adrenaline that had her screaming and shoving her attacker, then turning and racing through a darkness broken only by the starlight—and the sharp crack of the gun.

As Aurora ran through the stand of trees, she heard the zing of a bullet ricocheting past her. But she kept on moving, unhurt, save for the stinging slap of branches as they whipped her face and shoulders. Raising an arm to protect her eyes, she ducked around a thick trunk, only to hear another blast and feel the spray of flying bark.

Far too close, she realized, as a flashlight's beam

swayed through the undergrowth. Gulping deep breaths of air so cold her lungs stung, Aurora raced off once again. With terror riding her sore shoulders, it was impossible to move with anything approaching stealth. Leaves crunched and branches cracked or gouged, pulling grunts of pain she couldn't hold back.

As the trees grew thicker, the branches closed in on her, and the bright beam of the moving flashlight cast black shadows that lurched eerily beside her before, inevitably, joining with her own.

An instant later, she was falling, her foot snagged by the edge of a jutting rock. As she went down, her shrill scream slashed through darkness—the scream of a woman who knew she would never outrun the next bullet...

Nor the death that had stalked her so ruthlessly, so long.

Just a few more steps...

Adrenaline flooding his body, Dylan put on a burst of speed, pushing past both pain and his instinct for self-preservation and toward the black-clad figure whose flashlight led him like a beacon. Breathing hard and intent on her own quarry, the armed figure never saw him coming, never realized how dangerously close he was to striking from behind.

But he chased a moving target, an uninjured, agile stalker who stubbornly remained a few steps out of reach. Until the hooded assailant abruptly drew up short, weapon rising to take aim—even as Dylan shouted, "NO!"

Leaping toward her, he heard the deafening report, followed by what could only be Aurora's scream. A scream of pain and terror, from a woman who knew that she would die.

He collided with the shooter, both of them crashing to the ground. But the impact sent agony spearing through his rib cage, a pain so sharp and stabbing, he didn't dare to breathe. Still, he grappled with the struggling figure, his hand clamping over the gun as she tried to turn it on him.

"Dylan!" Aurora cried out from nearby, distracting the attacker enough to let him shift his grip.

There was another explosion, another female cry of pain, this time from the woman in black as she clapped a hand to her upper arm. Yet within an instant, she somehow managed to slam an elbow into his side.

A wave of dizziness sent the stars spinning and had him dropping the gun. By the time he dared scoop out a shallow breath, she had rolled to her feet and come up running. Running into the blackest patch of shadows.

Follow her. End this, finally.

But with the sound of another woman's weeping, he knew that even if he found the strength to give chase, he couldn't do it—not without risking all he had of Aurora.

Chapter 21

Thanksgiving morning

Under the watchful gaze of the bodyguard assigned to look after her, Aurora drifted into the employee dining room. Now that Misty Mayhew had been taken into custody, she felt safer than she had before, though neither she nor any of the ranch's other female workers showed any sign of a gunshot injury.

But as dark and confused as the night that she was shot had been, maybe Dylan had been mistaken and the bullet hadn't struck the shooter. Misty, Aurora was certain, though the conniving little schemer had so far admitted nothing beyond tampering with the electrical panel and "accidentally" replacing the contents of a certain white bottle on Aurora's cleaning cart with a solution containing a strong acid.

"I never really meant to kill her," she'd insisted, "only to convince Mrs. Perkins she was too incompetent to keep on staff. I swear it!"

Police chief Peters had insisted Misty's "mischief" was all about her desperation to pay off her debts—and snag the one man she'd been gambling could buy her way out of trouble.

A man who remained in the ranch infirmary, sedated against the pain of what had turned out to be three fractured ribs.

Blinking back tears at the thought of all he'd suffered, Aurora went to the table, which was beautifully but simply set for the employees' meal this afternoon. Already, she smelled the rich aroma of turkeys cooking in the ovens, the spicy-fruity scents of a half-dozen baking pies. Those smells were overlaid with memories from years past: her mother's glazed sweet potatoes, green-bean casserole and yeast rolls, her father's smile of contentment as he pushed back from the table and praised her mother by insisting, "You've outdone yourself again, dear."

Aurora dropped a folded paper into the top of the pumpkin that was the table's centerpiece before the tread of boots warned that someone was approaching. As she turned, her jaw dropped at the sight of Dylan coming toward her.

"You're up!" she said, recovering enough to smile nervously. "I'm so glad you're feeling better. I thought I might miss you."

Dylan didn't smile back. Instead, he scowled, which, combined with the boyishly tousled hair and the misbuttoned shirt, somehow only made him more appealing. "So Amanda was right. You *did* plan to leave, without saying one damned word."

At a look from her, the bodyguard gave a nod before discreetly stepping outside to guard the door.

"I've said goodbye," she told Dylan. "I told you last night—"

"After whatever was in that painkiller Levi gave me, I barely knew what *language* you were speaking. I only knew that when you held my hand, your flesh was warm, your pulse strong beneath my fingers. And your eyes were shining with— I could have sworn it was with a lot more than plain relief."

"It—it was," she admitted, overtaken by an echo of that riotous emotion. She reached out as if to touch him, reached so close she could imagine the prickle of the stubble darkening his jawline before she pulled back, then drew her shaking fingers through her own loose hair instead. "When I saw you wrestling with my attacker— I've never been so frightened. More afraid of losing you than I was of being killed. And then to hear that gun go off, to see her get up and run off while you— I was so damned sure she'd shot you, Dylan. And my heart—I swear that it stopped, until I saw you moving."

He took a step nearer, his expression giving way to anguish. "I thought you'd been hit, too. And I swore, Aurora, swore to myself that if by some miracle you made it, I would never let you walk away from me again."

She stared into his blue eyes, her pulse throbbing in her ears like thunder. "What choice do I have, Dylan? You know I can't stay here, that even with my ex dead and the family in disarray, they'd find a way to get to me—"

"You're right," he said. "You do have to leave."

"The helicopter's on the way. It should be here for me in—" she glanced at her watch "—about fifteen minutes."

Closing the gap between them, he took her hands in his. And her heart crumbled into dust, with the knowledge that she would lose the kind of bond that she had never even guessed existed, that even if she lived to be an old, old woman, she would never know its like again.

"But that doesn't mean," he told her quietly, "you have to go alone."

She shook her head, pain mushrooming through her

chest at his offer. An offer she could not accept. "You can't mean that. Dylan, you have a *family*. Right here. Do you have any idea what I'd give to see mine one more time?"

He grabbed the back of a chair with one hand, then gingerly lowered himself onto one knee.

"What on earth are you doing? You can't possibly mean to—"

"There's not much time, so are you listening?"

"Are you kidding? Crazy-hot cowboy down on one knee?" She sketched a check mark with one finger. "You've definitely got my full attention."

"I choose *you* to be my family, to be all the family that I'll ever need in this life. Because, whatever name you go by, I know exactly who you are. I know you and I love you, and that's the only thing that matters."

She shook her head, her eyes closing and the dust of her devastated heart blowing in the wind. "That's impossible. Dylan. You can't really know me. And what if something happens? If you change your mind?"

"That's fear talking, and I already know you're one gutsy woman. A Jersey girl, like you say, brave enough to testify against a mob boss and carjack some good old boy's pickup out from underneath him to come running to my rescue—"

"So Amanda told you about that." The memory heated her face.

"She certainly did." He grinned, grunting a little as he climbed back to his feet. "So don't tell me you're *afraid* to take a chance on me. I don't believe it any more than I believe you still have feelings for that ass who was your husband."

But she *was* afraid. Scared to death that Dylan would

grow to hate her once he realized all he'd given up for her. Not only the career and reputation he'd worked so hard to build, but all the relationships here on the ranch that clearly meant so much to him, relationships that would change and grow as he, too, grew to accept his Colton heritage, his sisters and his brother, maybe even to reclaim the name to which he'd been born. And then there was the money, all the money he'd be giving up for her. It might sound crass, but his share of his father's fortune could change his life forever, could enable him to achieve his every dream on a grand scale.

Telling herself she could bear even a lifetime of loneliness more than his eventual resentment, she swallowed hard and spoke past the pain knotting in her throat. "It's not that I'm not flattered by the offer, Dylan, but a quick fling's not the same thing as forever. And I'm pretty sure that you're confusing lust with—"

"Are you telling me you don't love me? That you risked your life, your freedom, everything you have to come racing back to face an armed assassin out of— What would that be? *Gratitude* for a good time?"

"I—I'd do the same for any of my friends."

"Friends?" he asked, the word dripping with disbelief.

"Good friends," she allowed with the smallest of shrugs before lying, "but no more…"

He moved to within inches, as he searched her eyes with a searing intensity that primed her every nerve ending, that had her heart pounding out a warning to turn away before he—

Too late, for as he pulled her in his arms and kissed her, all her objections, all her willpower ignited like a million tiny torches. Melting into his embrace, she kissed him back, her lips parting to his questing tongue, her hands stroking the hard muscle along—

He broke off the kiss to pull away, his teeth gritted in pain.

"I'm sorry," she told him. "I forgot about your poor ribs. And I—I forgot other things, as well. Things that you'd be giving up if you chose me."

"Do you mean a chance to father children?" he asked gently.

She shook her head and said uncomfortably, "It could be I exaggerated about that a little. But what if it did happen? What would we do then?"

He took her hand and stroked it, his callused fingertips gliding over smooth skin. "The best we could. Together. Just like every other couple. *If* you love me, that is."

Reasons clamored in her mind, reasons that she shouldn't. "What about your business here?" she asked. "About finding your mother's killer? Police chief Peters said himself, Misty might've been behind the recent attacks, but up until a few months ago, she was still halfway across the state gambling up a storm, with plenty of witnesses who can alibi her."

"I know that. And I'm sorry to be leaving without those questions answered." Dylan looked over his shoulder before lowering his voice. "I did speak to an old friend of mine, Slade Kent, of the Wyoming Bureau of Investigation. With police chief Peters's blessing, Slade's going to be coming to work here as a ranch foreman— and he's sworn he won't leave until he's shut down the mastermind once and for all. Because it's obvious we're going to need a professional to do it."

"And you're willing to walk away from all that?"

"I've told you, I can't stay here. I can't and I won't play the Colton, ever."

"Ever is a long time. Are you sure you—"

From outside, they heard the thumping beat of a descending helicopter.

"I won't change my mind about this. Or about you, either."

"Not even if they send us to—" As she leaned forward, her warm breath feathered a location into his ear. A location so remote, she'd never dreamed it possible, but not even the Australian Outback would seem empty if she had someone to share it with her.

"Not even if they send us to the moon," he promised. "Not as long as I can earn my keep with my own two hands…and know you love me, too."

"How *do* you know?" she teased. "Are you really that confident?"

"Confident enough," he said, turning from her to face the table, then reaching for the centerpiece and pulling it his way.

When he winced with pain, she chided him. "You really shouldn't—"

"What's this?" he asked, pulling out a slip of paper. The very same one she'd dropped inside only moments earlier. Making a show of unfolding it, he flashed that cocksure grin of his and read the two words. "*Dylan Frick.* I *knew* it."

Feigning innocence, she said, "How do you know that's my handwriting, cowboy? Maybe it's one of the hands who likes the way you look in your Levi's, or Mrs. Black's got roving eyes. The good one, let's hope."

He made a face, then hugged her to him carefully. "I'm pretty sure none of them dot their *i*'s with a heart."

"Come to think of it," she said, "*I'm* the one who's been noticing the way you look in those jeans—" And obsessing all too often on how much better he'd looked out of them.

"And the one who loves me?" he asked, abruptly growing serious. "Because you're right. This is for the long haul. I need you to be sure."

Studying his eyes, she read the hunger in him, the need to build a new life with her at his side. And seeing his vulnerability as well, how she could crush him with a single word if she chose. Still, she hesitated. "What about Amanda. Amanda and the others?"

"I know they hoped I'd stay, but they've given me their blessing. Levi even helped me pack a bag. So answer me, please, Aurora. You're going to have to say it."

Tell him no. Tell him now, her frightened brain was begging.

But her heart spoke even louder. "Then we'd better hurry, cowboy. Because, much as I love you, this is one flight we can't miss."

Still, they were delayed several minutes longer, as his strong arms encircled hers, and their mouths joined together. And in his kiss, she tasted life and love and passion…and all the hope she thought she'd left behind.

* * * * *

Don't miss the last story in
THE COLTONS OF WYOMING:
COLTON CHRISTMAS RESCUE
by Beth Cornelison, available December 2013

A sneaky peek at next month...

INTRIGUE...

BREATHTAKING ROMANTIC SUSPENSE

My wish list for next month's titles...

In stores from 15th November 2013:

❑ Cold Case at Camden Crossing – Rita Herron

& The Cradle Conspiracy – Robin Perini

❑ Justice is Coming – Delores Fossen

& Yuletide Protector – Julie Miller

❑ Undercover Twin – Lena Diaz

& Dirty Little Secrets – Mallory Kane

Romantic Suspense

❑ Colton Christmas Rescue – Beth Cornelison

Available at WHSmith, Tesco, Asda, Eason, Amazon and Apple

Special Offers

Every month we put together collections and longer reads written by your favourite authors.

Here are some of next month's highlights— and don't miss our fabulous discount online!

On sale 6th December

On sale 1st November

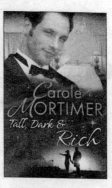

On sale 6th December

Save 20% on all *Special Releases*